WHAT PEOPLE AR

"This is a haunting, moving story that needs to be told. Be prepared for an emotional journey as the author, through careful weaving of personalities and events, takes you to the heights of laughter, to the deep love of friendship, and even to a turbulent, unsettling rage. *Then Came a Hush* is the story of how God's love brings healing to the hurting in a modern-day version of the Good Samaritan. It's the story of how God's love—lived out in His creation, His word, and His church—can bring freedom."

SUSAN BAKER, B.Mus., M. Mus.

Lindsay, Ontario

"If you have never known the intensity of spousal abuse firsthand, *Then Came a Hush* will provide you with a depth of understanding of various aspects of the abusive personality, as well as a profound compassion for the plight of one being abused. Waring's treatment of this subject engaged me in heart-racing reading as I was drawn into the secret life of Abby and Jake, and the natural consequences of the words said and actions taken between them. Not to be discounted is Waring's ability to present the intense inner conflict that Christians experience when they are on the receiving end of such abuse."

GAIL NICHOLSON, Certified Pastoral Counsellor
Coordinator for Living Waters, Peterborough, Ontario

"*Then Came a Hush* spoke to my Jewish roots, my experiences in life, and my love of the Lord. I was drawn into the characters' lives from the first page. Be aware that at times you will find yourself on the edge of your seat, hoping and praying for the characters as they come to life. I can only imagine how the author felt as she created each character with love, as she wove the tapestry of so many lives—intertwining them so seamlessly and then watching as they took on a life of their own. You are right there with them, laughing and crying through their joy and pain. The authenticity and depth of *Then Came a Hush* reveals God's never-ending capacity to bring healing in our lives."

SHARON BERMAN, Senior Fitness Specialist
London, Ontario

"*Then Came a Hush* is everything a good book should be—engaging, thought-provoking, memorable, meaningful...life-changing. The author has achieved a depth of emotion in her writing that is only found in the best of the best. I will delight in reading this book many times over. A sequel is a dangerous thing, sometimes better left to the imagination of the reader, but not so with *Then Came a Hush*. *Come Find Me* was a beautiful, moving, and well-written book; *Then Came a Hush* is a gem."

KATHY LE GRESLEY, Elementary School Teacher,
Lindsay, Ontario

"Ruth has done it again! The continued story of Evelyn Sherwood, her family, and her friends is so compelling that it draws you in to become a silent observer in the living room on Aspen Avenue, or in the car travelling to Pike Ridge. Great job!"

LAURA VAN ZANDEN, Bookkeeper
London, Ontario

"The anguished cries of those who are bullied, abused, shamed, manipulated, and hurting—emotionally and physically—have been heard compassionately in *Then Came a Hush*. Through telling, through truth, and through trusting people and God comes freedom and peace. Thank you, Ruth, for courageously supporting those who are victimized, and for shining the light of Scripture in a dark world...and doing it well."

TRUDYLYNN IRELAND (Chittick)
Ilderton, Ontario

"The author's description of the signs and symptoms of abuse—especially the loss of self-respect and self-trust that comes as self-confidence is eroded—was right on the mark and beautifully woven into the story. And she dealt with the abuser directly, sharing some of his history so that the root cause of his behaviour might be understood, yet she holds him accountable for his actions. There was absolutely nothing I would change given God's part in the writing of this book and Waring's willingness to follow His lead. I hope He leads her to keep writing!"

PAT MCCARDLE, BSCN, Trauma Therapist
Bethany, Ontario

Sequel to *Come Find Me*

THEN CAME A HUSH

RUTH WARING

Word Alive Press
131 Cordite Road, Winnipeg, MB R3W 1S1
www.wordalivepress.ca

WORD ALIVE PRESS
Just Write!

```
  ®        MIX
          Paper from
FSC    responsible sources
www.fsc.org  FSC® C016245
```

Library and Archives Canada Cataloguing in Publication
Waring, Ruth
          Then came a hush / Ruth Waring.
ISBN 978-1-77069-329-6
          I. Title.
PS8645.A745T54 2011   C813'.6   C2011-904341-6

Dedicated to
MARY
my sister and a survivor

I love you.

ACKNOWLEDGEMENTS

How can I begin to thank everyone who has encouraged me to write a sequel to *Come Find Me*? Many have supported me through e-mails, cards, and phone calls, and some have allowed me to intrude on their pain as I've researched for *Then Came a Hush*. "Thank you" does not seem to be enough, but the list is long, and the fear of leaving someone out hangs over my head. But you know who you are and you know how grateful I am for your encouragement in seeing this sequel birthed and nurtured into adulthood.

My wonderful husband Doug has stood in the shadows of this journey, praying for me and perhaps worrying a little, as I struggled with fear, frustration, and lack of sleep. But lovingly and willingly, he listened, questioned, challenged, and suggested, and even bought me a car adapter for my computer so that time would not be wasted on a three-day trip home from Florida!

I would be remiss if I failed to acknowledge Word Alive Press for once again coaching me through to the eventual release of *Then Came a Hush*. Caroline, Jen, Nikki, and Paul have been amazing. Without the encouragement and expertise of Evan Braun, the editing process would have been painful. He took a rough piece and polished it so it would sparkle! Thank you!

Without the input, suggestions, corrections, and patience of Kathy, Laura, Trudy, Susan, Sharon, Pat, and Gail, I would have helplessly floundered. The Rev. Warren Leibovitch, incumbent of St. Paul's Anglican Church in Lindsay, graciously allowed me to tap into his history and willingly shared many insights into the Jewish faith. And as I listened to a new friend, her tragic life story filled me with such sadness that I wondered if I would be able to do justice to the topic God had laid upon my heart.

Abuse is prevalent in our society and is often left untold and ignored, its existence even denied. Yet it is only when we are exposed to its horror that we can offer love, support, and counsel to the abused. God allowed me the privilege of insight as I struggled with *Then Came a Hush*. The title, characters, theme, and story had to have come from Him, since my finite mind and life experiences have not allowed me the insight with which I have been credited. Often I felt overwhelmed by the fear of failure as I wrote—the fear of failing to be authentic. I have never walked this road. For a time, I even refused to write. Yet through God's gracious leading, my friend Luella and I discovered—or rediscovered—1 Chronicles 28:20, and my writing took on new meaning:

> Be strong and courageous, and do the work. Do not be afraid or discouraged, for the Lord God, my God, is with you. He will not fail you or forsake you until all the work … is finished (NIV).

It is my prayer that God will use the story of Evelyn and Abby to encourage broken hearts and set the angry and fearful on the path of healing.

Ruth Waring
ruth.waring@gmail.com

Be still, and know that I am God:
I will be exalted among the heathen,
I will be exalted in the earth.

PSALM 46:10

TRUST

Their honking is heard across the sky,
Stretching their wings
In perfect form they fly,
Never faltering.

I STAND TRANSFIXED...

Do they know where they are going?
They follow without fear
They trust their leader, soaring,
Never doubting.

The time has come, a path they'll take
Perhaps to the unknown
Resolved, a decision they have made,
Never questioning.

I'M LOST IN THOUGHT...

Can I learn from these created beings
And leave my nest and fly
Over mountains high, over paths unseen
My trust unwavering?

I ponder this thought; weigh its meaning:
Do I step beyond my box
Trusting my Creator to do the leading,
My hand in His?

I'VE MADE MY CHOICE

My fears aside, a trust is found
My wings are spread. I'm ready
The Creator leads me, safe and sound,
Loving unconditionally.

Following my Leader, I will soar high
Sometimes faltering, often doubting
And at times even questioning, *Why?*
But I'll hold His hand ... and fly.

LIST OF CHARACTERS

Lewis Sherwood (Louie)	1921–1961
Evelyn Crawford Sherwood (Evie)	1925–
a.k.a Evlyna Lilach Cohen	
Bobby Jenkins	1921–1942
William Stewart Douglas (Wil)	1942–
Jacqueline Lucille Sherwood Douglas (Lucy)	1947–
Anna Evlyna Louise Douglas (Annie)	1969–
Jacob Sela Morsman	1879–1956
Christina Moses Morsman	1895–
Levi Yaacov Morsman, M.D. (Lee)	1920–
Cliff Moses (Uncle Mo)	1890–1968
Robert Adams (Rob)	1942–
Holly Adams	1942–1964
Bradley James Adams (B.J.)	1961–
Angelina Abigail Evans Waters (Abby)	1942–
Jake Waters	1942–

Joseph Crawford	1901–
a.k.a. Jóózsef Solomon Cohen	
Hannah Crawford	1906–1943
a.k.a. Hannah Adiva Feldman Cohen	
Rachel Crawford	1943–
Marek Aaron Feldman	1875–1906
Rachel Fraser	1883–
a.k.a. Rachel Lilach Feldman	
Ruth Norton	1907–
Edna Barnes	1915–
Hank Mason	1914–
Joshua Graham (Josh)	1935–
Jennie Graham	1938–
"Trickster"	1968–
a.k.a. Tricks, Tricksie, etc.	

PROLOGUE

Thystle Creek, Alberta
July 1, 1969

I t would just be for a short time, honest, Jake. I just need to see my mom and sisters." Abby tried reasoning with her husband, but Jake Waters shook his head in disgust.

"Are you deaf?" Jake turned slowly. His stone-grey face lacked emotion, but his threatening eyes shot invisible daggers. "The only thing you *need* is to grow up. You're a married woman and your responsibility is with me! How many years have we been married, and you still want to run off to *mommy*?" Sarcasm soaked Jake's words. "You're not going and that's final."

Jake slammed his fist on the table to punctuate his decision.

Abby ignored her husband's threatening response. "But, Jake, listen! Please! It's been more than nine months. Dad's really sick and Mom would be glad to have an extra pair of hands for a few weeks. Before we closed for the holiday, Josh okayed my time off at the Emporium and I'm not…"

"That's right, Abby. You're not…going!" Jake shouted, towering over his wife, spittle frothing from the corner of his mouth.

Abby watched her husband's demeanour change. His voice quieted and an abnormal calmness filled the room as he stared into her eyes. She watched the veins pulsate in his neck in tune with the opening and closing of his fist. His knuckles grew white and she knew she was in trouble.

"It appears you need to be reminded where your place is." His words sliced the air and hurled contempt. His movement was smooth and calculated, like a lion ready to pounce on its unsuspecting prey.

Abby knew what was coming.

"No, Jake, please! I understand. I won't ask again. I promise. You were right. I need to be here with..."

But Abby's words fell on deaf ears. She stood defenseless as the suddenness and brutality of her husband's first blow stunned her. Her head jerked to the right as his fist struck her left eye and cheek. She had been unprepared for the viciousness. Jake had never hit her in the face before. His aim had always been exact, premeditated, the results out of sight. Abby threw her arms across her face to protect it from further attack, exposing her arms to take the second and third blows. Jake's last strike spun her hard against the bedpost. Like a small dog helpless against the ruthless assault of its owner, she crawled across the bed, desperate to escape the abuse.

"You're...not...going!" Jake hissed and left her cowering in the corner of the bed.

PART
ONE

1

God is our refuge and strength, a very present help in trouble.
Therefore will not we fear, though the earth be removed,
and though the mountains be carried into the midst of the sea.

PSALM 46:1–2

July 5

The sun shone warm and high in a blue sky, a perfect day for a parade. Four days earlier, July 1 had provided a much-welcomed opportunity for the people of Thystle Creek to enjoy the break in their daily and weekly routine to barbeque hamburgers and hot dogs, drown themselves in lemonade, gorge on apple pie, and light fire crackers in the shape of schoolhouses and snakes. The holiday was over, yet every year the small town in northern Alberta united with Maudesville, its sister town to the west, to celebrate. Everyone would be there: children, parents and grandparents, aunts, uncles and cousins, and friends who only saw each other once a year. No one would miss it; no one would *want* to miss it—no one except Abby Waters. She had no intention of going to the parade or the picnic. Her eye was still swollen and the bruising had spread across her cheek.

The night of the attack had ended in a physical act that had, once again, left Abby violated and emotionally empty. The following days found her home filled with deafening silence, and on the day of the parade, when Jake had left a good three hours before the noon launch, Abby was glad. He would stay away the whole day, go to the Saturday picnic without her and, no doubt, make an excuse for her absence.

In earlier years, she had wished he would just hold her, tell her he was sorry, and never hit her again. But he'd never held her. He'd only pass the blame, making her responsible. He'd say, "If you'd just done as I asked…" or "You made me so mad…" His words would ring in her head for days, magnifying her years of guilt. Jake had never promised it wouldn't happen again. He would just disappear.

Abby had come to welcome his absence.

Taking advantage of being alone, Abby lifted a suitcase from the top shelf in their bedroom closet and began packing her personal things: her clothes, the necessary toiletries, her favourite books, and a few pictures. Her head throbbed and her ribs ached each time she bent over.

At least nothing's broken, she thought with a twisted sense of thankfulness. The swelling in her cheek persisted, however, and her left eye stung each time she blinked. *But the ice helps.* She released a helpless sigh.

Abby glanced at the melting ice cubes in a bowl on the bedside table and, involuntarily, her eyes turned to her wedding picture. She hesitated before picking it up. Her hand went to the image of her husband and tears blurred her vision. *Why did you have to be so cruel, Jake? I loved you so much.*

Placing the picture back on the table, apathy settled over her like a black cloud and she sat on the edge of the bed.

I have hidden the truth for too long, but…

"Jake beats me!"

Abby screamed the words as though her home was filled with a sympathetic audience, as though she had to hear the words to believe they were true.

"My husband beats me."

She repeated her words softly. Although they were therapeutic, Abby fell prostrate on the bed and let loose a gut-wrenching wail as she grieved the death of her marriage. She pounded the pillows with clenched fists, believing the very act itself would release her of any guilt.

Moments passed before short, breathless sighs replaced the frantic sobs.

Jake's always blamed me and I've believed him.

"Maybe before, Jake, but not now—not anymore."

Abby rolled on her back and stared at the ceiling. She yearned for a place void of pain, a place where, even for a moment, she would feel safe.

BE STILL.

Be still and what? Wait for another beating?

Abby knew that voice, or rather she sensed it. In the past, it had been her comfort, her strength, her hope that eventually Jake would stop, that eventually he would love her as a man was supposed to love his wife. But lately, it didn't seem to help. She had fallen into the enemy's trap, and she knew it. Her trust and faith in God as Sovereign Ruler had eroded. She felt her heart hardening, wondering if God really did care.

Stifling a yawn, Abby curled on her side, emotionally and physically spent. She closed her eyes and considered her future.

Can I do this? Should I do this?

Despite the rising doubt, she knew the answer. She had no choice. If she was to survive, she had to leave.

Fortunately, Abby's new life in Thystle Creek had renewed her inner strength. Her long-lost self-confidence had been restored. Her new friends and her position as store manager at Sherwood's Hardware Emporium had supported her growing confidence. She'd begun to like herself, to see herself as a person of worth, someone who could be a trustworthy friend, someone who could inspire others, as Evelyn Sherwood had inspired her. Evelyn had seemed to understand.

Abby lay curled in a fetal position on her husband's side of their bed. And with her last thoughts on her new friendship with Evelyn, Abby drifted into a fitful sleep.

The afternoon sun warmed her face and Abby woke with a start. The clock read 1:18 and Abby panicked. Throwing back a cover she had no memory of pulling over herself, she stood and fought a moment of head rush. She grabbed the suitcase from the bottom of the bed, lifted her jacket from the rack on the back of the bedroom door, and swung her purse to her shoulder. She stopped in front of a potted violet and smiled, admiring its profusion of purple blooms before lifting it from its draining dish. Over the eight months she'd worked at the Emporium, she had managed to keep back $139 from her paycheque and hidden it from Jake for an emergency.

My life has become one long emergency, she thought, shoving the bills into her jacket pocket.

In an act of resignation, she ran her hand down her husband's red plaid jacket.

"You never gave us a chance, Jake. We could've been so happy."

Her hand dropped to her side. She had been very wrong to think he would change, that a new start in Thystle Creek would erase the painful memories and heal the emotional wounds. He'd left her no choice. There was no other way. The abuse had to end. She needed to start a new life away from her husband, far away.

With suitcase in hand, Abby took one last look at the home she was leaving, turned, and shut the door behind her.

2

And the Lord, he it is that doth go before thee;
he will be with thee, he will not fail thee,
neither forsake thee: fear not, neither be dismayed.
DEUTERONOMY 31:8

The mile and a quarter walk to town proved uneventful. No cars passed her, bringing inquisitive stares. No children rushed by on bicycles, racing against the wind. Even the fields were empty.

I guess the whole town's at the picnic, she thought wistfully. *Even farmers.*

Yet the relief of not being seen on her walk to town suppressed her longing to be part of the celebration.

The annual picnic had been planned and talked about for weeks, maybe even months for some. She and Jake had been invited to join "Evelyn Sherwood and Company"—as Evelyn's daughter Lucy had tagged the group who would be gathering for supper when all the festivities were over. The invitation had come as a surprise considering the bad blood between Jake and Rob Adams.

Some people are more forgiving than others.

Abby picked up a dead branch and swished the tall grass as she thought about forgiveness. Jake and Rob had been friends since they were kids, but now they were staunch enemies. Jake had never forgiven Rob for marrying Holly, a girl who Jake had believed would be *his* wife one day.

Always the peacemaker, Rob had tried to repair the damage to their friendship and approached Abby shortly after she had become engaged to Jake.

"What do you think, Abby? Do you and Jake want to get married the same day as Holly and me?" Rob had asked. "It'll be two great weddings the likes of which this town has never seen before. It's sort of like killing two birds with one stone."

Abby stopped abruptly. The dead branch fell from her hand. The double wedding *had* killed two birds with one stone: Rob and Jake's friendship and her marriage. Somehow Abby didn't think those were the two birds Rob had meant to kill.

Kicking at a loose stone, Abby reflected on her husband's infatuation with Holly. Jake had loved Holly through his childhood and teen years, even after Holly had married his best friend, even after she'd given birth to a son.

Even after he married me, Abby thought sadly.

Despite the possibility of playing second fiddle, she'd married Jake, believing one day he would come to love her as much as he'd loved Holly. And she'd even loved him as he nursed a growing hatred for Rob after Holly's death, irrationally blaming Rob.

But reality had a way of blurting out the truth, and the truth found its mark as Abby stood facing the mountains she had come to love: *Have you wished that I was Holly all these years? Is that why you hate me so much, Jake?*

With vision blurred from unshed tears, she scanned the distant mountains and released a determined sigh.

I will be loved someday, Jake Waters. Someone will love me from the depths of his soul, and you will have lost it all. As though feeling her pain and crying for her, somewhere nearby a mourning dove sang its sad melody.

She drank in the surroundings, like a dog frantically lapping a roadside puddle after a failed rabbit chase. The acres of fields meandering to the foothills, the white flowers of northern bedstraw growing wild in the ditches, and the waterfall dropping from Miller's Mountain that, if she lingered, she could hear landing in the creek far below. She smiled, remembering Lucy Douglas sharing that it was on the smooth ledge overlooking Thystle Creek where Wil had kissed her for the first time.

She stood as one stands before unblemished art: breathless, in awe of such beauty. The Rocky Mountains had only been a place on a map, a place where snow never melted at the peaks, a place where cattle grazed in the valleys far below, serenading each other like gallant troubadours. As a young child in grade school, Abby would never have imagined that one day she would stand so close, looking up at such majesty. She inhaled the summer mountain air. It filled her lungs until they pressed against her injured ribs. She winced, screening her eyes from the sun sitting low in the sky. A worrisome glance at her watch revealed the time—3:15.

Abby hastened her steps. *I need to get to the bus depot.*

She had intended to leave while the whole town was at the fairgrounds, but her arrival in town coincided with a throng of people leaving Rosedale Park. She didn't recognize anyone, but she cautiously remained out of sight.

How come everyone's leaving before supper?

Abby remained on the opposite side of the street and worked her way toward the bus depot, fearing the possibility that Jake would show up at any moment.

Two women crossed over and walked in front of her.

"I can't imagine what I'd do if it was my little boy that went missing," one woman whispered, sharing her fears with her friend.

Abby listened.

"They say he's been gone most of the afternoon," the younger of the two women said. "Went down to the water with a man, and the man came back without him. Just left him there, alone, down by the water. Can you imagine?"

"Excuse me." Abby touched the one lady on the shoulder. "Is someone missing?"

The two women turned and looked at Abby. Sunglasses covered Abby's bruised eye, but not her cheek.

"Weren't you at the picnic?" the younger woman asked, staring at the bruises on Abby's face.

"I'm sorry. No, I wasn't." Abby slowed her step to put distance between them, conscious of the woman's stare.

"A young boy is missing," the first woman said. "I think his last name was Anderson, or Andrews… something like that. We're from Maudesville, so we can't be sure of the name. It started with an A. I do know that much."

"Would it be Adams? B.J. Adams?" Abby whispered, afraid to say it louder for fear she would be correct.

"Yes, that's it! Do you know him?"

But the question was put to Abby's back as she raced toward the bus depot. She knew the man the ladies were so quick to criticize had been Jake. She had to get rid of her suitcase; she had to get out of sight.

3

The wise shall inherit glory:
but shame shall be the promotion of fools.
PROVERBS 3:35

The grove of aspen trees just inside the entrance to Rosewood Park provided the perfect place to see and not be seen. Abby headed for them, keeping her head down. She avoided curious stares as she walked contrary to the flow of people leaving the park. The trees loomed ahead and she prayed she would reach them before being recognized.

Safely behind the bushes, Abby strained to listen as children and adults quietly followed the path through the wooded area. Whispers drifted her way.

"Mommy, do you think he fell in the water?"

"Will they find him before dark? I'm afraid of the dark."

"Mommy, why did that man leave the little boy?"

Replies held assurances that the lost child would be found, but Abby wondered if false hope was masking the worry and fear she read on the faces of the mothers. She couldn't help noticing how the last question had been left unanswered, for which she felt a strange sense of relief. Abby didn't want to hear another woman's disgust for her husband's irresponsible and dangerous actions.

Abby fanned away the mosquitoes from her face and checked her watch. 5:20. The sun had dropped behind the trees, but no one seemed to be rushing. Children held hands with their mothers, having left their fathers behind to aid in the search. There was no laughing or shouting out to friends ahead or behind them. No skipping or pushing or teasing. *It's like a funeral procession, but without the casket.* Abby shuddered at the thought.

In desperation, Abby pushed aside branches bursting with new buds and eased her way deeper into the woods.

On the backside of the wooded area, the empty park greeted her and filled her with dread. She knew the reason everyone had left, but despite that, she had wished the park to be full of people. She hoped that everything she'd heard had been a misunderstanding and that B.J. would be found sitting under a tree eating a popsicle. But that was not the case, and as Abby scanned the emptiness before her, she saw three women: Evelyn Sherwood, her daughter Lucy, and Christina Morsman taking shelter in the shade of a large Manitoba maple tree.

"How many hours has it been, Lucy?" Evelyn's question filled the air. With the wind in her favour, Abby didn't need to strain to hear Lucy's reply... and what she heard left her numb.

"A little over four hours, Mom. But don't worry. They'll find him. We've got a lot of men looking."

"But it's getting dark ..."

"I know, and I think we should go home. We can't do anything here and I need to get the baby out of the night air. Why don't we all go to your house, Mom, and wait—"

"No, you go ahead, dear. You're right. You need to get Annie away from the mosquitoes. I want—I *need* to wait here until they find B.J." Evelyn hung her head before continuing. When she did, her anger frightened Abby. "If only Jake had stayed with him! If only he had done what he promised to do. Why would anyone leave a child like that?"

Evelyn raised tear-filled eyes.

"I'm afraid that's something only Jake can answer," Christina responded slowly while Lucy settled Annie in her carriage. "Jake is a troubled young man. You already know that, Evie. What he does and why he does it … I'm not sure it's clear even in his own mind, but his actions raise a lot of questions."

The wind shifted and the voices drifted beyond Abby's hearing. She moved closer, cautious not to be seen, and watched Lucy take her mother's hands. They appeared to be praying as a short, stocky man came bustling across the open field.

"They found him!" the newcomer shouted. "They found him! He's all right. Doc Bailey and Doctor Morsman are with him."

Had the situation been different, Abby would have laughed aloud at the theatrics of this small overweight man. Instead, his news brought Abby to her knees.

"Seems he wandered downriver," the man said. "Slid off one of the embankments and rolled into the underbrush and thistles. Got quite a hit on the head, must have been out when they found him. He's covered with scratches and his left arm may be broken."

Abby cringed at the news and watched as the heavyset man accepted a chair.

"Seems we have another problem, though. Jake Waters has taken quite a thrashing from the young lad's father. Appears he's being held responsible for the boy's dilemma, leastwise that's what Mr. Adams is saying. When I last saw Mr. Waters, it appeared he needed some doctoring, too, but had refused it."

Abby couldn't listen anymore. Stepping backwards, she slipped deeper into the safety of the dense bushes and trees. Jake had done this! She raged against her husband.

Bad enough you beat on me, Jake, but to let that happen to a child …

Fighting off rising nausea, laced with shame and driven by disgust, Abby knew what she had to do, and the threat of her departure from Thystle Creek being discovered by her husband did not impede her.

4

But his [Lot's] wife looked back from behind him,
and she became a pillar of salt.

GENESIS 19:26

Abby never looked back. She couldn't. She feared what she would say—or worse, what Wil and the doctor would do. She just kept walking down the sidewalk, away from Evelyn Sherwood's front door, away from their questioning looks.

Her hand went to her left cheek. Had Doctor Morsman noticed the bruise? She hoped not. She knew she had taken a chance going to Evelyn's, but she'd hoped that the lateness of the evening and the shadows on the front step would mask her face. It had been hard enough going to her house, but to explain her swollen cheek... She shook her head and sighed. That would have been more painful than the bruise itself. But she had to know how B.J. was doing; she had to know before she left town.

Doctor Morsman's words rang fresh in her ears, confirming what she had heard earlier. "B.J.'s fine, Abby. He took quite a tumble down the embankment, but apart from some bruises and a few cuts, he'll be none the worse for wear in a few days." Abby appreciated that neither Wil nor Levi Morsman mentioned her husband's role in the young boy's disappearance.

Abby walked slowly down the path. *Why did you do it, Jake? You ignored your promise to Evelyn that you'd stay with B.J. Were you getting even?*

Abby did not want to believe her husband could be that vindictive, but there had been a history between her husband and the seven-year old, and Jake never forgot. And he never forgave; he had demonstrated his ability to hold grudges many times during their nine years of marriage. This left little hope that Jake would ever forgive the boy for the confrontation he'd endured with B.J.'s father over another incident at the creek earlier that spring.

"What's with you anyway, Jake?" Rob had shouted in Jake's face, poking his chest with an accusing finger. "He's just a kid and you scared the daylights out of him. Did you get some kind of charge out of sneaking up on him like that and then watching him fall into the muck when you scared him? Just because you yanked him out before he sank further doesn't make you a hero."

Jake's grin had infuriated Rob so much that Abby had feared the shouting would turn into a full-fledged brawl right in the middle of the Emporium.

"Back off, Rob. Ain't my fault your kid was horsing around where he shouldn't have been. You need to keep a better eye out and teach him not to be so careless. Kid needs a mother."

At the mention of Holly, Rob had grabbed Jake's shirt and screamed, "If I ever hear of you pulling a stunt like that again, I'll…"

Rob's whole body shook with rage. It had frightened Abby. She knew Rob well, but she had never seen him so angry. She'd stepped in, pleading with him to stop, and he had, but not before letting Jake go and pushing him to the ground. Towering over him, Rob had raised his fist. "I'm warning you, Jake," he'd hissed. "Keep your hands off my boy."

Abby could still hear Rob's threat. She could still see the hatred steaming from her husband's eyes, and she shook her head. No need to wonder what had become of their friendship.

She heaved a sigh as she glanced over her shoulder at the group still gathered in Evelyn's living room. She saw Wil and Lucy laughing, hugging one another, and she thought of her own marriage and her dream that Jake would learn to love her. But not long into their marriage, she'd realized she was in love with a dream, and time had turned that dream into a nightmare.

Her husband had lost control of his anger more times than Abby could have thought possible, and she had been the instrument of his venting. The beatings and ensuing bruises, his accusations, and his withdrawals all went hand in hand. And no one knew. She had managed to keep it a secret back home in Quebec.

Who would have believed me anyway? she thought as she walked away from the Sherwood home. *Certainly not Mom.*

Her mother had encouraged Abby to marry Jake once it was obvious that Rob and Holly were getting married. "He's a fine boy, Abby," her mother had said. "Just a little melancholy, that's all. Nothing a good wife won't fix."

With one last glance over her shoulder at Evelyn's house, Abby realized that despite her mother's opinion, she was now doing the right thing; she was leaving Jake. Shame had prevented her from explaining her predicament to Wil and Levi; she'd led them to believe she was going home for a visit to give Jake a chance to cool off, hoping maybe he would return to Quebec, too.

"What are you doing here?"

A voice startled Abby from behind and a hand yanked her into the shadows of the pine trees in the middle of Evelyn's front lawn.

"Jake! You scared me. I just—"

"Just what?" Jake's grip tightened around her already-bruised forearm. His voice whispered. His eyes threatened.

"You're hurting me, Jake!" Glancing at the front window, Abby took courage from her unseeing friends and yanked her arm free. "I just wanted to see how B.J. was doing. That's all." Abby rubbed her arm. "What are you doing here? Haven't you done enough damage for one day?"

The words were out before she realized what she had said, and she was not prepared for the pain when her husband seized her arm again. This time there was no opportunity to shake free.

"I'm sorry, Jake! I didn't mean that you caused the accident."

She winced as he tightened his hold and it was then that she saw the results of his fight with Rob. Fresh blood oozed from his nose, mixing with the crusty dried blood in the corner of his mouth. His left eye was swollen shut and appeared to need stitches.

"Jake, please, you're hurting me. All I wanted was to see how B.J. was after his accident, and th—that's what it was, Jake, an accident. You didn't cause it and Rob had no right to blame you. B.J. got lost and fell down an embankment, that's all. He just got lost."

Abby struggled to put conviction in her words, which seemed to pacify Jake. His grip lightened somewhat, but he didn't let go.

"Please, Jake. Let's just go. I need to clean those cuts."

With that, Jake released her and pushed her toward his truck, parked in the shadows down the street. Stumbling over tree roots, Abby rubbed her arm and prayed Jake wouldn't notice the missing piece of luggage when they got home.

5

Peace I leave with you, my peace I give unto you:
not as the world giveth, give I unto you.
Let not your heart be troubled, neither let it be afraid.
JOHN 14:27

July 6

Thystle Creek sat nestled between two small mountain ranges in northwestern Alberta and hosted three denominations each Sunday. Churchgoers would either resort to their cars—if distance demanded their use—or enjoy a casual walk to their preferred place of worship.

One such church sat back a hundred feet from the sidewalk, with the parking lot in the front and slightly to the left. Regardless of the season, the parking lot buzzed each Sunday with the noise of children running wild, calling to their best friends or playing catch-me-if-you-can while parents failed helplessly in their attempts to hush them. The pre-service gathering of adults often hovered at the base of the wide, white steps leading to double doors which were always open, weather permitting. A postcard scene, Grant Street Chapel welcomed everyone.

Evelyn Sherwood stood soldier-still at the bottom of the church steps, waiting. Whirlwinds of dust spun loosely around her feet as she glanced up at the grey, menacing clouds.

There's a summer storm coming, she thought briefly, then turned her thoughts to her own stormy dilemma.

With each passing moment, overwhelming anxiety threatened to break her resolve to join her family for Sunday morning worship. Memories surfaced of her only other church attendance, on the previous Christmas Eve, and her desire to repeat that early departure was far too tempting. But then she remembered the comfort she'd felt as she heard Levi's voice singing in the pew behind her and the encouraging smile from his mother, Christina. Evelyn almost laughed, remembering Mae Smytheson's boisterous greeting as her neighbour declared in disbelief, "Well, I'll be! I'd never have thought…Evelyn Sherwood in church… my, my." She recalled the friendliness Helen Broughton had shown her and their ensuing visit over a cup of coffee. Was that just seven months ago? So much had happened since then. These memories helped abate her growing fears, although the lateness of Lucy and Wil with little Annie aggravated her attempt at calmness.

Evelyn relived the memory of meeting her son for the first time—the young man she had called "friend" for over eight months. Rob Adams had come to Thystle Creek, and into her life, as a stranger—a widower with a little boy, both needing to start over. There had been an instant connection. Looking back on her early encounter with Rob, Evelyn could not put into words what it was that drew her to him. In a very short time, she had come to adore his son, B.J., and she saw in Rob strength of character, the likes of which any mother would be proud. The moment—the incredibly terrifying yet amazing moment—when Rob became aware of *who* she was filled her with such wonder that she knew it would live in her heart forever, as would Rob's face as she watched his eyes fill with tears of disbelief.

"You're…my…"

"…birth mother? Yes. I gave birth to you and hid it from the world, including my parents, my husband and my daughter.

"Rob, I have carried your birth deep in my heart, behind a very high wall. But I wasn't ashamed of you. You are an extension of my first love."

Evelyn stared past the growing crowd at the base of the church, lost in the memory of her son's words.

"I've never held any resentment against an unknown woman for giving me up. I have to admit, though, that I've often wondered what she was like, especially after I became a parent myself. But I've come to realize that no matter what happens around us, God is in complete control and He will work things out according to His own pleasure."

She marvelled at his wisdom and felt her chest swell with pride at being able to call him her son.

Then there had been the call to her father, but before Evelyn could dwell further on the broken silence of twenty-five years, a familiar red truck pulled up at the far end of the church parking lot, distracting her. She watched Abby open the driver's door, pause, then turn and hurry toward town.

Now that's strange. I wonder where…

"Hi, Mom. Sorry we're late—and of all days!"

Lucy's arrival distracted Evelyn and removed any apprehension she had been feeling about attending church. She linked arms with her daughter and smiled up at Annie snuggled in Wil's arms.

As the threesome moved up the steps, Evelyn turned her head toward the red truck. "Isn't that Jake and Abby's truck over there by the grove of trees?"

Lucy glanced across the parking lot as she made her way to the church's front door. "Yep. That's theirs, all right. It's normal for Abby to come by herself. Jake never comes. She must be here somewhere. Maybe she's inside already."

"No, she's not," Evelyn said. "She drove up moments before you got here, parked the truck, and then walked toward town."

"Really? Hmm…that's strange," Lucy said. "Oh well, I'm sure she'll show up eventually. Have you seen Rob and B.J.?"

"No, not yet," Evelyn said, pulling herself away from her concern about Abby. "I couldn't sleep last night and haven't had a chance to talk further with Rob. Did you get any kind of a reaction from him when I was on the phone with my father last night? And my father…oh my goodness, Lucy. There's so much to find out. Our call was very short, but it ended on the promise of another call soon, when it's not so late on his end. But I am concerned about Rob and how he's feeling."

Before Lucy could respond to Evelyn's concern, they arrived in front of the church nursery. Lucy greeted the workers with brief instructions regarding Annie's bottle, reminding them that she was a nursing mom and to hold back on the bottle, if possible. She kissed Annie, passed her to Katie Woodford, and watched as the young teen handed her to Jane Proctor. Then she wisely moved out of sight of her daughter.

Moms and dads waiting to pass their children into the protective care of the likes of Katie and Jane bumped into Evelyn and extended polite apologies. Children ran carefree on their way to their cherished teachers' Sunday School classes, oblivious to Evelyn's growing panic. Greetings from strangers and smiles from familiar but nameless faces added to her increasing and all-too-familiar desire to escape behind her protective wall. But she couldn't, or rather she wouldn't. She had awakened early in the morning with a new determination, a new desire to see life differently. She knew it wouldn't be easy. She knew she would take backward steps before being able to face all that the future demanded of her, but she had her daughter to think about, and now a son and grandson as well.

6

But my God shall supply all your need
according to his riches in glory by Christ Jesus.
PHILIPPIANS 4:19

Abby had seen Evelyn Sherwood standing by the church stairs, and for a brief moment—a *very* brief moment—she thought it strange. When Evelyn looked right at her, Abby knew she had to get out of sight. Yet children's laughter gave pause to Abby's hasty departure, and she chanced a quick glance over her shoulder.

Ruth Morton stood talking with Bessie Cribbs, who was struggling with a restless toddler. Another child clung to her skirt, playing peek-a-boo with Ruth.

It's like a big, happy family, Abby thought, and she knew she would miss it terribly.

Warm and inviting, the service always encouraged her. Pastor Cribbs seemed to understand her needs without ever being told. His gentle demeanour and tactful humour never failed to relax her despite the anxiety she sometimes felt in coming to church without her husband. And Pastor Cribbs never missed an opportunity to point out the need for Jesus in people's lives.

If only Jake had come.

For a moment, Abby squeezed her eyes shut, as though to block out the pain and failure of her marriage, then turned and headed for the bus depot.

With her emotions riding high, her thoughts turned to Lucy and Wil. Lucy had introduced her to Evelyn, and although Evelyn never attended church, that never seemed to inhibit their friendship. *She always had time for me. She seemed to understand. I know she must wonder why I didn't go to the picnic yesterday.*

"Hey, Abby, aren't you heading the wrong way?"

Jim Broughton's voice startled her. She stumbled over a crack in the sidewalk.

"Careful, there. You all right?"

Abby waved to Jim and Helen from across the road. "I'm okay, Jim. Thanks. I'm just on a quick errand."

Acknowledging their smiles, Abby pressed on, head down. Tears filled her eyes and she walked faster, fearing another chance meeting. As though to emphasize her fears, a car horn honked and Abby waved, realizing she didn't even know the names of the two women smiling at her as they drove past in the opposite direction.

Crossing Grant Street, she turned into Rosewood Park, glad to be out of sight from further inquisitive eyes. In an attempt to block out yesterday's failed departure, she focused on her immediate concern: the amount of money she'd left with her luggage in a bus station locker and how much of it she should spend. She had no idea where to go or how long the money would last.

Fear for her future and rage at her husband mingled as she relived the fight three days earlier. She had just wanted to see her mother for a few weeks! She gave in to the tears as they emptied onto her face.

I should never have questioned Jake. I should've known he would take my pleading as a challenge. Abby leaned against a tree. Instinctively, she rubbed her ribs, glad nothing had been broken.

The quietness of Rosewood Park magnified another painful memory, one more terrifying than the fight that had led to her black eye and bruised face. She pressed her hands to her ears, hoping to bury the memory deep into her subconscious, but a barrage of words continued to shout in her head. Abby trembled, remembering how her altercation with Jake in front of Evelyn's house had escalated into the morning hours when Jake had discovered the missing suitcase.

Images flashed before her and Abby quickened her steps, as though running would help her escape the memory. The images fuelled her anger and intensified her need to escape, to survive, but one look at her hands and her courage evaporated. Dried blood circled her fingers and filled the creases on her hands; despite her efforts, she'd failed to rub them clean. She needed water.

Panic filled her at the thought of being discovered in this state. She had to find a washroom!

Abby broke into a full run. She needed to get to the bus depot, she needed to get the next bus, she needed to get out of town in a hurry.

7

Peace, peace to him that is far off, and to him that is near,
saith the Lord; and I will heal him.
Isaiah 57:19

Sidestepping the growing crowd of moms and dads, Evelyn followed Lucy through the nursery corridor en route to the main auditorium.

"Will she be all right?" Evelyn glanced over her shoulder and watched an older woman snuggle Annie in her arms, cooing softly to the three-week-old infant.

"She'll be fine. Jane Proctor's a grandmother and has spent years looking after babies," Lucy said. "Besides, she's a retired paediatric nurse and has an amazing gift for settling new babies on their first visit. This is Annie's second visit, so she's an old pro at being separated from her source of food." Lucy laughed and looped her mother's arm in hers. "Honestly, Mom, she'll be fine. If there *is* a problem—and, no, there probably won't be, so take that look off your face—an usher will come and get me and I'll slip out to see what's up. Does that make you feel better?"

Evelyn shrugged and shook her head. The noise had crescendoed as people hustled past her and little children dodged the forest of adult legs. But turning Annie over to a stranger and walking away…the whole idea seemed preposterous.

"You were asking how Rob feels." Lucy's voice again broke through Evelyn's worried thoughts. "You don't need to worry about him! He's ecstatic. He has so many questions. I promised him we would all get together after service today. I've got a roast in the oven and I've invited Lee and Christina to join us. Hope that's okay. Rob's overwhelmed with the news that you are his birth mother and desperately wants to hear more from you. Trust me, he's thrilled. And to think little B.J. gets a new grandmother in the deal! And I have a brother, and a nephew—and a grandfather!" Lucy added, clasping her mother's arm.

A tap on her shoulder ended Evelyn's worried thoughts as she turned to receive a warm hug from Christina.

"How are you feeling?" Christina held Evelyn's hands and smiled sympathetically. "You must be a little overwhelmed, with all that has happened in the last twenty-four hours. Have you seen Rob and B.J. yet?" She squeezed Evelyn's hands before releasing them.

"No, not yet. I'm wondering if they'll even be here, what with B.J.'s injuries. I'd not be surprised if... what?"

Evelyn felt a hug from behind and turned to find B.J. smiling up at her.

"Well, hello there. We were just talking about you. How's that arm of yours?" Evelyn cupped her grandson's chin. "Looks pretty good to me."

"Oh, it's okay," B.J. said. "I'm glad it's not broken. Baseball starts next Saturday and I want to be part of the team. Can't look like a crybaby."

Evelyn smiled at his courage. She bent down to face the youngster at eye level. "Of course you don't, but I doubt very much the other boys would think you were a crybaby. I think they would see you as..." Evelyn hesitated. "...brave. You might even be their hero!"

B.J. cocked his head to one side. "You think so? Never thought of that. But I still wanna play ball."

"We'll have to wait and see," Rob Adams said, tousling B.J.'s hair. His soft voice brought Evelyn upright. "I think Doctor Morsman might have something to say about that, big guy." He winked at his son before turning to Evelyn. "Good morning, Evie... I mean, *Mother*." Rob leaned forward and kissed Evelyn on the cheek. "That has a nice sound, don't you think?"

"Yes, it certainly does, *brother!*" Lucy said with a smile. She eased an arm around her mother. "I like having a brother, and when Mom gets her breath, I'm sure she'll agree." She hugged her mother's waist. "But right now we need to find a seat before we end up sitting in the foyer."

Evelyn smiled at Rob as the small group, increased by two when her son-in-law and Levi Morsman joined them, walked into the main auditorium and found seats much closer to the front than Evelyn would have liked.

"Do we have to go so far in?" Evelyn whispered.

Before Lucy could respond, the organ began playing and Evelyn found herself reluctantly following Lucy into a pew just four rows from the front. A lady in the pew behind them leaned forward and welcomed her with a tap on her shoulder and a gentle smile. Evelyn recognized her as the grandmother of a youngster that attended *Just Evie*, Evelyn's story hour at the library on Thursday afternoons.

It was then that Evelyn caught sight of her neighbour, Mae Smytheson, who appeared to be in shock as she acknowledged Evelyn's slight nod. A woman well into her seventies, Mae had a well-deserved reputation for knowing everyone's business in town and having no problem sharing it with a willing listener.

"Here we go again," Lucy whispered into her ear. "Mae's going to have a free-for-all with this. Wish I could be a fly on the wall when she gets home to tell Charlie." There wasn't a person in town who didn't pity Charlie Smytheson and marvel at the number of years he'd managed to live with a wife who had more interest in other people's affairs than her own.

"Maybe he'll just turn off his hearing aid," Evelyn whispered back.

Lucy snickered and muffled her laugh in her mother's shoulder. "Hang in there, Mom. You'll be just fine with or without Mae's approval."

As the organ played, Evelyn suddenly remembered Abby. She scanned the front rows for her familiar face, but Abby was nowhere to be seen.

She's probably sitting behind me, Evelyn concluded. *Almost everyone else is!*

Her concern for her young friend diminished somewhat as a familiar voice caught her attention from the front. It was Wil. Why was he standing behind the podium? Lucy greeted her questioning look with a smile just as Wil invited the congregation to open their hymnals. Evelyn sheepishly accepted a burgundy-coloured book from her daughter.

The soothing music had the same effect on Evelyn as she'd experienced on Christmas Eve; it relaxed her despite the strangeness of her surroundings. Sitting to her left, Levi's voice once again could be heard in full harmony with the songs.

He's so unlike Louie, Evelyn thought as she remembered how her late husband had mimicked singers with all the gusto of a cat with its tail caught in a door. She almost laughed aloud, and then was sobered with a startling thought: *Why am I always comparing those two?*

To distract herself from such unsettled feelings, Evelyn focused on the words in the hymnal.

"What a friend we have in Jesus…"

She listened more from curiosity than a desire to understand, until she heard, "Oh, what needless pain we bear."

Needless pain! Is that what I've experienced all these years?

The distraction proved more disturbing than her previous thoughts of her husband and Levi.

Evelyn struggled as the long-silent voice surfaced.

You've carried this pain because of them!

Evelyn quivered and struggled as nauseous bile rose in her throat. Despite the argument put in her defense and the logic it seemed to suggest, she felt shame and regret. Painful memories of her life with Lewis rose before her as though on a screen for everyone to see. Memory after painful memory surfaced as she glanced in either direction for an escape. But there was none. She was too far from the end of the row. She was trapped.

BE STILL.

Evelyn turned slightly. No one was watching her. *Everyone's singing.*

I AM THAT I AM.

There it is again!

It was as though a gentle breeze brushed by her ear, or someone whispered a soft hush. Evelyn could not discern the words; there were no words to discern—just a feeling. She closed her eyes and breathed deeply. Her racing heart began to slow down and her hands no longer gripped the book as though it was a lifeline. She took a deeper sigh. Unexplainable calm filled her, and when she opened her eyes Cameron Cribbs stood before the congregation.

8

Now faith is the substance of things hoped for,
the evidence of things not seen.
Hebrews 11:1

An unassuming man in his mid-forties, Pastor Cribbs placed his Bible on the podium, scanned the crowd, and smiled. Evelyn watched the faces of those around her, and recognized, perhaps felt, the respect and love of his congregation. An unusual quietness filled the room; no one wanted to miss a word.

"Miguel de Unamuno once said, 'Those who believe that they believe in God, but without passion in their hearts, without anguish in mind, without uncertainty, without doubt, without an element of despair even in their consolation, believe only in the God idea, not God Himself.' Thought-provoking, isn't it? Where do you fit in? Are you a believer in God Himself? Or do you struggle with the faith one needs to believe in the God of these Scriptures?" He leaned his elbows on the podium and held his unopened Bible in his hands as he scanned the audience once again.

Stepping to the side of the podium, he held up a small jar of yellow seeds and dramatically quoted, "*If ye had faith as a grain of mustard seed, ye might say unto this sycamine tree, Be thou plucked up by the root, and be thou planted in the sea; and it should obey you.*"

Evelyn watched as the energetic pastor plucked an imaginary tree from one side of the podium and presumably planted it on the other side. Had she not sensed the seriousness of what he was saying, she might have thought his antics comical. Rather, she marvelled at the alertness of those surrounding her. Even Mae sat entranced, captivated by what she saw and heard.

Evelyn couldn't begin to understand what he was talking about, and as though aware of her confusion, Pastor Cribbs explained himself.

"Another way of saying this is that even if the amount of your faith is as small as this mustard seed," he held the jar above his head, "or a poppy seed—and we all know how small they are!—you can say to a mulberry tree, 'Go jump in the lake,' and it would do just that."

The congregation snickered. Evelyn watched, amazed at such a response.

"Now that I've got your attention, let's talk about faith," the enthusiastic pastor continued.

Evelyn listened as the rustling and quiet laughter ceased.

"You and I practise some kind of faith everyday and think nothing of it. You have faith to believe that your cars will bring you safely to church and I have faith to believe that you will come! You put a special kind of faith into practise when you believe I won't be long-winded, and I am trusting you'll stay awake just in case I am." The father of three teenagers and a toddler, smiled as he looked over his congregation. Evelyn noted how relaxed he was. "Nothing dramatic. Nothing profound. Just a simple faith we apply to our everyday life. Not the kind of faith that will allow us to transplant a tree on demand!"

Evelyn sat transfixed, listening to every word. Despite her lack of understanding, she found Pastor Cribbs's analogy and simple approach to the Bible fascinating. His warm, non-threatening voice held her attention. She watched him settle himself in front of the pulpit before continuing.

"In Hebrews 11, in the first verse, we read about another kind of faith: 'Now faith is the substance of things hoped for, the evidence of things not seen.' Another way of saying that is, faith is being sure of what we hope for and certain of what we do not see. Think about your Sunday dinner. You have faith to *believe* that the roast is cooking, even when you don't *see* the heat waves that cook it. Correct? But Hebrews 11 is not talking about the kind of faith we have when we hope our ovens won't fail us and our dinners will be ready when we get home."

He smiled and looked across the congregation.

"It's talking about a life-changing faith. A faith we receive only from God, not something we muster up within ourselves. It's a faith that allows us to believe the first words of this book—'*In the beginning God created the heaven and the earth*'—though we never saw the heavens formed. This God-given faith allows us to believe God's promise of a home in heaven, though we have never seen what heaven looks like. It allows us to believe in God's pardoning mercy, although there is nothing we can do to obtain it."

He tarried before continuing and Evelyn breathed out, not realizing she'd been holding her breath.

"These things are written in the Bible, but can we believe the Bible? More specifically, is this God-given faith enough to *trust* God's word? Folks, faith is a gift nurtured by the Holy Spirit. Trust is an action to substantiate the measure of that faith. Simply put, *faith* is believing that God is who He says He is and *trust* is the evidence of our belief that He will do what He says He will do."

Evelyn squirmed slightly, remembering the words Rob had shared the night before when he'd talked about B.J.'s accident and Holly's death: "I could have blamed God for Holly's death, even cursed Him, but both Holly and I had come to accept that He is sovereign and there's nothing so sweet in life than to trust Him for everything that touches you." Why she remembered his remarks, she could not fathom. They had just stuck in her head.

And now here she sat, listening to her first sermon, which happened to be about the very thing Rob had spoken of!

The depth and challenge of Pastor Cribbs's message increased and Evelyn felt overloaded, especially when she anticipated the upcoming interrogation from her daughter. She smiled inwardly.

Lucy cares so much. And so does Levi. No doubt he'll be wondering if I have any questions.

The morning ended with a return to the nursery to "rescue Annie from strangers," as Evelyn had quipped on the way up the church aisle. In the front foyer, Wil and Lucy's friends greeted Evelyn, having never met her before. She shook hands with spouses, grandparents, and newlyweds. Children smiled at her and she warmly greeted three teenage girls she had seen at the library just before school had ended for the season. She politely acknowledged an invitation to join a ladies Bible study—feeling more than overwhelmed by the idea—and graciously accepted a second invitation for tea from Helen Broughton. And then, of course, there was Mae Smytheson. Evelyn smiled at the prospects of a Monday morning visit from her inquisitive neighbour.

Overall, the morning had been nothing like her previous visit to Grant Street Chapel. She had actually stayed for the whole service, despite the unsettling questions that had surfaced.

9

When thou passest through the waters, I will be with thee;
and through the rivers, they shall not overflow thee.

Isaiah 43:2

Evelyn stood at the top of the stairs near the chapel doors and stared. The truck was still there and Abby was nowhere to be seen.

"Hi, Evie. About our get-together, how does next Wednesday sound?" Helen Broughton followed Evelyn's stare and saw the red truck. "Now, that's strange. We saw Abby walking toward town just before church. She said she was on a quick errand but would see us later, in church."

"An errand?" Evelyn's concern doubled and was soon picked up by her friend.

"Yes, I remember she waved to us after tripping on the pavement. I assumed she would do what needed doing and we would see her later, even if it meant being late for church. I never thought anything of it, but now that I see the truck and don't see Abby, I'm beginning to wonder where she was going, and where she is now."

Helen Broughton's remarks fuelled Evelyn's concern. She was about to walk down the stairs toward the truck when Levi met up with her.

"How're you feeling, Evie?" Levi asked, joining Evelyn on the church steps. "Overwhelmed? Ready to bolt like a deer caught in headlights? Evie?"

"Oh, sorry, Lee. I was just looking for Abby. Seems she was seen earlier today by the Broughtons." Evelyn nodded toward Helen, who had joined her husband. "They saw Abby walking away from the church toward town. Said she had an errand. I can't help but feel something's wrong. Would you walk over to the truck with me?"

"At your service, Madam." Levi bowed, teasing, but quickly changed his expression when he saw the look of concern on her face. "I'm sure everything's okay, but let's take a look."

Hesitating, Evelyn allowed Levi to hook her arm in his. She looked around to see if anyone had observed his affectionate behaviour, and locked eyes with Mae Smytheson. Evelyn cringed, thinking of the gossip that was no doubt going through her neighbour's head.

Levi nodded discreetly in Mae's direction. "Don't pay attention to her. If she wasn't talking about you, it would be someone else. Maybe even me." Levi grinned and clutched her arm in his.

The sun shone brightly in the noon sky, and despite the shade the trees provided, the truck shimmered with heat waves. They found the windows up and only the passenger door locked.

"Strange," Levi mumbled. "Why not lock both doors?"

Evelyn stood back, waiting while Levi opened the driver's door and looked in. He immediately turned and his face revealed the worry Evelyn had been experiencing most of the morning.

"Evie, there's blood on the steering wheel and the seat. Either Abby's injured or…I'm going to drive out to the farm." Levi peered across the parking lot and spotted Ruth Morton. "Ruth!" he called, signalling for her to come over.

Ruth owned the local strawberry farm outside of town, and when Abby and Jake had arrived in Thystle Creek needing a place to live, she had offered them the use of a small shack usually reserved for seasonal workers. In her early sixties, Ruth worked hard to maintain the business she and her late husband had started over thirty years ago when they moved to central Alberta, bringing with them one hundred strawberry plants and a lot of ambition. After Stanley Morton had succumbed to a rare kidney disease twelve years earlier, she'd hoped Jake would be a good asset come strawberry season. But his apathetic behaviour did not make him a "winner, in my eyes," as Ruth had shared with Levi not long after the young couple moved in.

"Hi, Levi, Evelyn. What's up? You both look way too serious for such a beautiful summer day." Ruth nudged Evelyn's arm endearingly, bringing a smile to Evelyn's face despite her inner turmoil.

"Ruth, have you seen Abby or Jake lately?" Levi asked, putting an end to the small talk.

"No, but they were at the picnic yesterday, weren't they?" Ruth paused before continuing. "Come to think of it, I only saw Jake." Her eyes darkened. "I saw Abby earlier this week. She was working in her little flower garden, the one out front. She's always trying so hard to make that little shack homey for Jake—although he never seems to notice." Another pause with a look of disdain. "We chatted for a bit and she told me how much she was looking forward to going on Saturday. First picnic and parade for her here in TC."

Ruth's casual abbreviation of her hometown would often bring a smile, whether one was hearing it for the first time or had heard it for many years. It was her trademark and no one questioned it.

There was no smile today.

Ruth frowned and Evelyn grew more uneasy. "I didn't see Abby in church today. Why is Jake's truck here?"

"I think there's been some kind of an accident," Levi said. "There's blood in the truck. Not a lot, but enough to warrant a drive out to their place to see if someone's been hurt." He turned to Evelyn. "Please apologize to Lucy for me. I may or may not make it for lunch. Oh, and if you see Doc Bailey, have him meet me there, would you? Ruth, are you planning on heading home now?"

"Why, yes I am. Do you need me to do something?"

"No. I just wanted to be sure someone was around, just in case..." Levi left his thoughts hanging. "Evie, don't look so worried. I'm sure everything's fine. I'll come over to Lucy's for coffee and dessert, I promise."

With that, Levi hurried toward his car. Evelyn noticed he kept his head down, avoiding the small group of onlookers that had gathered.

Evelyn turned toward the church and joined her daughter after an anxious look over her shoulder at the empty truck.

10

And the King shall answer and say unto them,
Verily I say unto you, Inasmuch as ye have done it
unto one of the least of these my brethren,
ye have done it unto me.

MATTHEW 25:40

The shack sat a hundred yards from the main house. Ruth Morton's husband had built the small living quarters hoping to encourage his migrant workers to stay on and learn a second trade after the short strawberry season ended.

Levi approached the blue-shingled shack, uncertain of what he would find within. The curtains were drawn and there was no sound coming from inside the small home. Despite the ominous feeling which was growing by the moment, a gentle smile crossed his face when he noticed the array of flowers planted under the front window.

Definitely Evie's handiwork.

He warmed at the thought of Evelyn and how his feelings for this strange and mysterious woman had captivated him so completely whereas all the other women in his past had failed miserably. *Except Leah*, he thought sadly, and for a brief moment he was a twenty-three-year-old med student in Toronto again.

His thoughts ended abruptly when he noticed the loose gravel scattered across the mat at the front door and the deep tire marks embedded on the gravel driveway.

Looks like Abby left in a hurry, he thought as he raised his hand to knock on the screen door.

Hearing no answer, he opened it, barely catching the door as it fell toward him, thankful that the bottom hinge remained attached to the doorframe.

"I wonder how long that's been broken," he thought aloud as he lifted the door back into its frame. Glancing back at Ruth, he remembered their earlier conversation about Jake's indifference, bordering on indolence. He shook his head, fighting off a feeling of disgust. He carefully held the screen, knocked on the inside door with his free hand, and waited.

He knocked again. "Abby? Jake?"

Ruth stood quietly to the side. "Maybe no one's home, Levi."

Levi pounded harder and hollered, "Jake! Abby!" He tried the doorknob. The door was unlocked.

Opening it slowly to preserve their privacy, Levi called again. "Abby, it's Doctor Morsman. Jake, are you here? Anyone?"

Having tagged along with Evelyn when she'd delivered some transplants from her garden earlier that month, Levi knew the layout of the shack. Abby had been excited to host two of her favourite people. Her words had been full of enthusiasm and delight, yet they had soured slightly as she'd apologized for Jake's absence. Levi had noted her choice of words and her hesitation in explaining Jake's hasty departure when they arrived, but he'd put his thoughts aside to enjoy the genuine excitement their visit had generated as Abby proceeded to give them a tour of her "little piece of heaven."

The shack only had four rooms. A bright kitchen with a spacious window over the sink faced west, overlooking the strawberry field and mountains in the distance. Floral wallpaper covered the walls and provided a cheerful setting for the small table and four chairs nestled in an alcove opposite the counter and window. The living room hosted a worn but clean sofa covered with an afghan Evelyn had given as a house-warming gift.

There was a blue plush swivel chair with a rip on the left side of the arm, and a television sat under extended rabbit ears, facing a well-used wood-burning stove. The curtainless bay window provided a natural ledge to display an array of African violets in assorted sizes and in various stages of profusion. Through a process of deduction, Levi concluded that the remaining two closed doors led to a bedroom and a bathroom.

Levi moved quietly through the living room, then stopped abruptly. "Ruth! Come in here!"

Jake lay on the floor in front of the sofa, his head resting in a pool of blood. He was unconscious.

Ruth's hands flew to her mouth. "Oh my goodness! Is he alive?"

"Yes, but his pulse is very weak. You need to call for the ambulance."

Before Ruth could turn, Levi grabbed her arm. "No! Wait! The ambulance transported Mrs. Hooper to Edmonton late this morning for her surgery. It won't be back yet."

He shook his head, frustrated at the inadequacies of the small town yet grateful that the small hospital servicing the surrounding communities was in Thystle Creek.

"Ruth, call Doc Bailey. If you can't reach him, drive to town and get him. I can't assume Evelyn found him after church and I can't move Jake alone. You need to hurry. I don't know how long he's been lying here, or if he has any internal injuries."

Ruth stumbled toward the door, her ears barely registering a muffled crunch of gravel as tires rolled over the driveway.

She didn't need to go to town to find Allen Bailey. His car had just stopped in front of the shack.

PART
TWO

11

I will praise thee; for I am fearfully and wonderfully made:
marvellous are thy works; and that my soul knoweth right well.

PSALM 139:14

August 2

J ake just lies in a darkened room, oblivious to the noise around him," Levi said. He and Christina had joined Evelyn for Saturday morning brunch in Evelyn's kitchen. "It's been almost four weeks since Doc and I rushed him to Edmonton."

Evelyn put fresh muffins on the table, momentarily distracting the three from their concern for Jake Waters.

"You can sure spoil someone with this kind of baking, Evie. No wonder my mother moved back to Thystle Creek! She still talks about her first visit, you know, and how she slurped her tea and embarrassed you." Levi reached for a warm muffin and winked at his mother.

"Hush!" Christina scolded. "What kind of a son tells tales about his mother? Shame on you. Don't listen to him, Evie. He's just trying to make trouble."

Evelyn welcomed the light-heartedness, as did Trickster, who had unearthed her favourite squeaky toy from beneath her blanket and dropped it at Levi's feet. Evelyn smiled as Levi threw the dog's toy into the hall.

Levi bit into the butter-soaked muffin and gave a thumbs-up to Evelyn. "How Jake survived that drive to Edmonton is beyond me, but Doc and I knew time was critical. As it turned out, we were right on the money. Jake had to have immediate surgery to ease the pressure on his brain. The surgery certainly saved his life, but he's still in a coma with no prognosis, either way. Time and patience will tell the story. It's a wait-and-see situation."

"How long can he stay in a coma without damage?" Christina asked as she toyed with the folded newspaper the trio had been reading moments earlier. The headline—*Neil Armstrong Lands on the Moon!*—faced her as she stretched her hands over the newsprint.

"That's a very good question, Mother, but I'm afraid I'm not qualified to give a good answer. Only a neurosurgeon can do that. However, I will say that the longer he's in a coma, the harder it will be for him to come out of it. But that's just a guess, and a poor one at that. Having said that, doctors have been known to sometimes offer pride-filled opinions, only to be countered by the Great Physician." Levi glanced at the folded newspaper. "You know, we can put a man on the moon 238,857 miles from earth, but when it comes to the human body, we are baffled."

Both women looked at one another and then stared at Levi, their expressions revealing their disbelief at what Levi had just declared with such ease.

"So, I'm detail-oriented." Levi smiled defensively. "I remember trivia." He paused, challenged by the sceptical look on Evelyn's face. "Besides, it was in the paper last week."

Levi continued on a more sober note as the women listened silently.

"Jake's injury could have been fatal had we been much longer getting him to Edmonton. From what we could piece together, when he fell backward toward the wood stove—that's where we found the blood—he turned slightly, probably in an attempt to avoid hitting it, but in doing so he inadvertently made a bad choice. When Ruth and I found him, it appeared he had come to, walked, or maybe crawled, to the sofa and sat for a few minutes. We found him on the floor in front of the sofa, and, as you know, he was unconscious."

Levi took a swallow of coffee.

"As awful as it sounds, it's a good thing he came to. In medical terminology, it's called a lucid interval, a period of consciousness before a coma returns. In cases of traumatic brain injuries resulting in a blood clot at the covering of the brain, the prognosis is better if the patient comes to rather than staying in a constant comatose state." Levi rubbed his fingers on a spot on his head just above the ear. "Jake hit his head right here."

Instinctively, Evelyn placed her index finger on the spot. "Isn't that the temple?"

"Not quite. A little further back." Levi reached over to Evelyn's head and placed his fingers on the correct spot. "Right here. An artery that runs beneath this spot is vulnerable to injury because this is the weakest part of the skull. Jake's injury resulted in an epidural hematoma, but fortunately time was on his side. The surgery proved successful, other than the fact that he's still in a coma. But he's breathing on his own. That's a really good sign that there's no underlying cause for the coma. If that's true, he should have no lasting effects once it ends."

"Whew! I feel like I've just sat in on a brain surgeon's lecture," Christina teased her son.

Evelyn smiled. "Have you been given any encouraging information?"

"I'm heading to Edmonton in the morning. I need to meet with the neurosurgeon who operated on Jake to get a full report. Hopefully, I'll bring home some good news."

"Is there any word about Abby?" Evelyn asked, changing the subject yet feeling a heavy sense of foreboding.

"No. It seems she's just disappeared. The police contacted her mother in Quebec, who said she hasn't seen Abby since she and Jake left for the West last October. Unfortunately, her prolonged absence has made her a suspect. At least, that's the buzz around town."

Christiana sat up straight, clattering her cup as she placed it in the saucer. "Nonsense. That wee bit of a thing wouldn't hurt a fly. Why, she brakes for butterflies, for goodness sake."

Levi smiled. "That may be true, Mother, but the police are only dealing with the facts. It looks like Jake's injuries weren't accidental, and Abby *is* missing."

"Well, it will take a lot to convince me she had anything to do with it," Christina said. "Until I hear directly from Abby, I'll never believe she would have done such a thing, unless…"

Evelyn waited for Christina to finish.

Levi broke the silence. "Mother, what do you mean 'unless'?"

"I can't help wondering if there's a piece missing in the proverbial puzzle," Christina said. "There's no question that we've all come to know and love Abby. She's a sweetheart and wants nothing more than to please. Can you honestly believe, even for a moment, that she's capable of harming Jake—unless she was provoked?"

Christina ended her thoughts quickly, as though the idea was unfathomable.

"Christina, do you think Abby did something to Jake in self-defense?" Evelyn spoke the words slowly.

Levi stood and walked to the back door to let Trickster out. The young dog made her way to her designated spot in the backyard, and in a few moments came bounding up the garden path again. Levi ushered her to the towel to dry her feet from the morning dew and reached into the cupboard for a treat.

"Are you suggesting that Abby struck Jake in an effort to protect herself?" Levi asked as he rejoined the women around the table.

Evelyn stood up, agitated. "We know Jake has a temper, Lee. That's a given. But would he hit Abby? Surely if he did, Abby would have said something."

Evelyn wandered aimlessly around the kitchen.

Levi hesitated. "Not necessarily, Evie. Everything I've read on spousal abuse shows that women are ashamed and often feel deserving of the abuse."

"That's ridiculous," Evelyn said. "Abby would never deserve—"

"I'm not saying Abby would ever deserve Jake's abuse, Evie, but it's a documented fact that abused women often live a life of guilt and shame."

Levi's interruption didn't sit well with Evelyn, but she let him continue as she paced in front of the kitchen sink.

"They become masters at hiding the physical evidence," Levi continued. "They may even live a double life rather than reveal what's happening behind closed doors."

Evelyn stopped pacing and turned to face Levi. "They wear a mask."

Her guests stared at each other as Evelyn returned to her chair, Christina reaching for her hand.

"I suppose that would be a good description," Levi said. "An emotional mask would definitely describe what a person uses to hide his or her pain from the world. But as you have experienced, it's quite futile, since the problem never goes away. It just gets covered up and the pain increases in intensity, resulting in further damage. From my personal and professional experience—"

"Please, Levi, must you always be so *professional*?" Evelyn removed her hand from Christina's. "Making those kinds of clinical comments proves you've lived a life absent of such debilitating pain. Yes, emotional masks hide pain, but it's a matter of survival." She glared at Levi. "It's either wear the mask or call it a day. I doubt you've ever experienced the kind of pain that smothers a person, almost chokes them. The kind of pain that's there constantly, that never lets go, that's never resolved. The kind of pain that can only be suppressed. Masks may be futile, Levi, but believe me, they are the lesser of two evils."

Evelyn didn't mean to lash out, but her words cut the air like a knife cuts soft butter. Lost in her own anger, she missed the look exchanged between Levi and his mother.

"I'm sorry, Evie," Levi said, reaching for Evelyn's hand. "You're quite right. I have no right to judge what a person does or doesn't do. Forgive me?"

The phone rang, startling everyone, even Trickster, who had curled up on her mat by the back door. The second ring found Evelyn on her feet, her head down to hide the fierce emotions raging within.

She picked up the receiver.

"B.J., how nice to hear your voice!" she said into the phone. "How's that arm of yours?"

"Doctor Morsman took out my stitches the other day. He says I'm back to normal," she heard B.J. reply. Evelyn smiled, imagining him waving his arm in the air to prove his point.

"That's great news. Did it hurt?" Evelyn asked, casting a cursory eye at Levi, who offered a guarded smile.

"Just a little. It felt like he was pinching me. But I didn't cry!"

"I'm sure you didn't. Would you and your daddy like to come for lunch today? I'll make your favourite sandwich. Grilled cheese, right?"

"Daddy has to go and help Mrs. Morton in the strawberry field. He says it's a busy time of the year for strawberry farmers and she could use his help. He was hoping you'd look after me for the afternoon. So, can I come alone?"

"Of course you can," Evelyn said. "And don't forget to bring your bathing suit. My lawn will need some watering. There's no sense wasting good water from the sprinkler, and I'm quite sure Trickster will join you."

At the sound of her name, Trickster yawned and stretched before ambling over to Evelyn, tail wagging in agreement, as though she understood what was in store for the afternoon.

"Sounds like you're planning a party," Levi jested as Evelyn put down the phone and filled in the blanks from her conversation with her grandson.

"So it would seem."

The tension returned, despite Evelyn's silent offer to top up their mugs.

"Oh, no thank you, dear," Christina said. "I'm afraid I'm well over my limit, and we must be going. We've intruded on your morning long enough."

"Christina, you're never an intrusion. Either of you," Evelyn added, offering a strained look at Levi. "I'm sorry, Lee. My words were hurtful. I'm just…I'm still dealing with my own mask."

"Anyone home?" a familiar voice called from the front door, quickly evaporating any lingering tension.

Christina smiled as Lucy's exuberance filled the room.

"I do believe you have a revolving front door, Evie," Christina joked.

"Making up for lost years," Evelyn responded as Lucy placed Annie in her arms.

Wil came in the door next. "And doing a fine job, I might add," he said with a wink at his mother-in-law.

"Here's your mail, Mom," Lucy said. "It looks like Ernie's getting a head start on his mail delivery. Guess he's trying to beat the heat. It's gonna be a scorcher today."

Evelyn transferred Annie to her other arm, took the stained envelope from her daughter, and placed it on top of the fridge.

"Christina, you must stay for a visit with Lucy and Wil. Besides, it looks like Lee has already decided for you." Evelyn smiled as she watched Levi open the door for Trickster, only this time going out with her, rubber ball in hand.

Relieved that the discussion had moved to simpler and safer subjects, Evelyn sat down to enjoy her daughter and son-in-law, granddaughter, and best friend. There would be no more discussion of masks or secrets or pain. Not today. Today she would enjoy her family, suppressing the gnawing remorse she felt over her angry outburst and her growing fear that there was something terribly wrong in Jake and Abby's home.

12

Hear my prayer, O Lord, and let my cry come unto thee.
Hide not thy face from me in the day when I am in trouble.
PSALM 102:1–2

Pike Ridge, Alberta

August 3

Where is it?" Jake's face burned with rage.

"I—It's getting fixed." Abby stumbled over her words and Jake pounced.

"Fixed! It wasn't broken! Where is it?" He towered over her, clenched fists shaking.

The first blow to her head dazed her. The second and third targeted her arm and back as she cowered to protect herself, and then in a moment of unnatural strength she shoved him.

"Get away from me, Jake! Leave me alone!"

Abby awoke, curled up in a fetal position. Her arms covered her face and head and she was sobbing. The dream had been too real, too exact. Her last encounter with her husband had invaded her subconscious—the one place where she'd felt safe, until now. She could hear Jake's screaming, her pleading, his accusation, her pointless explanation … she smothered her ears with her fists in an effort to drown out his voice. But there was nothing she could do to erase the sound of skin on skin as Jake's hand made contact with her face. Nor could she undo the push that had sent her husband stumbling backward, turning and falling against the corner of the wood-burning stove and dropping to the floor.

Throwing back the covers, Abby lay prostrate on the bed. She tried to pray, but God seemed too remote. Instead, she looked at her surroundings with a feeling of apathy. The sterile motel room offered little comfort. Worn drapes hung loosely at the window, offering the privacy she needed but no relief from the neon sign flashing steadily at night: WIND-IN-THE-PINES MOTEL, DAILY, WEEKLY OR MONTHLY RATES.

Her suitcase lay open on the round table in front of the window where she had dropped it four weeks earlier. The few clothes she had were scattered haphazardly over the nearby chair. A broken drawer sat lopsided in the four-drawer dresser that accommodated a warped mirror. The television sat on a table in the corner opposite the door, but there had been no reception since the day she'd arrived, even though she had mentioned it to the motel owner the very next day. As nice as he was, he'd made no effort to fix the problem and Abby had chosen to say nothing more. The only good thing about her accommodations was her bed—a firm mattress, clean sheets, and a warm blanket for cool evenings.

The receipt for her fourth week's stay lay on her bedside table and she reached over and picked it up. It read *Angie Evans*. Her full name, Angelina Abigail Evans, sounded far more impressive than just *Angie*. Her mother used to tell her she'd read the name in a book while she was carrying Abby and decided it would be the perfect name for a little girl. When Abby had signed for her room four weeks earlier, she had used her abbreviated maiden name. Looking at the receipt now, she realized how foolish her impulsive decision had been. She had made it very easy to be found.

Abby flicked the receipt back onto the table and shrugged with growing indifference when it fell to the floor. She scanned the room. The cobwebs that had greeted her earlier that month were no longer hanging above the doorframe, and she'd made sure no unwelcome visitors lurked beneath the bed or in the darker corners.

Home, sweet home, she thought painfully as she sat up and swung her feet to the floor.

As quickly as the flick of a light switch, Abby felt a wave of heat flush her face and she raced to the bathroom. She heaved into the toilet repeatedly, wiped her nose, and then sat hugging the bowl for several moments before daring to stand. When she did, she regretted the decision and hurled once again from an upright position into the waiting bowl. She carefully moved a towel to the floor and sat down once again, hugging the ceramic form that had suddenly become her new best friend.

Moments passed before Abby realized that whatever caused her disturbing wake-up call had passed. Nevertheless, she stood up gingerly. Moving to the sink, she hung her head close to the tap, bathed her face in cold water, and brushed her teeth to remove the sour taste from her mouth.

She studied her face in the mirror. Dark circles outlined her eyes, and her long brunette hair hung loose and limp over her shoulders and face. She ran her fingers through the tangles in a pointless attempt to loosen the knots.

Memories of her mother's words rang in her head: "Need to get rid of those tangles." In an instant, those long pigtails had disappeared with two snips of her mother's dressmaking shears. Her mother had insisted that the best way to deal with tangles was to cut them off. Abby had cried for days and refused to go to school until her mother promised never to cut her hair again—unless Abby asked her to do so. Abby never did. Her hair had not been cropped to her ears since the eighth grade.

In a flash, Abby made a decision. She'd already determined that to survive her new life, her new existence, she would need to change her looks. She had purchased a bottle of hair colour, which had sat on the bathroom counter for over two weeks; she hadn't had the nerve to use it, not until now. Rooting though her handbag, her hands found the object of her search.

Her manicure scissors were tiny but sharp, and Abby began the onerous task of cutting her hair. With each snip of the scissors, her anger intensified and she blamed Jake.

If he'd been the husband he should have been… snip *…I wouldn't find myself hiding in a motel…* snip *…in a remote town in the mountains…* snip, snip *…waiting on tables…* snip *…hoping no one recognizes me.* One last snip and she stopped.

"But he wasn't the husband I believed he would be, and I *am* here," she concluded, staring at the thin chunks of long hair scattered over the tiled floor and in the bathroom sink.

With new resolve, she reached for the bottle of hair colour.

An hour later, Abby raised her head and stared into the mirror.

Who are you?

She shook her head at the reflection. Running her hands through her hair, she forced back threatening tears. *It could be worse,* she thought, trying to convince herself that it was an improvement.

Instinctively, her hand went to her face and she stroked the ever-present blemishes, flaws Jake callously pointed out all too often. Holly's face flashed before her. She could hear her best friend's laughter and see her natural auburn curls bouncing on her shoulders with each laugh. Freckles covered her perfectly formed face despite her efforts to conceal them. They were her trademark, but Holly had seen them as a thorn in her flesh. Abby smiled, remembering her friend. She missed Holly despite the incurable obsession Jake felt toward her.

Abby lowered her face. She'd never had Holly's beauty or charisma. Her shyness proved more annoying to Jake than attractive, and even though she tried to be the wife she thought Jake wanted, he appeared blind to her efforts. Abby glanced in the mirror long enough to watch her eyes fill and the tears empty onto her face.

Her watch, a permanent fixture on her right wrist, told her she had a little over three hours before the noon shift at the diner. It was her first day at the new job. She crawled back into bed, glad of the thin blanket to help subdue the violent shaking that had invaded her body, and fell asleep.

13

I was not in safety, neither had I rest,
neither was I quiet; yet trouble came.

JOB 3:26

Mid-August

Almost a week passed before Evelyn remembered the envelope on top of her fridge. Her days had been full since her last visit with Levi and Christina. She had not resolved her inner emotions after her outburst, and she felt a twinge of shame whenever she thought of it. Rather than deal with the root cause of the unfortunate scene, she'd busied herself preparing her home for Rob and B.J.'s arrival.

Six days earlier, she had approached Rob with the idea of them living with her until he could find something permanent for himself and B.J. Evelyn had no idea how long their stay would be.

"Evie...Mom," Rob had said, clearing his throat. He had hesitated in the use of Evelyn's maternal title. "B.J. is over the moon about living here, and to think you would want us to stay until we can find our own place seems...well, that's beyond generous."

"Nonsense, Rob. It's August. School doesn't start for another three and a half weeks. B.J. can stay with me while you help Ruth with her

strawberries—which, by the way, goes beyond generous, too." Both
had smiled. "Besides, I need help with my garden, and that son of yours
seems to have grown a green thumb. If not, he's doing a pretty good job
pretending."

Evelyn had leaned forward and whispered, "Personally, I think my
garden is just an excuse for B.J. to play ball with Trickster. Anyway, as far
as I'm concerned, it's a win-win situation, Rob. You and I have a lot of
catching up to do and I need to make up for lost time with my grandson.
You'd be doing me a favour."

Rob had conceded with a hug and a *you-win* smile. "I'll accept, but
you have to let me look after any repairs on the house, cut the grass, and
pay my share of the expenses." He'd given her a wink, accentuating the
dimple in his cheek. "But you can do the gardening."

Warmed by the memory of Rob's conditions, Evelyn poured a glass
of lemonade and, with the neglected envelope in hand, headed for the
garden. Her smile turned to laughter, which sparked Trickster to race
ahead, almost tripping her as they aimed for her favourite spot under the
aspen tree.

"Easy, girl, my hands are full."

With the mild scolding delivered, Evelyn settled in her chair and
opened the mysterious letter while Trickster settled at her feet gnawing
on a stick.

Evelyn stared at the piece of paper in her hand. The envelope had fallen to
the ground, receiving Trickster's immediate attention. She stretched her
nose and chin across the length of the envelope, then flipped on her back
to attack it further. Coming quickly to her feet, she shook her fur coat,
grunted, and returned to her stick.

Evelyn sat quite still, oblivious to Trickster's antics. She raised the
letter from her lap and began reading it again.

Dear Evelyn...Evie,

I feel I must ask you at the beginning of this letter to keep it a secret. Please, don't tell anyone you have received this from me. It's important.

I left Thystle Creek without saying goodbye to you. Yes, I know I spoke with Doctor Morsman and Wil, but it wasn't right that I didn't speak to you, personally... to thank you. Something has happened. I can't come back to Thystle Creek, ever, but I just wanted to thank you for being a good friend to me. You helped me find something I'd lost: my confidence and self-respect. It kind of slipped away without me realizing it was gone. But when I met you, I saw something in you I didn't have. I know you're not a churchgoing person, and I could tell that you had some problems, but I could also tell that you were very caring...you cared about me. I just wanted to thank you for that.

I can't tell you where I am. I might not stay here, but then again, circumstances might make it possible. I have a job and some money saved from working for Josh at the Emporium, so I'm okay for a while. Hope you don't mind me sending this note.

Well, thanks, again.

Abby

"Anyone home?"

Evelyn folded the letter and put it in her apron pocket. "I'm in the garden, Rob. Pour yourself some lemonade and come join me."

Rob reached down and picked up the empty envelope. "Did you drop this?"

"Thanks," Evelyn replied, her heart racing as she folded the envelope and put it in her pocket. "Where's B.J.?"

Her son pulled up a second chair beside Evelyn and stretched his long legs. She smiled as Trickster attacked his shoelaces with killer instinct.

"Go get 'em, Tiger." Rob laughed, swishing his feet back and forth.

He turned to Evelyn and paused, filling the air with an unnatural calm. Evelyn waited. In the months she had known Rob as a friend, she had come to appreciate his frankness and honesty. Somehow she knew the next few minutes would bring a strain on their relationship; after all, they were no longer friends, but mother and son. Seconds stretched into minutes and Rob looked away, watching Trickster yank and pull the laces she'd managed to untie.

"Evie…"

Evelyn greeted her son's smile with a nod. They had an accepted yet unspoken understanding that Rob unintentionally floated back and forth in addressing Evelyn.

"I asked Lucy to entertain B.J. for a couple of hours so we could talk." Rob looked toward the end of the yard. "Those trees are beautiful," he commented absentmindedly, as though needing a distraction from the impending conversation.

"Lewis loved them. He used to stand at the base of them and look up. I'm sure most of the time he was praying—probably for me." She studied her son's face, sensing a struggle within.

"Evie, I'm worried about Abby."

Evelyn sighed, relieved to some degree without understanding why. "In what way?"

"Her absence. No one seems to know where she is and the gossip train in this town is going full steam ahead with all kinds of stories and accusations… she wanted out of the marriage, she had hidden anger issues, she missed the picnic to plan her attack on Jake. Things like that. It makes me furious! People don't even know her, but they've all got an opinion that they have no problem sharing."

Evelyn sat very still, conscious of the letter in her pocket but bound by Abby's request for secrecy.

"Rob, I've lived long enough to know you have no control over what people think or say—"

"That's the whole point. I *can* control what people say! I should be speaking up in her defense, but I don't. That's the problem. I keep silent. I should be reminding people of the kind of person Jake is, how he's treated B.J. in the past, how he's so totally unreliable, and how he seems to be unable, or unwilling, to accept responsibility for what he says or does."

Moments passed. A blue jay screeched its call, only to be echoed by a second one high in the blue spruce.

"I feel as though I'm betraying a friend," Rob continued, his agitation giving way to guilt. "My silence seems to contribute to the accusations, even support them, but the truth is I'm just not sure myself. I'm not sure that she didn't do something to Jake."

He leaned forward, elbows resting on his knees. His fingers stretched open and closed while Evelyn helplessly watched her son struggle with the guilt he had just confessed.

He turned his head sideways and asked, "Has Lee given you any more information on Jake's condition? Is he out of the coma?"

"I don't know. I haven't seen or talked to Levi for a week." Evelyn ignored Rob's raised eyebrows. "I'm quite sure that if his condition had changed, we would have heard by now."

"Probably."

The silence returned until Trickster jerked her head up and raced to the end of the yard, yelping at a small rabbit that barely managed to escape to safety under the fence.

"Think she would have killed it?" Rob asked. He meant Trickster.

"One never knows. She's an animal … she just doesn't know it."

Rob smiled and Evelyn relaxed, glad the tension had been lifted, but realizing that neither one of them had appeased Rob's feeling of guilt.

14

But there is forgiveness with thee, that thou mayest be feared.
I wait for the Lord, my soul doth wait, and in his word do I hope.

PSALM 130:4-5

August 19

N ana, can I play with Trickster in the backyard?"
Evelyn sat, coffee mug in hand, remembering her grandson's request moments earlier. It wasn't just the request; it was what he'd called her. It was a first and she relished in it: *Nana.* She smiled. No cathedral choir could have brought greater sound or pleasure.

My long lost son has a son, and he just called me Nana.

The mid-August sun was slow in drying the dew permeating her garden, but the dampness had not stopped her, and she'd released B.J. and Trickster to run off their early morning energy.

Having Rob and B.J. living with her had provided another strike against the menacing wall that had stood for too many years. *They've helped me see the other side,* she thought.

"I feel blessed," she whispered as she stood at the screen door watching B.J. race around the yard, chasing and hiding from the dog. She loved him and her heart ached with overflowing joy.

Yet, despite the unspeakable pleasure B.J. and Rob were bringing to her life, Evelyn struggled quietly with the guilt of their very existence. *What would Lewis have thought had he known?* The question was permanently engraved in her mind, and it surfaced more insistently each day as she watched her grandson interact with his father and Trickster.

Then her thoughts turned to Levi and their possible future. Her face revealed her inner thoughts: profound happiness mixed with sheer terror.

How could Lee have feelings for me, knowing my past, knowing how I deceived Lewis, knowing how I've lived such a double life?

Don't get your hopes up! You're only kidding yourself.

For the first time in many weeks, the accusing voice evaporated any thoughts of happiness. A portion of the wall surrounding her heart rebuilt itself.

Evelyn set her cup on the table and sought out her journal and the Bible Levi had given her for Christmas. Throughout the few weeks she'd been attending church, she had yet to feel comfortable taking notes but had no problem underlining verses as she listened. Alone in the privacy of her bedroom, she would ponder over what she'd heard and often worry if she remembered Pastor Cribbs's exact words.

Wanting to keep an eye on B.J., Evelyn sat at the small table under the kitchen window and flipped through her coiled journal, pausing at an entry.

> Sunday, July 27, 1969—Neil Armstrong landed on the moon a week ago!

Evelyn smiled at that moment in history before continuing:

> Pastor Cribbs said we are to put our hope in God's Word, that whoever finds God, finds life. How do you do that? He said hope is like taking the first step even though you can't see what's coming next, like walking out of a dark forest or landing on the moon. You know you have to take that first step to get out, so you just put one foot in front of the other and trust, even though you're not

sure where the next step will lead. Makes sense, I suppose. I wonder what Neil Armstrong was thinking when he opened the hatch and took his first step toward the moon's surface. What was it he said?—"That's one small step for man, one giant leap for mankind."

One simple act and the world is changed forever.

With pen in hand, Evelyn watched her grandson race around the garden, hiding from her dog.

One simple act and my *world has changed forever. An infant son I relinquished to another and a grandson I never knew existed are now part of my life.*

Evelyn closed her eyes and sighed at the wonder of such a gift. *I suppose I have to admit my life has changed since I met Christina… and Lee.*

She finally found the current entry and read:

> Pastor Cribbs said, "It's a lot easier to say, 'Don't get
> your hopes up…'"

Her heart quickened as she marvelled at what she had written a few days earlier in contrast to the taunting she'd just heard in her head.

> Pastor Cribbs said, "It's a lot easier to say, 'Don't get
> your hopes up, in case there's disappointment.' Some-
> times we choose our pain rather than risk the possibil-
> ity of having our hopes dashed. It's hard to hope." Can
> I dare hope?

The back door flew open and her grandson's laughter ended the moment. Evelyn smiled and welcomed the distraction, closing her Bible and journal.

"What monster is chasing you two?"

Out of breath, B.J. laughed and reached for Trickster's towel.

Evelyn smiled. *Got him trained nicely.*

"You two hungry yet?" she asked. "It's going to be lunchtime before you know it, and you still haven't eaten breakfast. Trickster certainly needs a treat."

With the mention of a treat, Trickster raced across the kitchen. Her world revolved around the promise of food.

"Seems your new friend is trying to tell you something," she said.

Evelyn and B.J. laughed as the young dog circled and bounced in front of the cupboard that contained her food.

"Nana, I think Trickster is my best friend."

Evelyn ruffled her grandson's head and reached for the coveted box of treats. "Well, Bradley James, there's no doubt she thinks the same thing about you."

B.J. cocked his head to one side and frowned. "My mommy used to call me that. Daddy never does. He started calling me B.J. when Mommy went to heaven."

Evelyn bent down to face her grandson, wiping away a single tear from his eye. "Adults can be pretty confusing sometimes. But there's one thing you can be very sure of. Your daddy loves you very much. He might just be leaving your full name in a special place in his memories for a little while longer."

"That's okay. I can wait." B.J. grinned shyly. "I kind of like being called B.J. Sounds important, don't you think?"

"Absolutely!"

Evelyn watched her seven-year-old grandson devour a bowl of cereal, marvelling at his wisdom.

15

O Lord, how manifold are thy works!
in wisdom hast thou made them all:
the earth is full of thy riches.
PSALM 104:24

September brought the beauty of the fall season in more abundance than Evelyn could ever remember. The last of her summer blooms filled her garden as though each flower knew the season was coming to an end and its last curtain call had been made. Walking her garden path, Evelyn noted that the baby's breath bordering it had grown in profusion, duplicating the previous summer when she had extravagantly planted seeds for Lucy's garden wedding.

Seems they were able to reseed themselves, contrary to the norm.

To her right, multiple shades of blue felicia, lustrous pink coral bells, and lavatera huddled at the base of the swamp milkweed. White shasta daisies thrived in the sunlight against the side fence, and white and pink peonies had doubled in size at the back of the yard, their green foliage filling in places where tulips had grown earlier in the season.

I'm gonna miss this, Evelyn thought, feeling a sense of melancholy as she scanned her garden. As if on cue, a robin landed on a branch of the hackberry tree directly in front of her.

"How come you're still here? Don't you know all your friends have headed south?"

In answer, the red-breasted robin lingered overhead momentarily before flying to the birdbath at the far end of the garden. Watching its flight, Evelyn recalled wondering why Lewis had put the birdbath so far from the house, but as the years passed she'd come to understand. The distance from the busyness of the house allowed the birds to frequent the water, not only to drink when the summer heat prevailed, but to splash recklessly without fear of human intrusion.

Studying the robin, Evelyn marvelled at the beautiful creature, having witnessed many times its instinctive ability to protect itself from the more aggressive blue jay. As in the past, she watched in amazement as the robin puffed itself to almost twice its size, keeping a blue jay at bay and forcing the loud-crowing jay to watch and wait its turn before submerging its body in the fresh water. The lone robin sprinkled its head one more time before taking off.

In wisdom you made them all. The earth is full of your creatures. Evelyn repeated the words she had read earlier that day as she watched the robin take flight and wing past her, swooping momentarily as though to say, "See you next year."

There was no denying that her rejection of God as the loving, supreme Creator had been challenged over the summer months. Evelyn had experienced a new awareness, a new peace, a strange presence, especially as she enjoyed her garden; yet she still held back. Still held on to her doubts. Still debated over and over in her mind that a loving God would not permit a war such as the world had witnessed almost three decades earlier. A war that redefined the brutality and depravity of the human mind. A war that saw the mass extermination of twelve million Jews.

How can a God who created such beauty be the same God who inflicts such cruelty on His so-called chosen people? Is this the God Levi is desperate for me to know personally?

Evelyn stared at the blue jay sprinkling its head and back repeatedly, allowing her mind to drift away from her disturbing thoughts to consider her feelings toward Levi. Her heart swelled. "I believe I'm in love with him," she whispered, sharing a secret with the bird at the end of the yard that was occupied with pruning its wet feathers. The words that her heart had been refusing to hear reverberated in her head. "I'm in love with Levi!" She smiled again at the formal use of his name. But the words that should have brought her much joy almost stopped her heart from beating. There was Someone keeping them apart, and she knew it was his God.

Go ahead. Love him. You can pretend you love his God. He never needs to know how you really feel.

Revulsion filled her and she shuddered at the suggested deception— at the evilness the deception personified. In all her years of battling the inner taunts, the accusations, the discouragements, she'd never tagged them as *evil*.

"Hello! You home, Mom? Annie wants her Nana!"

Lucy's voice broke through Evelyn's dilemma and, as so often in the past, she welcomed the distraction.

"I'm in the garden."

"No surprise there!" Lucy quipped as she greeted her mother and plunked Annie into her eagerly waiting arms.

"My, she's getting big. What are you feeding her beyond your own supply?" Evelyn asked as she jostled Annie high above her head.

"Just some Pablum, but not a lot," Lucy added emphatically. "I've still got lots of milk and she seems quite content. I'm only giving her a little Pablum at night, and that helps her get through until six. I'm good with that. What brings you out this far into the yard? Usually I find you balancing a coffee mug in one hand and a book in the other, curled up in your favourite chair."

Lucy nodded toward the house where Evelyn's patio furniture always welcomed visitors.

"Just enjoying my garden. It won't be long before the first frost takes the blooms and I have to start putting things to bed for the winter. I just can't think that far ahead yet, although from the look of the sky earlier this morning, winter's not far away."

"Yuck! You can't be serious. I can do without that…forever!"

Excited by the animated response, Trickster dropped a mud-soaked ball at Lucy's feet. Backing up, head down with her rump in the air, the young dog's eyes darted from side to side, ready to race after it.

"Go get it, girl!" Lucy obligingly threw the ball to the far corner of the yard, bouncing it off the birdbath. Then she turned to her mother with a more sombre remark. "I can't seem to get Jake out of my mind, or Abby for that matter. Is there any word on Jake's condition?"

"Well, actually, there's good news and bad news. Christina called last night to tell me that Jake came out of his coma."

"Christina called? Not Lee?"

Evelyn ignored her daughter's question. As with Rob, she did not intent to involve Lucy in her disagreement with Levi, a disagreement that had never been resolved, only ignored. Sundays brought polite conversation about the weather and Jake, but apart from that, there had been no surprise visits, no drop-ins with Christina, no phone calls, no *anything*. Levi had stopped communicating with her, and after her morning revelation, her heart was filled with questions and fear.

"Apparently," Evelyn continued, despite her inner turmoil, "Jake just opened his eyes, looked around, and went back to sleep. Lee told Christina that's pretty normal."

"What's normal?" Lucy heaved Trickster's ball in the air, sending her yelping to the back of the yard.

"It seems patients are only awake for a few minutes the first days out of a coma, but the duration gradually increases. That's the good part. The bad news is that he doesn't seem to recognize where he is—other than the fact that he's in a hospital. He can't remember what put him there and, worse, he has no memory of his life."

"What! He doesn't know who he is?"

"Apparently not. Coming in and out of natural sleep, he's been confused, speaking incoherently…he's very agitated. The doctors sedated him just enough to keep him quiet until his body heals, but he's not able to remember anything beyond waking up in the hospital, let alone what happened to him."

"Jake has amnesia?"

"So it would seem." A restless feeling settled over Evelyn and she handed her granddaughter back to Lucy. "Have you seen Rob lately?"

"Yeah, he dropped by after school on Monday. Seems rumours are flying high with Abby's name attached to them. He told me that he talked to you about them and feels a sense of responsibility to set people straight…"

Evelyn remained quiet. A second letter had arrived from Abby two days earlier and Evelyn had read it with great alarm. Her thoughts drifted to the main thrust of the letter:

> …so now I'm going to have a baby. I have wanted a child for over nine years and now, when I didn't think things could get any worse for me, they just did. When I counted back the weeks, I figured it was the last time… well, you know… with Jake, and it was anything but loving. Funny how things work out. He never wanted a child, and here I am carrying his and he'll never know it. The more I live apart from Jake, the more I realize how much was missing in our marriage. He's not the husband I thought he'd be. People don't know the real Jake.

"…and when he admitted he had his own doubts about Abby, I found it hard to believe, since he's known Abby all his life. Surely Rob must have had some inkling as to the kind of person Jake was. I mean, look how he treated B.J. That kind of person doesn't just happen. He must have had problems simmering under the surface for years. Don't you think? Mom? Hello, earth to Mom!"

Evelyn smiled apologetically. "Just taking it all in. You've raised some valid questions, but I suppose Rob's the only one who can answer them."

"Did I hear my name?" Rob approached through the garden gate and received the usual wagging-tail greeting from Trickster. "Hiya, girl."

"Hi there yourself, big brother! How did school go today? Where's B.J.?"

Evelyn smiled at Lucy's intentional mention of their sibling relationship.

"School went just fine, thank you very much!" Rob said. "It's the end of the first week and I've already determined that I've got a good class this year, and if that's not good enough, I'm on full-time. Got the news early this morning."

Rob greeted his mother with a kiss on her cheek.

"That's wonderful! Congratulations!" Evelyn and her daughter both chimed their excitement, laughing at the coincidence of the timing.

"As to where B.J. is, he's gone frogging down by the creek with Bruce Malcolm and his son," Rob said. "Gotta get the last few trips in while they can. But going back to *my* question…didn't I hear my name mentioned earlier?"

"Well…I…"

Evelyn glanced at Lucy with raised eyebrows. "I believe Lucy is trying to say she has some questions to ask you about Jake, so Annie and I are going for a walk. You two can talk."

Smiling encouragement to her daughter, Evelyn took Annie from Lucy and headed toward the birdbath, promising her granddaughter stories of red-breasted robins and bossy nuthatches, and chanting the black-capped chickadee's song, *Chick-a-dee-dee-dee. Chick-a-dee-dee-dee.*

"You know, Annie, when we watch a flock of chickadees in the winter, they're like little children playing in the snow."

Evelyn snuggled her granddaughter, kicking Trickster's ball along the way, much to the delight of both child and pet. A quick glance over her shoulder made her wonder how her son would respond to the news that Jake was awake.

16

Thou art my hiding place; thou shalt preserve me from trouble;
thou shalt compass me about with songs of deliverance. Selah.
PSALM 32:7

Pike Ridge, Alberta
October

With the third month passed, Abby felt the nausea easing. Mornings no longer found her hovering over the toilet bowl. She discovered that dry crackers appeased the mid-day hunger, so she always made sure a supply filled her apron pocket while at work.

"Angie, can you do a double shift for me tomorrow? I'm heading to the big city to stock up on supplies before the first heavy snow. I may be late getting back."

Hank Mason stood head and shoulders over Abby, wearing a stained baker's apron and a chef's hat. His stomach indicated years of bad food and too much beer, but his boisterous and infectious laugh made up for his overindulgence.

"Sure, Hank. I'll let Edna know I won't be home for supper tomorrow night, but I can tell you right now, she's not going to be too happy with you for asking." Abby shook an accusing finger at Hank, scowling in anticipation of her landlady's reaction. "She's fussing over me as if I was *her* daughter and I was carrying *her* grandchild."

Abby laughed, remembering how Edna Barnes had started to pamper her the day she'd moved in, and even more so once she'd learned Abby was expecting a baby. Under the guise of being lonely and needing the company, Edna had befriended Abby, showering her with such love that Abby found it difficult to express her gratitude.

"Oh, her bark is worse than her bite, if you'll excuse an old man an old expression." As an afterthought, Hank added, "Edna should have married me years ago, when she had the chance. I proposed right after the bewitching hour one summer night. She said she needed to think about it."

His charm and wit brought a smile from those sitting nearby enjoying his Friday special: apple dumpling and ice cream with caramel sauce.

Hank rolled his eyes and sighed. "I'm still waiting. Stubborn woman!"

With that, he headed back into the kitchen, grumbling some inaudible words that left his audience wondering how many years ago the proposal had actually been made.

The day ended and Abby felt a sense of relief. But despite her weariness, the acceptance and love she enjoyed from her two new friends overshadowed any physical limitations she experienced at day's end. Hank's offer of a job had come just as her money ran out, and it had been Hank who'd suggested talking with Edna.

"She lives alone and has a heart as big as this whole province," Hank had said. "Besides, her house is huge, and since she never married me— or anyone else, for that matter—she may be happy to have someone to fuss over."

Abby smiled at Hank's wisdom as she enjoyed the brisk walk to her new home on the outskirts of Pike Ridge. Heading out of town, she turned the corner and was greeted by a burst of wind. It was cold and she put her head down, pulling her scarf tighter around her neck and head. She had three more blocks to go before reaching Edna's long walkway and she increased her pace, bucking the wind with all her strength. But neither the weather, the long walk home from the diner, nor the extra hours she worked gave her reason to complain. Not ever. Not for a moment. Thanks to Hank's overly protective nature and Edna's unlimited generosity and gracious hospitality, Abby had come to regard the small town as home.

A three-hour bus ride west and slightly south of Thystle Creek, Pike Ridge sat in a remote valley just inside the border that divided Alberta from British Columbia. The small town of four hundred residents offered very few, if any, luxuries. It had a general store not unlike Sherwood's Hardware Emporium, but on a much smaller scale, providing life's simple necessities—hardware supplies, a limited selection of paint and wallpaper, basic food staples, bolts of fabric and the required notions, and an abundance of canning supplies for the very industrious. More importantly, the general store provided a place to meet and exchange the latest news and gossip.

Hank Mason's Grill and Diner provided another meeting place. On any given day, breakfast saw most of the booths filled with townsfolk enjoying coffee and small talk. Abby seldom experienced this collection of people since her shift started at the lunch hour and went through to supper. Sometimes it even went beyond, depending on how busy it got or if Hank needed her to stay for some reason. Despite the long days, Abby never ceased to thank Hank for her job, and he never seemed to be able to thank her enough for her faithfulness and willingness to fill in on short notice.

Abby almost skipped as she headed up the walkway to Edna's veranda. The fall had arrived sooner than expected and, despite the promise of a long and challenging winter, Abby felt a deep sense of relief that she had a place to live beyond the motel that had been her home for over a month. For the first time in a very long time, she was happy.

Hank and Edna had been a gift and she knew where the gift had come from. God was in her life, there was no questioning that, but Abby still struggled with the distance she felt between the One who unquestionably loved and protected her and the reason He had permitted her husband to abuse her.

I won't go there, Abby determined, and she quarantined the memories of her husband in an isolated place, a place she seldom, if ever, visited except in her dreams.

Hot chicken soup awaited her when she got home, despite Edna's absence. Homemade biscuits and milk completed her supper and Abby pampered herself with a second helping. With her milk topped up and two chocolate chip cookies wrapped in a serviette, she headed toward the stairs that led to her two rooms on the second floor.

When Edna had wholeheartedly agreed to having Abby live with her, Abby had no idea what space would be hers. She learned that, in anticipation of her arrival, Edna had burrowed through two bedrooms of "stuff that's been there since my parents were alive," but nothing could have prepared Abby for what awaited her when she followed Edna to the second floor that first day. Edna had ushered Abby into a large room, opened the windows, pushed back the drapes, and just smiled.

Beautiful mahogany pocket doors joined two rooms. The first was a sitting room with a walnut desk and chair, a sofa, and a floor model radio. The separate bedroom was furnished with a four-poster bed, a dressing table with matching dresser, and a working fireplace. Both rooms housed identical windows that stretched from the floor to just below the ceiling. Ecru lace curtains and floral drapes blocked the summer heat, but did not prevent the light from filtering in and bouncing off the crystal sconces that graced the fireplace wall.

Abby had stood speechless, slowly easing her suitcase to the floor. She'd moved slowly to the centre of the room, appreciating the lush woollen rug beneath her feet and noticing an array of clothes spread out on the bed.

"Freshly washed, ironed, and smelling like new," her new friend had declared. "My mother was tiny, just like you. She threw nothing away and the trunk in the attic is full of clothes that haven't been good to me. I'm on the plump side, took after my father's sister."

When she'd left Thystle Creek in July, Abby had never considered where she would go or what clothing she would need come winter. What did not fit in her suitcase had been left behind. Apparently, Edna had sorted through the trunk and found all that Abby needed until she could afford her own things.

Edna had rambled on as she fussed, shook, and smoothed whatever her hands touched, shushing Abby's attempts to express her thanks and appreciation. Just as she'd left Abby to settle in, Edna had paused. "We need to finish that haircut; I'm pretty good with hair shears. Mustn't use just any scissors. No, sir, you can ruin a nice head of hair in a flash! Whenever you like, I'll tend to that for you."

Her smile had been so understanding that Abby just stood there and soaked in the love and attention she desperately needed.

She'd have made a wonderful mother. I wonder why she never married, Abby thought as she slipped her flannel nightgown over her head and stood by the fire Edna had prepared. She turned and scanned her rooms. *This is my home. I'm loved. Accepted. No more bruises. No more threats. No more self-doubt.*

Abby breathed a sigh of wonder at how quiet and content her life had recently become.

Hearing the front door open and close in the downstairs hall, she prayed that Edna would accept the brown envelope containing Abby's rent money, the envelope she'd left propped up against the cookie canister in the kitchen.

A gentle noise outside her door brought a sigh from Abby. She didn't need to turn around, but she did. The brown envelope had been gently pushed under her door, unopened. Her rent money had been returned.

Abby left it on the floor, yielding to Edna's generosity and firm refusal to accept money from her. Instead, she opened a small cardboard box that contained writing paper and envelopes and sat down on the floor by the fire. With her milk and cookies close by, she began a letter.

> Dear Evie,
>   I wish you could meet my new friend. Your kindness to me is mirrored in her...

17

The heavens declare the glory of God;
and the firmament sheweth his handywork.
PSALM 19:1

Thanksgiving Saturday

Trickster raced to the front hall in response to the doorbell, circling in excitement and yelping at the unseen guest. Thinking it would be Lucy and Wil arriving several hours early for turkey dinner, Evelyn wondered why they rang the bell. She scooped up the dog, opened the door, and stood and stared.

"Good morning, Evie."

Evelyn continued to stare. In a matter of seconds she relived her recent revelation of growing love for Levi and wanted to shout it at her visitor, but wisdom—and perhaps cowardice—left her speechless.

"My mother told me, in no uncertain terms, that it was time you and I had a talk," Levi said. "And you can just imagine how my mother would have said *that.*"

Evelyn smiled, knowing.

"But if you're busy or would rather not…"

"No, no, I'm—I'm just happy to see you."

"You are? Even after all these weeks? It's been a lousy two months, at least for me—not sharing your garden, I mean." Levi stumbled over his words, bringing a flush to his face. "Did you really mean you were happy to see me?"

"Yes," Evelyn whispered shyly. She was not prepared for Levi's embrace.

Stepping into the open doorway, he wrapped his arms around her and held her quietly until Trickster's pain-filled yelp brought closure to the moment. Releasing both of them, Levi tousled Trickster's head.

"Sorry, girl. Forgot about you." Turning to Evelyn, he asked, "Would you be interested in a walk?"

At the sound of the word, Trickster squirmed from her arms and ran to the wooden tree stand that held her harness and leash.

"Now you've done it!" Evelyn said. "You've said the magic word. How can I say no, now? Let me get my jacket. You can have the honours of putting the harness and leash on this overzealous animal. And good luck … she never stands still for me."

2–2–2

Rosewood Park loomed in the distance, full of colour and majesty. Levi never ceased to marvel at how God's handiwork thrilled him each season. He often thought of those he called the less fortunate, those who lived in the warmer climates and never saw the palette of colours across parts of Canada in the fall months. Gorgeous. Breathtaking. Awesome— although he reserved that last word for God. There was never the *right* word to describe it, and he believed, until his last breath, he would never find the right one. He just stood and drank it in, as a parched tree drinks from an overflowing stream after a long drought.

He sighed audibly as he parked the car and turned off the ignition.

"Evie, how can you deny God when you look at what He has created?" His eyes filled and he smiled. "According to Thomas Aquinas, God reveals Himself through nature, so to study nature is to study God. But better still, the *Bible* says that God reveals certain truths about Himself through nature—and I know how much you love nature. Your garden testifies to that! How is it that you continue to fight the One who not only created the beauty that surrounds you, but the One who has been faithful in loving you despite your anger toward Him?"

Levi stretched his arms over the dash of his car as though to embrace the forest of trees. He hugged the steering wheel before turning his head to face the woman who had stolen his heart.

Evelyn turned slowly from the window as she opened the car door. "Let's walk."

Trickster raced ahead, chasing anything that moved—leaves, twigs, a squirrel that was unfortunate enough to be caught between two trees.

Evelyn laughed at Trickster's futile attempt. "She needs to get out more."

"Good thing she can't understand you," Levi responded, fully aware that she had avoided, if not ignored, his earlier question.

"What makes you think she can't?"

On cue, Trickster bounded up the path toward them, dropping a well-chewed stick at Levi's feet as if to say, "Throw this. I need the exercise."

For several minutes, the routine of dropping the stick, throwing the stick, and chasing the stick distracted Levi from fulfilling his mother's demand: *Go and talk to Evelyn.*

Reaching the open field where the annual picnic had ended with B.J.'s disappearance and eventual discovery, Levi headed to the nearest picnic table. Tipped on its edge in anticipation of the winter deluge of snow, Levi set the table upright and gallantly offered Evelyn a seat.

It was time to talk.

18

A good man out of the good treasure of the heart
bringeth forth good things:
and an evil man out of the evil treasure
bringeth forth evil things.

MATTHEW 12:35

H er name was Leah Dupuis. She was my wife." Levi looked into Evelyn's eyes and spoke softly. "A while ago, you said you doubted I've ever experienced the kind of pain that sometimes smothers you. Well, I know that kind of pain, Evie." He paused to let his words sink in before continuing. "It's a part of my life that I need—no, I *want* to share with you."

Levi sat close to Evelyn on top of the picnic table, stretching his legs over the bench while Evelyn sat motionless, her arms locked across her chest. Seconds lapsed into minutes with only the rustling of leaves breaking the silence as Trickster repeatedly tumbled head over tail, oblivious to the emotional whirlwind Levi had created.

"Where is she? Wh—where is Leah now?" Evelyn remained still, staring across the open field, watching her dog burrow in the fallen leaves.

"She died in Auschwitz."

The nonchalant words covered emotions that, had they surfaced, Levi would have ended the conversation then and there.

"Auschwitz?" The word had an evil ring to it and Evelyn shuddered. "How? I don't understand."

Levi smiled a weak, yet sincere smile. "I'm sure you don't. I've sort of dumped you into the middle of my story. Perhaps I should back up a little. Leah and I met in Toronto during our first year at university. We both set our sights on medical school. At first, we were just friends, in and out of the same classes, sharing lunch schedules, debating new theories and cheering football games—all the normal things friends do together. Our second year changed all that. We fell in love and realized we were probably in love long before we were ready to admit it. We were married during Hanukkah in December 1941. I was twenty-one, she was one year older—well, actually just a few months. On paper, she was twenty-two when we were married."

Levi shut his eyes momentarily and then turned to Evelyn.

"Much like you, Leah was an only child who'd never seen snow-capped mountains." He paused, remembering the story Evelyn had told him about her first experience seeing the Rocky Mountains and how she'd stared, speechless at the expanse of mountains and valleys. "Like you, she was born and raised in Toronto. She attended synagogue, went to school, learned to play the flute and the piano, played hopscotch, and went to day camp in the summer where she broke her arm in a high jump competition. We often talked about our parents, since they both came into their marriages with different faith backgrounds. Her father was a Gentile who converted to Judaism, as did my mother. We were both raised Jewish. Her father was a dentist and her mother was an amazing cook! And boy, did we ever eat during Shabbat! Three festive meals in twenty-four hours! Her parents became my temporary family while we courted and then finally wed. They're gone now, but I loved them very much."

Levi smiled, remembering, and for a moment succumbed to a memory that the years had committed to a special place in his heart.

"I suppose Leah did all the things any normal girl living in Toronto would do, like visiting Niagara Falls. But unlike most girls her age, by the time she was in her mid-teen years, she had crossed the Atlantic several times. The spring of 1942 was her last crossing... when she left for England."

Levi struggled with this last remark, knowing it was responsible for the bile that had suddenly moved from his stomach to the back of his throat.

Evelyn sat motionless while Levi continued.

"Leah was exceptionally smart and would have been an amazing doctor. She'd planned on further studies in internal medicine once she graduated. In March of '42, word came that her mother's parents were desperate to leave Paris. They owned a home just inside the occupied zone of the Nazi regime and, with what was happening in Poland and the other Eastern European countries—Jews were disappearing by the hundreds every day—they feared for their lives. Leah's parents were not well enough to travel on their own and, as an only child, the responsibility fell to her to bring them home to Toronto. Plans were made for her to stay with her father's half-brother, Harry Rosenberg—he lived outside London and was too old to fight in the war—and wait for her grandparents there.

"At first I was unsure. After all, there was a war going on in Europe, and England was in the middle of it. But Leah had a mind of her own: determined, brave, and confident, and she loved her grandparents very much. With great reluctance, I finally agreed. She left right after her final exams and flew to England to wait for their arrival. Her grandparents never showed up."

Levi stopped talking. He slid off the picnic table and shoved his hands deep into his pants' pockets. He took a few steps, then turned and looked at Evelyn.

"Leah knew Paris well and was determined to find them. Her grandparents lived not far from the Eiffel Tower. She'd visited them often as a teenager and she spoke French fluently. Because of his military background, her Uncle Harry had connections with the French Resistance and the underground railway. So he arranged for Leah to travel into France under their protection. With their aid, she was to return to England with her grandparents.

"How she managed to cross the channel, travel down through the occupied zone, and make it all the way to Paris, I have no idea, but she did. I can only assume the French Resistance made it possible. The last letter I received was postmarked Paris. She said, 'I've found my grandparents. Having a good visit. Hard to believe it will be over soon.' According to Uncle Harry, it was a coded message she would've been instructed to use to let me know that she would be leaving Paris immediately.

"It's strange when I think about it now—as I've done many times over the years. As determined and brave as she was, and as confident in her ability to bring them home as I was, we were both very naïve. As most Canadians, we had no idea of the evil that lurked on the other side of the ocean. Canada was not at war with Germany at that point, and I suppose we both felt a false sense of safety."

Levi turned to face Evelyn.

"Leah and her grandparents became victims of the Vél d'Hiv Roundup in July that year. After being held in the Drancy transit camp outside Paris, they were shipped by rail to Auschwitz and never survived."

He stopped talking, then quietly added, "Soon after she'd arrived in England, she'd learned she was carrying our child."

Evelyn didn't move. Breathing was difficult. She watched Levi pace in front of the picnic table, heard his words, and desperately fought an overwhelming need to retch. How could she have been so insensitive? A wife. A child. Lost to the horrors of war. And she thought she had a burden to carry!

She reached for Levi's hand. He stopped pacing and stared at her.

"Lee, I don't know what to say. I…"

"I'm sorry to unload like that, Evie. It's been a long time since I've talked about Leah. I'm sure you never saw *that* coming."

"I feel overwhelmed with grief for you … and I feel … such shame for my own self-indulgence."

"Don't feel guilty—please! We've all experienced our share of grief and pain. I suppose it's how we handle it that counts."

Evelyn started to speak, but Levi continued. "I miss Leah to this day, but the pain is gone. I have wonderful memories, but they are not shrouded by overwhelming anguish; I released my anger and hate a long time ago."

Levi sat down beside Evelyn and unconsciously scratched Trickster's head as she lay curled up in Evelyn's lap.

"I'm going to say something that you may not understand," he said. "In fact, I'd be surprised if you did. I've come to accept God's sovereign will in my life. As much as I don't understand it, I have to trust God to do what needs to be done to accomplish His purpose for my life, which ultimately is for my good. *'He will perfect everything that concerns me.'*" He leaned against Evelyn. "That's in the Psalms. I have no idea why God allowed Leah and our child to die; I'll never know this side of Heaven. And I have no idea why God never brought another woman into my life before now. I've lived a very quiet but fulfilled life for the past twenty-five years, and just when I thought my life was complete, God surprised me with *you*."

Unable to look at Levi, Evelyn squirmed, waking her sleeping dog. Trickster shook her coat and jumped down to sit at Evelyn's feet. "Was it your God's will that you gave me this wonderful animal?" Evelyn asked, shying away from his last comment that, although thrilling her heart, terrified her at the same time.

"Perhaps. I do know that it has brought *you* immeasurable pleasure, and that has brought *me* immeasurable pleasure. From that, I believe God smiled on us both, or should I say on the three of us?"

Levi's easy reference to God proved unsettling for Evelyn. There was still so much for her to resolve on her journey of discovering God, as Christina had recently pointed out.

A gust of wind blew across the open field, giving her a reason to end their time together. Recalling that Lucy and Wil would be arriving soon, Evelyn lifted Trickster into her arms.

"I think we should head home. I'm sure the turkey is ready to come out of the oven." She turned toward the car. "Thank you for your honesty, Lee. I admire you very much for being so strong and confident in your belief in God."

With that, Evelyn turned and walked to the parked car, warmed by Levi's presence beside her as he slipped his arm around her waist.

"It's nice to be talking again," he said.

Evelyn just smiled. Her heart was calm. There was no taunting, no accusations filling her head. There was a calmness she had become accustomed to, a calmness she welcomed but could not explain.

19

The simple believeth every word:
but the prudent man looketh well to his going.
PROVERBS 14:15

Early November

Lucy kept Wil's supper warm, steaming it over a pot of boiling water while he finished raking the last of the fall leaves. Giving Annie her only bottle of the day, Lucy watched her husband from their daughter's bedroom window, hoping he would be in before Annie fell asleep. Dragging mounds of leaves to the roadside was burdensome and she felt sorry for him. She'd even offered to help, but was secretly glad he'd discouraged her.

"It's too cold for Annie to be out here, and besides, you hate raking leaves!" he'd quipped.

He'd been right. Even at a stretch, she was not a lover of cold weather, blaming her mother for the inherited gene.

"He knows me too well, Annie," Lucy whispered into her sleepy daughter's ear.

Setting the empty bottle aside, Lucy acknowledged a well-timed burp with a smile. Nursing Annie had been the highlight of her motherhood thus far, and she dreaded the prospect of stopping. However, the last month had produced all the signs of teething: drooling, feverish moods, and wakeful nights. She'd said to her mother earlier in the week, "I'm afraid the writing is on the wall. It won't be much longer until Annie discovers she can bite whatever she puts into her mouth."

Her mother had laughed at Lucy's descriptive fears, but Lucy felt a door closing and it saddened her. Still, she took comfort in knowing that Annie would not be their last child.

"Well, Little Lu, looks like your night-time bottle is empty and you're ready for bed. Daddy will come in for his goodnight kiss just as soon as he's finished." Lucy tapped on the window and raised their five-month-old daughter for Wil to see. "Wave to Daddy. Say night-night."

Settling Annie came easy and Lucy returned to the kitchen. Thoughts of having a second child hovered over her more than they did with Wil, but Wil had made a good point. "Annie's not six months old yet, Luce. Let's enjoy her for a while before we add to the family." He'd seen her look and wisely added, "But hey—if it happens, it happens."

Lucy smiled at how her husband had hugged her with his last remark. She couldn't help hoping it *would* happen.

"What do you think of Jake staying at Ruth's when he gets out of the hospital?" Wil asked once he had washed up and seated himself in front of his meatloaf, mashed potatoes, and green beans from their summer garden. "Hmmm, this is great, Luce! Looks like the beans froze well."

Startled by what she thought she'd heard, Lucy ignored Wil's compliment, turned from the kitchen sink with a jolt, and in doing so dripped sudsy dishwater on the floor. "What did you say?"

"The beans froze well."

"No, no! Before that … about Jake."

"I ran into Ruth in town this afternoon." Wil swallowed a forkful of potatoes. "Apparently, Jake is improving and will be discharged sometime early in the New Year. Ruth seems to think she can look after him, 'now that he's a new person.'" Wil quoted Ruth with facial expressions that momentarily brought a smile to Lucy's face. "It seems she didn't have a very high opinion of him before his injuries, but now 'he's so polite and cordial that he's really nice to know.'" Again the mimicking. "Since this revelation of the new Jake Waters, Ruth's been visiting him on a regular basis."

"Do you think his amnesia will last? I mean, how long can a person forget who he is, where he's from, and how he ended up in the hospital— let alone that he's got a wife somewhere? Does Ruth really think she can look after him, and more importantly, trust him?"

"She's actually looking forward to his coming home, but she did say on the side that she hopes he never rediscovers the old Jake. She said he's kind and thoughtful. The old Jake was never like that."

Lucy rolled her eyes and turned back to washing the dishes.

"About the amnesia," Wil continued, "I'm not sure even the doctors know how long he'll be without his memory. It was strange visiting him last week. I really didn't want to go, but Lee encouraged me to visit. I think it was some kind of test to see if Jake would recognize me."

Wil soaked up the gravy on his plate with his last slice of bread.

"It was so weird," he said, swallowing a mouth full of the soggy bread. "When I walked in and said hi, it was like we were complete strangers. I could see on his face he had no idea who I was. Apparently, Rob had paid him a visit a few days earlier—again, at Lee's request. Rob told him they were childhood friends, grew up in Quebec, and married two women who were best friends in a double ceremony. When he mentioned Holly, Jake never flinched. That was the big clincher for Rob. No one knew more than Rob how much Jake despised him for marrying Holly. He never blinked when Rob told him he was married to Abby, either, but Rob never told him that Abby was suspected of being the culprit behind his accident."

"Oh, come on, Wil! Please tell me that gossip has stopped."

"Actually, it's not gossip. It's the direction the police are taking. Josh was telling me that they paid him a visit the other day and asked him all kinds of questions about Abby. Did she ever talk badly about her husband? Did she ever wish she wasn't married to him? Was she an honest employee? Things like that. Of course, Josh had nothing but praise for

Abby. Always considerate. Always on time for work. Never once had he heard her speak ill of her husband, and he said so. But Abby's nowhere to be found and, as strange as it sounds, the police are concerned about Jake's safety once he's released from the hospital."

"That's ridiculous!" Lucy retorted. "Abby did not deliberately hurt Jake. We all know that!"

"But the police think otherwise. I suppose they're just looking at the evidence, Luce. You can't fault them for doing their job." Wil emptied his coffee mug, pushed back his chair, and stretched his long legs under the table.

Lucy took Wil's plate and gave him a disgusted look. "Well, if I ever hear from her, I'm going to tell her to keep on going."

"Hey, don't look at me like that! I'm just an innocent bystander delivering the latest news."

"I'm sorry, Wil, but this is just plain ridiculous."

"I can't agree more, but as far as people are concerned, that doesn't change the obvious: Abby's missing, Jake's in the hospital and is now suffering from amnesia. And the police are on the hunt for Abby."

With that, Wil raised his eyebrows and shrugged. He turned and headed toward Annie's room, leaving Lucy staring at his back and fuming at her husband's seemingly apathetic behaviour.

20

Be careful for nothing; but in every thing
by prayer and supplication with thanksgiving
let your requests be made known unto God.
PHILIPPIANS 4:6

December 10

Evelyn and Levi sat mesmerized by the fire as flames bounced and flickered behind the glass screen. Trickster's rhythmic snoring broke the tranquility, only to be matched by the gentle ticking of the wall clock in the front hallway. The subdued voices of Rob and B.J. filtered up the basement stairs as they rummaged through cardboard boxes looking for any sign of Christmas decorations, their distant laughter accentuating the quietness of Evelyn's living room.

Despite the hypnotic effect of the fire and the comfort of Levi's arm as they sat on the sofa, Evelyn's inner turmoil mounted.

"You're leaving first thing in the morning? Why Ottawa? And at this time of year! I'm surprised a medical conference would be planned so close to Christmas."

"I'll only be gone a week—ten days at the most," Levi said. "Besides, Ottawa is enjoying an unusually mild fall. Winter hasn't officially arrived via the calendar and Christmas is still two weeks away, despite the anxious searching going on downstairs." He smiled as he nodded toward the basement doorway. "Having B.J. around is a reminder of what it was like to be a kid with Christmas just around the corner. No doubt he's already written out his wish list."

Her curiosity piqued by the broken silence, Trickster rose from the comfort of her favourite spot by the fire, stretched, and sauntered over to Levi's outstretched legs. Rolling on her back, she nudged Levi's foot to procure her favourite pastime: a belly rub.

"I swear if this dog could talk, she'd demand a full head-to-tail massage!" Levi laughed at his own humour, only to have it rejected by Evelyn as she sat up and faced him with an accusing look.

"Don't change the subject, Lee. Winter may be late in coming for Eastern Ontario, but we've already had snow! Surely you haven't forgotten—again—how quickly a storm can come here! I'm sure if you try hard enough, you'll remember these conversations from last year. We can have sun one day and a deluge of snow the next! I—your *mother* would hate to have you stuck somewhere and spend Christmas alone. Flying into Edmonton is one thing, but the drive here can be treacherous. I can only imagine how Christina would take to the idea of your being stranded somewhere."

Levi drew up his legs and interrupted the massage he had been administering to Trickster, much to the dog's dismay. Grunting her disapproval, the disenchanted pet moved to her former spot in front of the fire.

"Evie, it's just a few days," Levi reiterated. "Your fears, and my mother's, are getting the better of you. Don't you know that *fear is false evidence appearing real?*" Levi smiled at the old saying his father had said to him when he'd faced his first surgery. "You're both worrying needlessly."

He moved to draw Evelyn closer to him, but Evelyn stood abruptly.

"You're—you're impossible!" she exclaimed and left the room.

The fire crackled and startled Trickster. "Well, girl," Levi sighed, "I suppose I should go and smooth things over."

Trickster crooked her head to one side as if to say "Good luck." Levi laughed at the dog's apparent insightfulness. But his laughter ended when he found Evelyn standing, arms folded, staring out the back window.

"Evie?"

"The last blooms are buried." Evelyn's voice was distant, almost void of feeling. Her hands reached further up her arms until she hugged herself.

"Evie, what is it?" Levi moved slowly, his physician instincts heightened by Evelyn's body language.

"Nothing, really." She continued to stare out the window. "Just that I'm missing my garden already and longing for spring."

"I know how much you love your garden, but there's more. I can feel it. Your comments a moment ago about winter and Christmas just don't add up. It's not like you. What aren't you telling me?" Levi placed his hands on Evelyn's shoulders and turned her to face him. "These tears are not for your frostbitten flowers. What's going on? Is it my trip? I hope it's because you're going to miss me."

He offered Evelyn his handkerchief, but she pulled away and blew her nose. "Of course I'll miss you, Levi."

"Wha—Levi? What happened to 'Lee'? Come on, Evie, what's going on?"

Evelyn avoided his second attempt to embrace her and walked to the kitchen table. She slowly sat on the chair facing the front window.

"This time of the year can be beautiful, can't it?" Evelyn's eyes revealed her inner torment and her struggle to find the right words. "I know I'm sounding unreasonable, Lee, but it's not you. It—it's my father."

"You've spoken with him recently?"

"No. I've only had two very short conversations with him since my initial call. The last time we talked—well over a month ago—he told me my mother had died not long after I left home. I'm afraid I didn't take that news very well. I hung up before he had an opportunity to explain. I've not spoken to him since, but with Christmas coming, I can't help thinking about him and wondering what…"

B.J. burst into the kitchen encumbered by a large cardboard box and headed for the kitchen table.

"Hey, Nana, look what Daddy and I found on a shelf in the basement. We found it way up behind the empty fruit baskets and old paint cans. Daddy says it looks like it's been there for years—even longer than

I've been alive!" B.J. gently placed the dusty box of Christmas ornaments on the kitchen table. "He said to be very careful because they look like they're very precious to someone."

"Indeed they are." Rob smiled at Evelyn and Levi, acknowledging their silent amusement at B.J.'s choice of words. "These ornaments *are* very precious, and fragile," he added, "and I bet if you ask Nana, each one of them has a story."

"Really? How can this glass heart or this wooden sleigh have a story?"

Despite hearing the light banter, Evelyn sat staring at the box, fighting the desire to take one sweep with her arm and send it crashing to the floor.

"Look, Daddy, this silver ball has some writing on it. It says, 'Baby's first Christmas.' And this heart has words on it, too. 'I'll love you forever, Lewis.' Yuck!" B.J.'s face matched his expression. "That's just mushy stuff. Who's Lewis anyway?"

Evelyn didn't move; she just sat there, the silence punctuated by the rummaging of paper as her grandson dug deeper into the box, ignoring his unanswered question. Levi and Rob each took the ornaments and read the inscriptions.

Meanwhile, Evelyn sank further into a world where life held promise and love ruled the moment.

$$\rightsquigarrow$$

"This is for you, Evie, girl. I can't wait 'til Christmas Eve."

Lucy had been in bed for hours, the kitchen was clean, and Lewis had built the perfect fire. Evelyn curled up with a book on the sofa, feeling blessed beyond words.

She took the small parcel from her husband's hands and looked deep into his eyes. This would be their third Christmas Eve to exchange tree ornaments and she felt a surge of guilt for having delayed in buying his. She struggled with weak excuses: there had been the barrage of Christmas baking, the already clean house needed further cleaning, the tree needed to be decorated, and the turkey needed to be picked up…and, oh, the endless Christmas shopping that needed to be done. The excuses seemed to justify her procrastination, but in those few seconds, they all seemed insignificant. Why hadn't she taken the time?

"Christmas Eve's five days away, Louie. I haven't bought your ornament, and yet, from what I can feel in this parcel, there's more than one in it." A tear fell on the tissue paper in her hands.

"Oh, don't go getting teary-eyed on me. I can't help feeling like a kid this close to Christmas. You and Lucy and I are going to have another member of the family next spring and I want to celebrate it now. Can't you give an expectant father some privileges?" Louie grinned sheepishly.

"Oh, Louie, it's beautiful!" Evelyn held the silver ball by the gold ribbon and read the inscription. "'Baby's First Christmas.' But aren't you a little premature? I mean, he or she isn't even born yet!"

Evelyn laughed at her own words and the idea of a preborn getting a Christmas ornament.

"Who says we have to follow all the rules? Open the second one." Louie paced in front of Evelyn with all the energy of a four-year-old on Christmas morning. "This one says it all, Evie. I can't say it any better."

The red heart would have looked like a Valentine had it not been for the green holly entwined on the edges. The inscription left Evelyn speechless as she lifted glassy eyes to her husband and welcomed his embrace. And with all the fervour of a new husband, Lewis whispered the inscribed words between each kiss, "I'll love you forever."

$$\backsim \!\!\! \backsim \!\!\! \backsim$$

"Look, Daddy, it's snowing!" B.J. ran to the back door with Trickster at his heels, barking to be free. "Let's go, girl, it's snowing!"

Wrestling a coat and hat onto his son, Rob laughed as he released both dog and child to the elements. "I'll put the kettle on. This day demands hot chocolate. Any takers?"

Rob's innocent question sparked Evelyn's re-entry to her current world and she rose to the occasion. "Absolutely, Rob. There's a lot to think about over the next few weeks." She placed the two ornaments in the box and closed the lid. "Did you know Lee is going to Ottawa tomorrow for a medical convention? We'll just have to hope that the mighty hand of winter doesn't hit too soon, and that he'll get back before the historic digging-out begins."

Levi joined in the laughter, but his look told Evelyn that their conversation wasn't over yet—just postponed.

21

Trust in the Lord with all thine heart;
and lean not unto thine own understanding.
In all thy ways acknowledge him, and he shall direct thy paths.
PROVERBS 3:5–6

Pontypool, Ontario
December 19

The Good Grain Company elevator towered over the low-lying shrubs like a friendly giant keeping a watchful eye for intruders. Levi turned east and drove his rented car parallel to the train tracks, thankful for clear roads and that Ottawa's first winter storm had not taken up residence in Pontypool. Houses spotted the hillside until the road reached a tee intersection and came to an abrupt halt.

Right or left?

Levi searched the road, hoping for human intervention and direction, but all was quiet. He looked at his watch, supposing 6:30 was a little early in the morning for most folk to be out and about. He shrugged, resigned to the uncertainty of his predicament. The only landmarks he knew to look for were a bakery and a grain elevator.

Well, I've found the grain elevator. Where's the bakery?

Still on the outskirts of the village, Levi turned right, choosing not to cross the train tracks. His choice proved correct. Less than a quarter of a mile ahead, he found the general store, and two doors down, he found a bakery. Or rather, his nose found the bakery.

Parking across from the building that exuded the succulent aroma of freshly baked bread, Levi read the sign:

CRAWFORD'S BAKERY
BAKED FRESH DAILY:
BREAD, ROLLS, MUFFINS, COOKIES AND MORE.
OPEN 7:00 A.M. CLOSED SUNDAYS.

He glanced at his watch. Only five minutes had passed since his last look and he sighed, realizing just how early it was and how far he'd travelled. He was tired. The last conference session had ended close to ten o'clock and by the time he'd said his goodbyes and found a ride to catch the last Toronto-bound bus, it was past eleven o'clock. He'd been glad to skip the pre-dinner outing, opting for a nap in anticipation of the five-hour bus ride ahead of him.

The bus station in Toronto had sat vacant except for a bleary-eyed ticket agent, a young couple asleep in a corner of the waiting room (with backpacks and sleeping bags piled next to their semi-comatose bodies), and a lone janitor who had taken the liberty of isolation to stretch out on a bench, his right hand holding his broom.

Renting a car had been easier than Levi had thought, but finding directions to an isolated, unknown village named Pontypool had proven onerous. By 5:10, with map in hand and a heart full of gratitude that the storm had swung south, Levi had headed east on a seemingly endless stretch of highway. A station on the radio had kept him awake, allowing his robust voice ample opportunity to break the solitude. He surprised himself at how well he knew the words of the music designed for teenagers.

He'd arrived in the obscure hamlet with little to no difficulty, but now weariness overcame him. He leaned back and closed his eyes. He was asleep in less than a minute.

With the engine turned off, the cold air soon permeated the car and woke Levi. When he looked at his watch for the third time, it read 7:15. He rubbed his eyes and stretched his long legs as best he could, considering the cramped quarters. A light snow had covered his windshield while he slept.

When Levi turned to look in the direction of the bakery, the lights shone from the inside and reflected off the white dusting on the sidewalk. The sign on the door read OPEN.

Well, here goes.

Reaching into the back seat, Levi opened his briefcase, lifted a folder from it, and closed the lid. Fighting apprehension, he opened the car door and stepped into the fresh snow.

The bell above the bakery door had an antique look and announced his arrival. It was only a matter of seconds before Levi heard a male voice call from behind a partially closed door, "I'll just be a minute. Help yourself to a cookie on the counter."

Levi promptly obliged his unseen host.

With growing expectancy overcoming his fear, Levi looked around and found everything in meticulous order. Fresh cookies and a variety of muffins lined trays in a closed window display on the front counter. Multiple loaves of bread filled wooden shelves behind the cash register, sharing space with sweet rolls of various sizes. Levi shook his head, marvelling at the quantity of baked goods and could only imagine that some unearthly hour had witnessed the inception of such a display.

"Can I help you?"

Levi turned abruptly and was greeted by an elderly man sporting a baker's hat. He stood taller than Levi, wiping his hands on a flour-dusted apron. Sprays of flour accentuated the permanent smile lines etched on his face. His deep voice hinted of an accent, giving it charm and dignity.

"Please excuse my appearance. I'm not used to such an early customer." The baker removed his hat and gave it a shake before putting it on the shelf next to where he stood. "Most folks around here don't darken my door before nine. You just passing through?" He gave a robust laugh. "Forgive me, but no one passes through Pontypool. They either come for a visit, or don't come at all, unless to buy my baking." He launched into another hearty laugh. "Sorry. I'm such a rambler, but I've given up trying to turn over a new leaf. I learned a long time ago to accept myself for the person God made me to be and trust the rest of the world to do the same."

Levi laughed at this gentle man's engaging humour and liked him immediately. He thought of Lucy and his encounter with her on the path behind the Emporium in his early days in Thystle Creek, and he knew he was in the right place.

He was looking at Lucy's grandfather.

"You're quite right on both counts. God has certainly given us our own individual identities," Levi extended his hand, "and Pontypool is *certainly* off the beaten path. I'm Levi Morsman, Doctor Levi Morsman."

Flour dusted the air from the baker's feisty handshake. "Nice to meet you…Levi, if I may? This small village doesn't stand too well on formality. I'm Joseph Crawford. Some folks call me Mr. J., others Joseph, but the young'uns, they call me Gramps, especially when they want to sample the latest goods!" He gave another hearty laugh and Lucy's face flashed once again before Levi's eyes. "Now, there I go again, rambling on nonsensically to a total stranger. How can I help you? Need some fresh bread as you pass through town?"

"Actually, Mr. Crawford…Joseph…I've always preferred skipping titles and I'm not sure why I used mine now."

Levi paused to let the moment pass. He glanced toward the closed door and noticed for the first time the framed scripture verse. The embroidered words said, *"Trust in the Lord with all thine heart; and lean not unto thine own understanding. In all thy ways acknowledge him, and he shall direct thy paths"* (Psalm 3:5–6). His eyes dropped, and before raising them again, Levi committed the conversation to the God who had brought him here in the first place, to the One who had never failed him.

"Joseph, I'm on a mission, and I believe I have arrived at my destination. Is there any possibility of putting the CLOSED sign on your front door for half an hour? I think what I have to share with you will not take much longer, but it may require some privacy."

Joseph frowned for the first time. "Can I ask what this is about?"

Levi thought for a moment. He wanted to say, *"I'm in love with your daughter, and I want to take you back to Alberta for Christmas to meet your grandchildren and great-grandchildren,"* but he thought better of it. Instead, in the most impersonal tone he could muster, he said, "I've come to talk to you about your daughter."

"My—my daughter. You know my daughter?"

Joseph stumbled forward and leaned on the counter. Levi jumped to assist him and slid a nearby stool closer. Waving aside the need for the stool, Joseph shook with emotion. Tears mingled with the flour on his bearded face, and he smiled.

"You know my daughter?" he repeated, motioning for Levi to flip the OPEN sign on the door.

⁂

"I was with Evelyn when she made her call to you back in early July," Levi concluded, half an hour later. He had been very selective in mentioning grandchildren and great-grandchildren, assuming that Evelyn had already told her father he was a grandfather and great-grandfather.

"We were all there, including my mother, Christina. She's become a wonderful friend for Evelyn, encouraging her and challenging her as Evelyn continues on her quest for God—you'd have to know my mother to understand that."

Joseph's eyes appeared blank, as though he had been lost somewhere along the way. Levi wondered how much the older man had absorbed. Moments passed before Levi spoke again and, when he did, he realized that the familiarity and light-hearted conversation they had been enjoying just minutes earlier had ended.

"Mr. Craw... Joseph, I know this is a lot to take in," Levi said. "I'm not sure how much Evelyn has shared with you over the past several weeks. She's been noticeably silent about her conversations with you."

Evelyn's father turned to look at Levi. His eyes held many questions.

"Lucy and Rob—my grandchildren. Correct?"

Levi nodded. He watched the face of his new friend digest this affirmation and quietly thanked God for planting in him the desire to come to Pontypool.

Resting on the stool, Joseph leaned on the counter with his forearms and released a long sigh. "We have spoken only twice, and at times I've wondered if I dreamed it all. Other than knowing I have grandchildren, she has shared nothing of her life with me." Sadness filled his face. "Our last conversation ended when Evelyn learned her mother had died a year and a half after she left home."

Levi nodded. He could well imagine how Evelyn would struggle with the guilt of never having seen her mother before she died, let alone sharing her past with her father.

"After learning of her mother's death, Evelyn stopped all communication. I've heard nothing. It's almost as though she's afraid to ask. Certainly, it seems she's afraid to share what has happened in her life these past twenty-five years. There's so much I need to tell her…" The older man's voice trailed off. He lowered his head and sighed. His eyes were full when he finally looked up at Levi. "It's been quite a shock to know my daughter is alive, Levi, and to learn that I have grandchildren. As much as my heart yearns to hear my daughter's voice again, I have left it to her to communicate with me. But tell me…you have come a long way…is your concern for my daughter personal or professional?"

Joseph's troubled look startled Levi. "Oh, it has nothing to do with my being a doctor, if that's what you mean. Let me assure you, your daughter's in good health. She loves being outdoors in the summer—in fact, she almost lives in her garden, but she dreads winter. She's already worrying about me being stranded far from home for Christmas. Northern Alberta can be unpredictable when it comes to winter storms. No, Evelyn's in fine physical health." Levi paused. "Joseph, I care deeply for your daughter, but my primary concern is her relationship with you. If Evelyn is in need of healing, it's centred on her father. And that's what brings me to Pontypool. I have a request."

"What do you want from my father?" a new voice demanded, startling him.

Levi turned, then gulped and stared at the newcomer. Wiping her hands on a bib apron, a woman came forward, folding her arms over the floured spot her hands had created.

Apart from the obvious difference in age, the woman standing before him could easily be Evelyn's twin sister. Evelyn's voice, her hair, her arched eyebrows when she disapproved of something…it was all mirrored in the face of this woman who stood glaring at him. But unlike Evelyn, this woman's boldness left Levi speechless.

"Perhaps I need to repeat my question," she said. "What do you want from my father?"

"Forgive me." Levi stumbled for words. "You took me by surprise. I thought your father was alone."

"Well, he's not!"

"Rachel! Your manners, please!" Joseph Crawford reached for the woman's hand. "This is Doctor Morsman…Doctor Levi Morsman…he's brought news of your sister."

"Really! My sister! How quaint is that? We haven't heard from her for more than two decades, and then, after turning my father's life upside-down with a simple phone call, she drops off the face of the earth. Now a stranger arrives with news. Seems like the prodigal has sent a messenger."

"Actually, Evelyn has no idea I'm here," Levi assured her.

Rachel harrumphed, setting the tone. The room resounded with an uneasy quietness. Only the soft voice of another woman, not unlike Levi's own mother, broke the silence.

"Take no mind of my granddaughter, Doctor Morsman. I'm afraid my namesake comes by her boldness honestly."

Standing in the doorway to the bakery kitchen was a much older woman. She had a smile that melted the air of hostility birthed by her granddaughter.

"…but she means well," the elder Rachel added, walking to where her granddaughter stood next to her father. Patting her granddaughter's cheek, she turned back to Levi. "You must be hungry, and since we have closed early we must take advantage and have some tea. Yes?"

Levi could only nod.

22

Be not forgetful to entertain strangers:
for thereby some have entertained angels unawares.
HEBREWS 13:2

December 22

I 'll get it, Mom," Lucy called from the kitchen in response to the
telephone.

Glad she didn't have to hurry—and even more so for Lucy and
Annie's early morning visit—Evelyn stretched from her stooped position to admire her handiwork. *Nice fire,* she thought as she smoothed
out her housecoat, pausing to brush at the streak of soot she managed to
get on the front of it. She missed Levi for more reasons than she wanted
to admit, but keeping a fire going was on top of her list! She smiled at
her own presumption as she stared at the fresh flames, appreciating the
warmth that slowly invaded her living room.

*I really have missed him. It's been over ten days and not a word. I wonder
when…*

"That was Levi," Lucy announced, wiping her hands on a tea towel as
she came to deliver the message. "Apparently, he got in late last night, but
he's coming over with Christina and some friends from out of town. I've
put fresh coffee on and…"

"Wha—did you say Levi's home? He's coming here? With strangers?" Evelyn glanced down at her soiled housecoat. "Now?"

Fighting rising panic, she hurried across the living room, running her fingers through her hair en route.

"I'll just be a minute, Lucy. Perhaps you should put Trickster out and then dry her feet when she comes in. Don't want her jumping on anyone with dirty paws."

Lucy nodded, masking a snicker behind the tea towel as her befuddled mother bumped into the edge of the coffee table as she paused in mid-flight to ask, "Did you say you made fresh coffee? Good. Maybe you should put on the kettle, too. Christina loves her tea. Thank goodness I made those muffins before you came!"

"Mother, just go and get dressed! I'll handle things here." Lucy laughed as Evelyn turned and headed for her bedroom, almost tripping over Trickster.

"Come on, Tricks, better keep out of her way if you know what's good for ya. You need to get your outdoor visit over with before Lee gets here."

Trickster raced to the front door.

"No, no!" Lucy said. "He's not here yet, but he will be soon. Let's get your *has-to* over with before our company arrives. Seems we're going to entertain some strangers."

Several minutes later, Evelyn stood in the kitchen doorway wearing a matching skirt and sweater that accentuated her figure, which most women her age would envy. Her walnut brown hair hung loose on her shoulders and she smelled like her garden in the throes of summer blooms.

"Wow! You look nice, Mom. And you smell good, too. New outfit?" Lucy teased.

"Not really, but thank you, dear." Evelyn brushed off her daughter's light attempt at humour. "Did you put Trickster out? Is the coffee ready? What about the kettle?" She paced in front of the kitchen sink. Taking a fresh apron from a drawer, she slipped it on, smoothed it out, then immediately took it off and put it back in the drawer. She stopped suddenly and frowned. "Where's Annie?"

"For goodness sake, Mom! You're more nervous than a newborn calf. You need to relax." Lucy pulled out a chair by the kitchen window. "Sit!"

Then, in a knowing manner, she held up her fingers to itemize each question Evelyn had asked.

"First, Trickster's in the living room looking out the front window, waiting. All I had to do was say, 'Lee's coming,' and she raced off to her favourite chair."

We have something in common, Evelyn thought, smiling inwardly. Her demeanour began to relax as she focused on the bond between Levi and her dog. She stared out the window at the fresh snow, remembering the summer day Levi had delivered Trickster to her front door. Levi had begged her to stop crying, but she hadn't been able to.

Even now she cringed at the memory, and yet it had its sweet side, too. Trickster had been a birthday gift. Levi thought she'd be lonely when Lucy and Wil got married, so he'd placed the young pup in a cardboard box on her front doorstep, rung the doorbell, then hid behind the grove of birch trees on the front lawn.

Evelyn closed her eyes and could almost hear Levi's voice when he'd brought the box containing her soon-to-be-inseparable pet in from the threatening rain.

"...and the coffee is made and the kettle is on for the tea, and I've just fed and changed Annie and put her down for her morning snooze. Poor thing, her gums are red and she's gnawing on my knuckles every chance she gets."

Evelyn turned from the kitchen window. "I'm sorry, Lucy, did you say something? I was just watching...oh my goodness, he's here...*they're* here."

Evelyn watched as Levi held the car's back door open and offered his assistance to the unseen visitor. Christina, already waiting on the sidewalk, smiled and waved enthusiastically in the direction of the house.

"She must be one of Christina's friends visiting from the coast," Lucy surmised as she returned Christina's gesture. "She seems a lot older, don't you think? Although it's hard to tell from this distance."

Evelyn strained to see the face of the visitor as Levi walked to the other side of the car and opened the back door. Gasping, Evelyn backed slowly away from the kitchen window and fell into the chair she had been sitting in moments earlier, staring as the foursome moved in the direction of her front door.

"Mother, what is it?"

But Lucy's concern abated somewhat when Trickster's yelping filled the house in response to the front doorbell.

"I'll go. You stay put." Frowning, Lucy glanced over her shoulder before heading for the front door, hoisting Trickster into her arms.

23

Thou hast turned for me my mourning into dancing:
thou hast put off my sackcloth, and girded me with gladness;
Psalm 30:11

E velyn watched her daughter leave the kitchen, panic enveloping her. Her heart beat wildly in her chest, pulsating blood to her head. She felt faint and yet knew she couldn't allow herself that privilege. Voices carried from the front hall into the kitchen, voices she knew, voices she hadn't heard in over twenty-five years—and her mind raced back to a memory buried deep behind her protective wall.

"I'll never forgive you for this. Never! This is your God's fault. I hate Him!"

Her world spun with the memory of what she had said to her father as a child, and further turmoil engulfed her when she remembered how she'd refused to listen to the one person who seemed to understand her.

"Bubi, I just don't understand. Why is he doing this? Why do we have to leave?"

"I can't answer that, at least not in a way you would accept. All I can say is that your father and mother are doing what they believe to be the best possible thing given their circumstances."

"Do you agree with them?"

"It doesn't matter, child. I must comply and so must you."

"But I won't! I can't. I don't agree with what they've done. They've just turned their backs on their faith and are choosing to believe in something that's completely opposite to all they've ever believed, all they've ever taught me. How can I comply?"

Her grandmother removed her pearls and placed them around Evelyn's neck.

"These pearls may break, may even be lost, but the memory of them will always live in your heart. Just like your life here. You will never forget it. It's sealed in your memory forever. But you have to choose, my dear Evlyna. You have to choose how you move ahead: with sadness, for sure, but determination, or with bitterness and resentment. Perhaps these pearls will help you choose."

And she had chosen. She had complied; she'd had no choice. They'd changed their names and moved. Evlyna Cohen had become Evelyn Crawford, and her beloved grandmother had surrendered her husband's name of Feldman to Fraser. But despite the wisdom offered by her grandmother, resentment and anger toward her father had escalated through her teen years and overflowed into her adult life; she had complied, but there had been a price.

Now Evelyn sat in her empty kitchen, terrified at the very thought of her father's presence in her home. Yes, there had been a couple of phone calls over the past six months. Yes, there were days when she wanted to turn back the clock…

But life isn't like that. You can't undo what's been done!

Evelyn considered the events of her past. Over and over in her mind she heard the unspoken words she had wanted to say to her grandmother, words of malice and contempt that came from being a child: "I'm sorry, Bubi, I'll never forgive him."

And she never thought she would, not until July, when she'd first called her father.

Trickster's excitable barking and her daughter's unbridled laughter engulfed the house and broke Evelyn's painful reverie.

"Really!" and "Wow, I've gotta phone Wil!" resonated in Evelyn's ears as she sat immobile in her chair, absorbing her daughter's excitement. Trickster's barking accelerated, matching Evelyn's heartbeat as her hands grabbed at her skirt, crunching then smoothing then crunching again. Her mind raced, listening, imagining, fearing. And then he was there, her father, standing in her kitchen doorway, filling it with his large frame.

"Evlyna," he whispered.

Evelyn heard her father speak her real name and, in an instant, her heart melted. She had forgotten the sound: the Polish accent, the husky voice he'd used when he'd gotten impatient with her as a child, the teasing tone when he'd chanted, "Lyna, Lyna, my little Evlyna." He hadn't called her Evlyna since the day they'd taken the train from Toronto to start a new life in the small, obscure village at whose name most people smiled. Now he stood in her kitchen doorway, arms outstretched, whispering *Evlyna*.

"Papa" was all she could say as she ran and buried her face in his chest. His embrace held her strong and hard as she sobbed deep, gut-wrenching, painful sobs that shook her body. Only when her father gently pushed her from his embrace did she acknowledge her grandmother.

"Bubi! Oh, Bubi!"

As her grandmother embraced her, Evelyn felt the arms of her father surround them both and the three became one as their sobs echoed throughout the house.

Blowing her nose first, Lucy passed around the tissue box. "At this rate, we won't need to wash our faces tonight. Even Trickster seems to understand that something monumental is happening."

The adults turned to the family pet, which had been standing near the front door, tail between her legs, whimpering.

"Come here, girl. There's someone I want you to meet," Evelyn called, and Trickster raced to Evelyn's waiting arms.

24

Ointment and perfume rejoice the heart:
so doth the sweetness of a man's friend by hearty counsel.
PROVERBS 27:9

Pike Ridge, Alberta
December 22

Feigning nonchalance, Abby listened to the conversation between Hank Mason and Jimmy Mitchell as she cleared and then reset the diner's few tables for the Sunday morning regulars.

It had been a long day. Abby could go home once the tables were set, and Hank and Jimmy's conversation seemed to make the time go faster. Not for a minute did she think she was being rude by eavesdropping. Not at all. The diner never provided privacy, and most conversations were open for public scrutiny. Besides, Jimmy had a special way of telling his stories and she often repeated them to Edna over hot chocolate and raisin toast, adding the necessary drama to accompany the details.

Peddling custom-made brushes, personal care products, and household cleansers, Jimmy travelled from town to town in northern Alberta picking up the latest and tastiest bits of local news. Abby had learned this quickly in her first week; Hank had warned her that Jimmy had a need to share anything and everything he heard, whether he had a willing audience or not. Today's discussion had piqued her interest more out of boredom than anything else, especially when she heard "Thystle Creek" mentioned.

"Yep, seems he's out of a coma, but doesn't know who he is," Jimmy said. "Leastwise, that's the latest news I'm hearing."

"Where'd you say he lived again?" Hank asked, wiping the black and white mosaic countertop that had previously held two orders of his evening special.

"Thystle Creek. The town's in a buzz. Seems the police think his wife beat up on him and took off. Headed back to Quebec, they think."

The room spun. The Christmas lights edging the diner's large front window blurred and became one large mass of colour. The darkness moved in slowly, like a black veil drifting in a gentle breeze and then landing. Abby sank to the floor. The tray of clean silverware clattered beside her, its contents scattering in all directions.

"Angie!" Hank yelled. "Jimmy, go get Edna, and hurry!"

The smell of stale tobacco and skunky beer stung Abby's nostrils. She had no idea where she was, but she knew she was going to be sick ... and soon. Arms held her back as she struggled to sit up. She opened her eyes to peer into the face of her landlady.

"Edna ... I—I'm gonna be sick!"

"Quick, Hank! Give me a bucket."

Heaving into an old spittoon, Abby closed her eyes and gave in to her body's need to cleanse itself. After repeated retching, she fell back, weak and distraught. Where had that come from? She forced herself to think, mindful of Edna's endearments and Hank's hovering. Jimmy's words resonated in her head—"Seems the police think his wife beat up on him and took off"—and she heaved again, this time from fear.

"Poor thing," Edna whispered to Hank, who stood by helplessly with his hands deep in his pockets.

"She hasn't been sick for a long time," Hank responded, shaking his head. "Not sure when it's supposed to stop, but I figured somewheres before now. Ain't that right, Edna?"

"As if I can answer that question, you old coot! But you're right about one thing, it's been a good while since I've seen her so poorly. Any idea what caused it?"

"None. Jimmy and I were talking—or should I say Jimmy was talking—and the next thing we knew there was silverware all over the floor and Angie had collapsed."

"Well, she doesn't appear to have harmed herself or the baby in the fall, but I think it would be a good thing if she took tomorrow off."

"But it's my busiest day of the week and I've got no one…"

"Shame on you! This child needs rest and I'm going to see that she gets it! Whatever caused her to faint may very well make a return visit."

Hank opened his mouth to say something, but Edna's look froze him in mid-thought.

"You're just gonna have to find someone else," she insisted.

"Okay," Hank conceded, shame burning his face. "I'll see if Maggie can fill in. Didn't give myself time to think it through. You're right. Angie needs to take the day off. I'm sure she'll be fine come Monday."

Abby lay still on the bed. She had time to think while overhearing the conversation between Edna and Hank. It didn't take long for her to realize that she was lying on a cot in the back room of the diner where Hank often spent the night when he'd had too much to drink and didn't want to drive home. The bedding had not been changed in—Abby didn't want to think how long, but it had served her well.

Jake was alive. Abby sighed, not sure if she was feeling relief that she hadn't killed him or frustrated that, regrettably, he wasn't dead. She felt immediate remorse for thinking the latter, but had to admit it terrified her knowing what she'd done and how determined her husband would be to find her and make her pay. Then she remembered Jimmy's words: "Seems he's out of a coma, but doesn't know who he is."

The faint smile was not missed on Edna.

"Now, that's the face I like to see. Whatever came over you, child?"

Abby made an attempt to sit up. "Not sure, but I think it's passed. I should get back to work."

"Nonsense. You're coming home with me right this minute. The diner's closed—"

"That's right, Angie," Hank interrupted. "I've locked the door and we're closed until tomorrow."

"And you won't be coming near this place until Monday. Never mind giving me a hard time." Edna raised her fingers to Abby's lips. "That's the final word. Right, Hank?"

"Absolutely. You need to take care of yourself and that little young'un. Maggie will look after things tomorrow."

"That settles that…now, where's your coat?" Edna said. "We're going home."

PART
THREE

25

Peace I leave with you, my peace I give unto you:
not as the world giveth, give I unto you.
Let not your heart be troubled, neither let it be afraid.

JOHN 14:27

Christmas Morning

Evelyn sat bewitched, her legs curled under her as she stared out her darkened living room window. Fresh snow filled the air, settling over the ground and surrounding the trees and shrubs. Christmas morning greeted her with quiet reverence. If she could put a sound to falling snow, today it would be a full orchestra. Her love for classical music was a close second to her love for reading and she smiled at the idea of violins, cellos, and violas playing with majesty and power to greet the morning.

Unable to sleep, she had moved from her bedroom to the warmth of the living room, grateful that the coals from the previous evening's fire had responded well to the addition of wood with very little prodding. The fire crackled and bounced, reflecting hypnotically in the darkened window.

What is it about a fire? Evelyn wondered as she fell under its spell.

Trickster lay curled up at her feet. Evelyn smiled. How she loved her dog! An impulsive caressing of Trickster's ears was greeted with a groan—known only to the canine world—and a long, slow stretch exposing a furry tummy that demanded equal attention.

Evelyn laughed. "You're one spoiled dog. You know that, don't ya?" Her vigorous rubbing produced further groans, no doubt of appreciation.

Lost in the silence, her thoughts returned to something that had filled her head in the early morning hours, awakening her from a sound sleep: everyone she cared about would be under the same roof.

All I need is Lucy, Wil, and little Annie to arrive and the day will be complete. What have I ever done to deserve this?

In a room illuminated only by flickering fire, the haunting question struck Evelyn with such force that, for a second, she gasped for breath. She shook her head in a desperate attempt to loose herself of the answer; nothing she could ever have done would have made her deserving.

She looked at the fire, at her sleeping dog, at her Bible that had fallen to the floor. She glanced at Lewis's chair, his desk, at anything that would prevent her from going down the dangerous path her meandering thoughts provoked. But thinking of Lewis was a mistake; a great sadness surfaced when she remembered how excited Lewis had been after purchasing their house.

"Think of all the children we'll need to fill these bedrooms," he'd speculated with child-like enthusiasm.

The memory hung in the air like a black cloud ready to empty its contents on unsuspecting picnickers. There had been no more children after Lucy. Evelyn had slowly filled the rooms, converting one into her library, which faced the morning sun. An old chair sat by the window, and many mornings would find her curled up with a book, escaping her current world by living in another.

A second room had become a sewing room, housing a large wardrobe filled with yards of material, patterns, and notions that had created the clothes Lucy wore as a child. Sewing offered her the isolation she craved, filling the long days when she wasn't working at the library. As yards of material slid beneath the needle, she often remembered her mother, but as often as those memories had surfaced, she'd never been prepared for the emotional setback they represented. With each memory, harsh words invaded her thoughts—words that had been spoken in anger, anger that had never really been directed at her mother.

The third room had been Lucy's, just across the hall from the master bedroom. Conveniently located, both Lewis and Evelyn had shared the wakeful nights of their new baby's fitful crying. For Evelyn, nursing had been the only option, and she'd welcomed Lewis's attentive support during those stressful months of early parenthood.

When Rob and B.J. had moved in with her in September, she'd decided to relocate to the spare bedroom on the main floor, just off the living room—the one Lucy had claimed when she was fifteen. This move had initiated a purging of all the rooms to provide extra space for her son and grandson. She'd given little girls' dress patterns and bundles of material with child-like designs to Mae Smytheson to disburse among her three daughters and their growing families. But the thinning of books had proven more taxing, since every copy was attached to a memory. Evelyn felt the burden of deserting her old friends lift when they'd found a new home at the town library. In the end, Evelyn had considered it a long-overdue job well done.

Dismantling the bedroom she'd shared with Lewis had been another matter. Memories had led to tears, and tears to regrets and hours of fighting the battle of guilt. Yet when the day had finally come when the room stood empty, Evelyn smiled through her tears. She and Lewis had shared this room for fifteen years and, despite the pain and anger the walls had often witnessed, she came to believe that Lewis had loved her and that he knew she'd loved him. Acknowledging that had brought closure and she'd carried the last of her clothing to her new bedroom on the first floor.

Stretching her legs slowly, not wanting to disturb Trickster, Evelyn remembered the day Lewis had convinced her of the need for the addition.

"We're not going to need it yet, Evie," he'd said, forcing an unnatural frown to prove and support his point. "But some day when we're older and greyer—and very much wiser—you'll be thank'n me. And you'll be glad you don't have to climb those stairs every night or every time you need to visit the water closet." He had a twinkle in his eye. Nothing had stopped him, not even a bathroom on the main floor.

She sat quietly reminiscing and missing her husband more than she had in a long while. Trickster yawned and slipped to the floor. Stretching her legs to their fullest, she lay prostrate in front of the fire, resting her head on her extended leg. Watching her dog settle into a deep sleep, Evelyn smiled at an old adage—*Let sleeping dogs lie*—and gently stepped over her snoring pet to poke the fire, placing another log on the fresh flames.

Closing the hearth screen, she turned and found her father watching her.

26

Watch and pray, that ye enter not into temptation:
the spirit indeed is willing, but the flesh is weak.
MATTHEW 26:41

Do I love my father? Aren't you supposed to love your father?

These questions startled her as she watched her father walk slowly toward her. Her life slid into slow motion as she searched her memory. Had she said, "I hate you"? No. She'd said, "I hate *Him.*" She hated God, not her father, and for some strange reason she was relieved by that. It was easier to hate a God she couldn't see than her own father. Anger? Yes. Hatred? No.

Since her first contact with her father in July, Evelyn had lived and re-lived her younger years—when happiness radiated in their small apartment above her father's bakery, when music and laughter bounced off the walls, when God was someone to fear yet worship at the same time. Her childhood memory of God had faded over the years, to be replaced by a detached indifference in which it was easy to erase His very existence, or at least any adoration for a Supreme Being she may have felt in her younger years.

As this older version of a man she'd once known closed the short distance between them, a realization struck Evelyn: *I don't hate him, but I don't know him, either.* Her childhood memories saw her father as a robust, smiling man, always laughing and joking with his customers as flour dust floated off his apron and hands. He'd seemed to tower over most men and Evelyn had worshipped him, until that fateful day when her life, as she had known it, had ended.

"May I join you?" her father asked.

Unnerved, Evelyn only nodded and watched her father ease himself into Lewis's favourite chair.

Lewis would have liked him. Surprised at the fleeting thought, Evelyn returned to the sofa where she had sat curled up moments earlier. This time, she sat straight, her hands in her lap as she watched the fire, hoping her father would speak first.

He did.

"This Christmas brings me much joy. I am sitting across from my daughter, who has been absent from my life for many, many years."

His words unsettled her but she smiled politely, allowing him to continue.

"The house is still asleep and my aging years don't allow me the privilege of sleeping late," he said. "When I heard the fire crackle, I knew you would be up, or at least hoped it would be you."

Joseph turned toward the grey window, now less dark than when Evelyn first stoked the fire.

"Don't you find falling snow captivating?" he asked. "It's so silent, and yet I can't help hearing music."

Evelyn gasped. "Like a symphony," she whispered, stunned at how alike they were. Did she want to be like her father?

"Exactly! Noisy snow," Joseph laughed. "Sounds like an oxymoron."

Moments passed and Evelyn welcomed the silence. She watched Trickster move shyly toward her father and half-smiled. "She's good with strangers."

She stopped in her tracks. *There, I've said it. My father's a stranger.*

Her father nodded as he scratched Trickster's ears and back. "I may be a stranger, but I believe I've won her over."

The small talk ended when her father eased his attention away from the dog.

"We need to talk."

"I wondered why her letters stopped. I just assumed my move to Thystle Creek was the reason. But apparently not." Evelyn lowered her head as she struggled with her words. "I—I never opened any, you know, but I've kept them all…the letters, I mean." She raised her eyes and looked directly into her father's. "Every one of them." Her voice faded.

Her father smiled, but said nothing. Moments passed. The mantel clock ticked, seemingly in tune with Trickster's snoring.

"And I—I have a sister?" Evelyn's voice broke. It was too much. She rubbed her eyes and slowly moved her fingers over her face and forehead, dragging them through her hair. "My mother died giving birth to a sister I never knew existed."

She heard her words and sat numb, staring at her father. For a moment, she wished he was a vision, a dream that would disappear like vapour in the wind. But he sat there, motionless. Was *he* remembering? After all, it was his wife who'd died. Was the pain still there? Was he angry at his God for allowing her death? The questions bounced in Evelyn's head like a tetherball spinning wildly around a pole.

Finally, the tension erupted and Evelyn began pacing in front of the fire.

"My mother's dead," she whispered, her hand resting on the mantel. She suddenly realized what her choices had deprived her of: her mother's forgiveness and love, her father's gentle words and compassion, her grandmother's quiet but strong demeanour.

She turned limp arms toward her father and fell into his lap, choking out the sobs rising in her throat. Suppressed for years behind her impenetrable wall of protection, tears of grief and guilt fell freely until her body shook uncontrollably. Begging for forgiveness didn't seem to be enough. The wasted years screamed at her and she muffled her agony and shame in his arms.

Evelyn raised her tear-stained face. "Can you ever forgive me?"

"Not only can I…I have, as did your mother…a very long time ago."
Joseph cupped her face with his large hands. "We understood your anger,
although it saddened us greatly. You were just thirteen when we turned
your world upside-down, and when you fell in love and…and my, how
very impulsive you were going off to Halifax like you did!" He laughed
slightly as he wagged his accusing finger at her. "But we understood."

He gently released Evelyn and held her gaze before continuing.

"Evlyna, reliving the pain of our past offers no opportunity for peace.
The only good thing about a difficult past is what we can learn from it. But
we must look ahead. Looking back only builds on our regrets. I learned
a long time ago that God is always present. He knows where we've been
and where we're going, and I take great comfort in this."

Evelyn stiffened and withdrew her hands from her father's.

"My dear, dear Evlyna, we are not here to debate your belief in God
or our Messiah." He leaned back in his chair, a gentle smile covering his
face. "Let's leave that for another time. The day is dawning and your family
stirs upstairs. Today we must prepare for a great Christmas celebration as
a family. We are restored and our wounds will heal. Tomorrow…tomor-
row we can talk. But today," he smiled, closed his eyes, and lifted his head
upward, "today we will celebrate our reunion."

Evelyn's grandmother stood quietly in the doorway, thanking God for
His goodness as she watched this new beginning for an estranged daughter and her father. She smiled as Evelyn rose to greet her.

27

Turn thee unto me, and have mercy upon me;
for I am desolate and afflicted.
PSALM 25:16

Pike Ridge, Alberta

Christmas Morning

A nd here I am carrying his baby," Abby spoke softly, resting her hand on her swollen abdomen. She sat cross-legged on the floor, her back resting against an antique Victorian side chair belonging to Edna's grandmother. She stared into the fire, desperately wanting to enjoy the contentment the rays of warmth provided, but struggling with what she had just shared. Following her collapse at work three days earlier, Abby realized it was time to be honest with her new friend. She owed her that much, as well as Hank, although Abby had determined her conversation with Hank would have to wait.

"I'm sorry I've not been honest with you." Abby looked at Edna as a guilty child looks longingly at a parent for forgiveness. "I hope you don't think less of me."

Abby smiled at Edna's attempt to wave away her apology.

"I have to admit," Edna proceeded with obvious care, "I've wondered about the baby's father and often considered asking you about him, but I felt it wasn't my place to pry."

Abby smiled, responding to Edna's forthrightness. "I've rehearsed over and over in my head what I would say had you brought it up. I always hoped it would never need to be shared. Now you know the truth—the whole story. The abuse. The accident. Why I had to change my name, even why I cut and coloured my hair."

Abby ran her fingers through the new hairstyle Edna had created for her the first week she'd moved in, a style she had come to love.

"When I heard Hank and Jimmy talking about Thystle Creek, I couldn't help listening," Abby continued. "Then I realized they were talking about Jake! When I heard that he had to have brain surgery because of me, that it left him with amnesia and that the police thought I'd tried to...well, the next thing I knew, you and Hank were hovering over me in his back room."

Abby's cup of hot chocolate rested on her distended belly and jostled slightly as her unborn child made itself known. Both women smiled at the distraction. Until Abby had shared her story, they had been enjoying a light-hearted morning of wrapping Christmas gifts and watching the light snow mantle the Christmas lights on the edge of Edna's porch.

Abby's story had changed the mood dramatically.

She ran her hand over her stomach, feeling the pressure of her baby against her hand. "I wish I could say this baby was conceived in love, but I can't. The last time we...he forced himself on me the night I asked to go home to visit my parents. He said 'No' and I made the mistake of challenging him."

Abby paused, head down. The fire sparked and crackled as both women sat quietly, pausing in their giftwrapping.

Breaking the silence, Abby's sigh bordered on defeat. "Edna, I don't think Jake knows how to love. He never had a good relationship with his father. In fact, I never once saw them doing anything together, like playing ball or going fishing. He didn't have any brothers, only a little sister, nine years younger. Jake used to say she was an accident. His mother always seemed so sad, almost afraid that if she spoke, she'd be repri-manded like a child speaking out of turn, and Mr. Waters always looked cross at her. They never went to church as a family, although sometimes Jake's mom would slip into the back of the church once the service start-ed. She'd always leave before the last song was finished. Thinking back on it, I can't help wondering if she was afraid of her husband. And if she was, I can certainly empathize with her."

Abby faltered.

"I can't help wondering if Jake's father was the wrong kind of role model," she said. "Maybe that's why Jake was so abusi…mean to me. Anyway, it wasn't a happy home. You know how you can *feel* happiness and love in a house? Well, it just wasn't there."

Abby paused before adding, "And then, of course, there was Holly."

Edna frowned. "Holly?"

With mixed emotions, Abby told the story of her husband's first—and, she believed, his only—true love.

"She was always present in our home—in our lives—always in the middle of everything. It took the last attack for me to realize that Jake had *never* loved me. He resented me. I wasn't Holly. She was dead and he was stuck with me. I thought moving to Thystle Creek would be a new begin-ning for us, but we weren't there very long before I realized he wasn't in-terested in a new beginning. He was just following Rob. He had no inten-tion of making a fresh start; he just wanted to make Rob's life miserable. I was just excess baggage."

Edna's words were slow in coming, but when she spoke, Abby heard words that offered healing, if not a solution. "Child, there's no excuse for a man to beat on a woman. None whatsoever. Jake may not have had a happy upbringing, he may not have had the best father in the world, and he may not have gotten the woman he loved—although he must be blind not to see what's been in front of him all these years—but what he *did* have was a choice. And he chose wrong. Dead wrong. I heard somewhere that life is not made of the dreams we dream but the choices we make, and Jake made a bad choice. A very bad choice." Edna hesitated before continuing. "I'm not much of a praying woman, child, but I'm pretty sure the big guy up there is watching out for you and that little one you're carrying, regardless of how it was conceived."

Edna cleared her throat and shifted her position. Abby had never heard Edna talk about God or praying or religion, and she couldn't help laughing at how ill at ease Edna appeared.

"Sorry, Edna, I love you for saying it, but those last words—the praying part—sounded strange coming from you, and I love you even more for saying them. I *do* believe in God, even though I'm convinced He's too busy with other things to focus on my problems. I will say, though, that I'm glad He brought you into my life."

"Well...well, that's just fine, just fine by me. You're like the daughter I never had, thanks to Hank Mason, that pigheaded old coot, and I'll see that no more harm comes to you."

Seized by a cramp, Abby groaned and extended her crossed legs in front of the fire before rising. Her face took on a more serious look. "Edna, I'm not sure I can stay here much longer. You don't know Jake. If he begins to remember, nothing will stop him until he finds me." Abby circled her hands on her belly. "And not even this child will stop him from—"

"Enough talk like that! You're not going anywhere and no harm is going to come to you or that baby. If I can't prevent it, you can be very sure Hank will. He's big enough, brazen enough, and intimidating enough to scare anyone. Now, let's finish wrapping these gifts for that pigheaded old coot." They both laughed. "We need to deliver them before he starts his Christmas Day brunch without us, and with that little belly of yours, you can play Santa!"

Giggling and laughter filled the home that had become a refuge for Abby, but she still harboured the fear of discovery, knowing in her heart that she might soon have to leave.

28

In thee, O Lord, do I put my trust:
let me never be put to confusion.
PSALM 71:1

Three hours later, Abby held her unborn child's new teddy bear close to her chest. It fit nicely under her chin and she closed her eyes, breathing into the body of the stuffed animal, cradling her head in its soft fur. It was a Christmas gift from Hank that had shocked both Abby and Edna.

"I don't believe he's ever bought a child's toy," Edna had whispered when Abby unwrapped the package. Abby laughed outright when Hank dubbed the tiny gift "Fearless."

"Such a big name for such a little bear," Abby had taunted, wagging Fearless in front of his face, much to Edna's delight and encouragement.

"Now wait a minute," he'd responded defensively. "Little bears grow up and *become* fearless."

His look had proven his point, and yet he'd squirmed in protest when Abby hugged him and planted a kiss on his whisker-covered cheek.

Resting the stuffed toy against the footstool in front of her, Abby curled up in her favourite chair, her outstretched legs and extended belly covered by the lap blanket Edna had given her for Christmas. With pen in hand and paper resting on her lap, she considered writing her mother.

Throughout the months she had been living with Edna, she'd suppressed the nagging guilt that she had not informed her mother that she was no longer living with Jake and that she was about to be a mother herself. But after the information she'd learned from Jimmy Mitchell, she came to a conclusion: *What she doesn't know, she can't repeat. I'll call her once the baby's born.* So instead, two words stared at her from the notepaper: "Dear Evie."

As much as she enjoyed writing to Evelyn, even that task proved difficult. With all that had happened over the previous few days, she found it hard to know what to say. Should she tell her she knew about Jake and his amnesia? Should she ask if the police really suspected her of hurting Jake on purpose? Should she tell Evelyn what she'd told Edna? Should she even tell Evelyn about Edna and where she was living now? In previous letters, she had referred to her "new friend," but it had ended there. She was very careful not to refer to her whereabouts in her letters, but after talking with Edna earlier that day, and then with Hank later, she began to wonder if she should include Evelyn.

After several attempts, Abby deferred the task and instead let her mind wander to the afternoon, to the laughter that had followed the small gift exchange. For the first time since she'd met Hank five months earlier, he'd been speechless when she'd given him the multi-coloured scarf she'd knitted throughout the fall. She smiled, remembering how he'd stuttered a *thank you* that caused Edna to burst out laughing and Abby to hold her sides as a fit of laughter cramped her abdomen.

Abby's gift for Edna had been nothing special in Abby's opinion, just an earthenware coffee mug, but the way Edna had carried on, one would have thought she'd received fine china, laden with gold and fit for a queen. Edna had hugged her, holding the embrace longer than usual. When Edna released her, Abby saw Hank wipe a tear from his eye and Abby quickly turned her head aside, not wanting to embarrass him.

I think he still loves her, Abby decided as she stretched her legs to release an annoying twitch in her side. *I wonder why they never married.*

But marriage doesn't always work out, she thought sadly, thinking of Jake.

She pressed on her lower back and tried to stretch the cramp that was spreading to her lower abdomen. *I shouldn't have eaten so much food, but it's hard to resist Hank's baked beans and homemade bread.* She decided a visit to the bathroom might alleviate the persistent discomfort.

Minutes later, Abby stood in Edna's kitchen doorway. Edna sat at the kitchen table reading a two-day-old newspaper, humming a Christmas carol, and drinking coffee from her new mug. She looked up.

"Abby?" Concern filled her voice and etched her face.

"I think I need to see a doctor. This cramping started at Hank's and it's getting worse. I don't know what labour feels like…" Abby faltered, then burst into tears. "But it's too early. I'm only six months."

Edna jumped to her feet, knocking her new coffee mug to the floor, breaking it into three pieces.

She held Abby briefly in her arms, then took command of the situation.

"Let's get you upstairs to bed. No, wait! On second thought, no more stairs. You come with me into the spare room. The bed's just as soft and I'll be able to keep an eye on you. Meanwhile, I'll call Doctor Crombie…"

Abby jerked to a halt. "Edna, I've never been to Doctor Crombie and—"

"Hush. Don't you worry none. Ken Crombie is a very good doctor and we need to make sure we keep you and that little child of yours together for a few more weeks." Edna paused. "I suppose a little longer than that would be better, but in any case, you need to get off your feet and I need to call Ken."

"What do you mean, he's got the flu?" Edna's frustration and worry escalated to such illogical proportions that she felt foolish about her impatience. "I'm sorry, Betsy. I didn't mean to sound so inconsiderate. I hope Ken will be feeling better soon. Does he know of another doctor in the area? Edmonton is too far to travel and this young thing may be headed for early labour if something isn't done to stop it."

"Hang on a minute, Edna. I'll see if Ken's awake."

Edna waited for a few moments, then heard Betsy Crombie return to the phone.

"Ken says there are two doctors in the area besides himself. Malcolm Ancaster is west of here by three hours, just over the border into British Columbia, but he's on a cruise in the Caribbean. Took his whole family for Christmas. The other doctor's in Thystle Creek. He replaced Doctor Bailey a while back. Ken's not sure of his name, but says we have Doctor Bailey's home number. Would you like me to call him for you?"

"Oh, please do, Betsy," Edna said without hesitation. "Let the new doctor know that if he needs to stay over, I've got lots of room here. And please, tell Ken I hope he gets better soon. Can't have our only doctor for miles around getting sick, can we?"

Edna laughed nervously, still feeling a bit embarrassed by her outspoken reaction earlier. Before hanging up, she added, "Hope to hear from you soon, Betsy."

29

Behold, thou art fair, my love; behold, thou art fair...
Thy lips are like a thread of scarlet.
SONG OF SOLOMON 4:1, 3

O ven-roasted turkey, apple bread stuffing, lots of gravy for the smashed potatoes. Can't get any better than that," Wil declared jokingly as he and Lucy arrived at Evelyn's home laden with gifts and, of course, Annie. "Hope you've got cranberries, Evie."

Wil kissed his mother-in-law and wished her a very merry Christmas.

"Wouldn't be Christmas without them," Evelyn replied shyly, conscious of her father and grandmother watching from their vantage point at the kitchen table.

Wil turned to his wife's great-grandmother and, in a way known only to Wil, bowed majestically. Taking Rachel's hand, he kissed the top of it. "And to you, my dear, newly acquired great-grandmother-in-law—whom I'd love to call Bubi—warmest greetings on this wonderful, sunshiny Christmas Day."

"Oh my goodness! Have you ever heard such outright—and excruciatingly painful—flattery?" Lucy hugged her great-grandmother, kissing her gently on the cheek. "Don't listen to him, Bubi, he's only making noise."

"Ah, but such a nice noise!" the elderly woman responded, a distinct twinkle in her eye. She turned to Wil. "And yes, you most certainly may call me Bubi. I would like that very much."

Lucy kissed her grandfather. "Merry Christmas, Zaida. Welcome to our winter wonderland."

Joseph stared. "Zaida?" he whispered.

Lucy smiled. "Yep, I've been doing my homework. Zaida is Yiddish for *grandfather*, right, Mom?"

Evelyn smiled at her father and grandmother, wiping her hands on the front of her apron. "Lucy is determined to learn as much as she can about her Jewish heritage and, no doubt, will be picking your brain, Bubi, for information about our ancestors in Poland."

"Ah, such *shtik naches*!" Rachel said, sharing a little Yiddish with Lucy. "My great-granddaughter brings me such great joy."

Evelyn continued to busy herself at the kitchen counter, making sure the potatoes were boiling, the gravy was simmering, and the turkey was waiting to be carved. Her heart almost burst as she listened to the long lost voices of her past fill her kitchen. Tears threatened to spill on her cheeks, but had she let them, she knew they would have been tears of *shtik naches*.

The doorbell broke the moment and Trickster, content to remain far away from the hot kitchen, bounded from her chair in the living room and reached the front door just as Lucy did.

"Come here, girl." Opening the door, Lucy bent down and picked up the wiggling dog that immediately squirmed and leaped from Lucy's arms as Christina and Levi stepped inside. Bouncing like a yo-yo on the end of an elastic band, the dog yelped an ear-piercing greeting.

"Nice to be loved so much, hmm?" Lucy remarked, cocking her head to one side.

"Indeed." Levi winked, bending down to scratch Trickster's head.

"Smells delightful," Christina said. "Somehow that word seems inadequate, especially if one stops and thinks about the work behind this wonderful aroma." She handed her gifts to Lucy and allowed her son to help her with her coat. "Your mother's idea of an early dinner is wonderful. Gives everyone lots of time to relax and enjoy the day!"

Christina leaned into Lucy's ear and, grinning like a schoolgirl holding the secret to ageless bliss, whispered, "I'm very anxious to get to know your great-grandmother."

Lucy smiled. "Go on into the kitchen. Mom's anxious to see you. I think she might need some moral support. Wil's being a goof, as usual!"

While Christina headed toward the kitchen, Lucy took the gifts into the living room. When she stood up from placing them under the tree, she all but bumped into Levi.

Levi extended his hand to Lucy when she lost her balance. "Sorry, Luce. Didn't mean to startle you." He nodded his head slightly in the direction of the kitchen and lowered his voice. "I just wanted to see how things are *really* going. I've not had a chance to talk with your mother since the shock of her father and grandmother's arrival a few days ago. Seems there's a lot of flu going around and I've been called in all directions."

Lucy smiled before linking her arm in Levi's and heading toward the front hall. "Actually, things are pretty good, all considering. Rob just told me that when he came down earlier this morning, he found Mom, our grandfather, and Bubi talking quietly in the living room. He said that from the look of their empty coffee mugs, they'd been up for a while. If Mom heard him, she never let on. He sensed the need for privacy and left them, but that ended when B.J. bounded in, ready to devour anything under the tree that looked like it might be for him."

Levi smiled. "Can't say I blame him. It *is* Christmas Day and he's done well waiting this long, especially with all the additional excitement."

Lucy released her arm and headed toward the kitchen, only to be greeted by her mother.

"Wondered where you two got to. Merry Christmas, Lee."

Evelyn politely acknowledged Levi's kiss on her cheek as she observed Lucy's quiet exit to the kitchen.

"Haven't seen much of you these past couple of days," she said once they were alone. "I thought maybe after your *surprise*, you might have skipped town."

Although accusatory, Evelyn's voice held a sly lilt. Her eyes never left Levi's. Alone in the hallway, yet never far from the escalating noise in the kitchen, she welcomed the warmth of Levi's arms.

"You mad at me?" Levi asked, releasing her from his embrace but still clutching her arms.

Evelyn felt comfortable with Levi's open display of affection—though she was always relieved when it wasn't witnessed—but she was startled by his question.

"Mad? How could I ever be mad at you for bringing me the best Christmas gift I could possibly have—apart from Annie," she added, not wanting him to let go of his arms. "My father and Bubi have come into my life again, thanks to you. Mad at you? How can I ever thank yo—

The kiss was so sudden that, had it not been for the wall, Evelyn would have landed on the floor. Her world spun as she responded to the demand the kiss provoked.

An instant later—or was it an eternity?—she stood breathless, staring into Levi's eyes.

"We'd better join the others," Levi said.

He laughed, leaving her alone in the hallway, smoothing her apron and gulping for air.

30

For unto us a child is born,
unto us a son is given.
ISAIAH 9:6

Midafternoon found Evelyn's living room scattered with torn
wrapping paper, ribbons, empty glasses, and an assortment
of gifts ranging from extravagant toys for B.J. and Annie to
more subdued gifts for the adults. Small plates, having once held Christina's Christmas cake, sat void of all but crumbs, and coffee mugs were
left empty on the end tables. B.J. lay stretched on the floor in front of
the fireplace, content to play with the model train marked "CP Railway
Lines, Pontypool"—a gift from his great-grandfather while Christina and
Rachel elected to sit by the living room window, away from the confusion, quietly sharing their love for and pride in their late husbands.

Unanimously voted to kitchen duty by the women, Rob, Levi, and
Wil had retreated to the kitchen an hour earlier—but not before threatening to devour a third piece of pumpkin pie, the likes of which Rob
declared he'd never tasted before. Rumblings and laughter drifted from
the kitchen as the three flicked damp tea towels at each other, eventually
congratulating themselves on a job well done. Clean silverware, neatly
stacked dishes, and various pots and lids sat on the kitchen table waiting
to be put away, and several damp tea towels lay strewn over the backs of

chairs. With Annie asleep in Evelyn's arms, father, daughter, and grand-daughter sat on the sofa, unaffected by, and perhaps even oblivious to, the tomfoolery going on in the kitchen.

"She was beautiful, Zaida," Lucy spoke softly, holding the framed picture of Evelyn's mother that Evelyn had received from her father earlier in the afternoon.

Joseph stroked the glass and sighed. "Indeed, she was beautiful, and I do believe your mother has followed very closely in her footsteps. Much better than the alternative." He winked at Lucy and tapped his chest to prove his point. He laughed aloud, then quickly lowered his voice when Annie flinched in her sleep. "Sorry, little one. Forgot how loud my voice can be."

He continued, with less intensity: "My Hannah was soft-spoken, and when she did speak, she chose her words carefully. I never could win an argument, not with my Hannah. She'd just smile, pat my hand in mock sincerity, and let me *think* I'd won." He turned to Evelyn. "Remember her books? Too many to count. She loved to read, didn't she?"

Evelyn nodded slightly, fully aware of her own love of books and the library still bursting at the seams on the second floor, despite the recent purging.

"It was never hard for you to get two or three stories out of your mother at bedtime. I was always the old ogre who broke it up with, 'Our little Lyna needs her rest.'"

Memories and sounds filled Evelyn's head. Her mother's quiet voice. Her lavender cologne, sprayed sparingly on the handkerchief tucked in her sleeve. The way her hair fell from behind her ear when she laughed at the funny stories she'd read. How she used to whisper, "Just one more story" when her husband tried to put a kibosh on their bedtime reading.

"So your mother certainly has no resemblance to me," her father said. "Nor does she have my boisterous voice, unlike your Aunt Rachel, who takes after my side of the family, poor child!"

Although his remark brought Evelyn back from her musings, her inner turmoil surfaced in a question. "What's she like...my sister?"

"Rachel? Oh my! How does one describe a walking ball of fire? Living, breathing, loud, demanding, and often too hot under the collar for her own good. Poor Levi met her and stood speechless while Rachel all but threatened him for invading our world."

"Did I hear my name?" Levi stood beside the trio holding a tray of fresh coffee and more of his mother's Christmas baking: brownies, shortbread, butter tarts, and chocolate-coated almond wheels.

"Oh my goodness!" Lucy exclaimed. "More food. I'm gonna have to jump up and down a little to make room." She uncurled her legs and stretched them before standing.

Placing the tray on the coffee table, Levi pulled up a chair. "Well, the kitchen is done. At least the dishes are washed, but the pots and pans await your attention on the kitchen table, Evie. I'm unsure where they belong, and Rob and Wil proved useless in that department. When the last pot was dry, they feigned exhaustion, but strangely enough found they had enough energy to chase Trickster around in the fresh snow. Seems your favourite pet enticed them outdoors and they fell under her spell."

"What! My dad's outside...without me?" B.J. leaped to his feet, almost tripping over his own stash of Christmas gifts. "Nana, can I leave this stuff here so I can go outside and play with my dad and Uncle Wil?"

Before Evelyn could reply, her grandson had his snow pants, coat, and mitts in hand and was halfway through the kitchen. Evelyn shook her head and smiled, but before anything could be said about the child's energy, Levi resumed the conversation about his encounter with Rachel Crawford.

"I think she thought I was going to kidnap your father, Evie. I was questioned, challenged, and evaluated with the skill of a sergeant major." Levi laughed at the memory. "But that wasn't the real shocker. When she first spoke from behind me, I turned and almost fell over. There *you* stood, only a few years younger. She really is the image of you."

Evelyn winced, regretting asking about her sister. She could not equate the idea that she had a sister and that they looked alike. It seemed surreal, unfathomable. Shifting a hungry baby to Lucy's waiting arms,

Evelyn stood, bringing closure to the topic of her sister and welcoming the excuse to leave the room in response to the ringing of the telephone.

Moments later, Evelyn stood in the kitchen doorway, concern covering her face. "Lee, Doc Bailey wants to talk to you. He says it's important."

Evelyn waved at her daughter and father, who watched from the living room window as she and Levi pulled away from the curb heading west. At first, she'd feigned reluctance at the thought of going to Pike Ridge when Levi invited her to go with him, citing the fact that it was Christmas Day and she couldn't leave her family. But in her heart, she had known better. The prospect of having Levi all to herself proved irresistible.

She could still hear Lucy's encouraging words. "Go, Mom! There's no one he'd rather have to keep him company. I'm sure you two can find something to talk about."

Her smirk had caused Evelyn's face to flush.

"Don't worry about this end," Lucy said. "We'll just have a party without you, won't we, Bubi?" She'd linked arms with her great-grandmother, who had unexpectedly overheard the conversation from the kitchen doorway.

Evelyn remembered her grandmother's knowing smile, her warm, penetrating eyes and quiet nod as she acquiesced to Lucy's suggestion. She remembered feeling a sense of awe looking at the family's matriarch and how beautifully she had aged. She hadn't realized how much she'd missed her grandmother. She hadn't been able to resist the urge to hug her, whispering a thank you.

31

By the word of the Lord were the heavens made;
and all the host of them by the breath of his mouth.

PSALM 33:6

The early snowfall had subsided while Evelyn and her family enjoyed their early turkey dinner, but the blinding rays of the late afternoon sun proved troublesome. Levi remained quiet for the first hour, struggling with the brightness, but as the sun's strength diminished, he relaxed and so did Evelyn.

"Seems the young lady is experiencing what might be early labour signs. According to Doctor Crombie's wife, the mother-to-be is just ending her sixth month."

"Can you stop the contractions if they're premature?" Evelyn spoke softly, remembering the two babies she'd lost.

"Depends."

"On what?"

"Oh, things like a recent fall or accident. Maybe it's just abdominal gas from something she's eaten, or perhaps she's been on medication that could precipitate early labour. On the other hand, she might just be suffering from good, old-fashioned Braxton Hicks contractions."

"Which are?" Evelyn adjusted the sun visor.

"Practise for the real thing," Levi laughed, then drew on his professionalism. "A woman can experience Braxton Hicks as early as the second trimester, but they're more common in the third. The muscles of the uterus tighten for about thirty to sixty seconds, or for as long as two minutes. I had a patient who experienced them around her twentieth week and was having ten or more contractions per hour. It wasn't painful, just bothersome, but it did go on for days. That's rare. Usually fewer than four per hour is considered okay. If our young lady is fortunate, this might be all she's experiencing, although the real litmus test will be whether she's dilating." Levi looked at Evelyn, who stared straight ahead. "Now, isn't that the doctor talking?"

She turned to him and smiled.

"She might simply be dehydrated," he continued. "That's often a cause for BH contractions. She may just need some fluids and bed rest. If that's the case, all we'll have had is a nice Christmas Day ride—just the two of us." Levi reached over and took Evelyn's gloved hand. "I can't think of a better way to spend Christmas, can you?"

Evelyn shook her head, left her hand in his, and remained silent.

Appreciating the warmth of Levi's hand, she glanced out the window and watched the snow blow across the open plain like gentle waves rolling in the open sea. For a moment she found herself grateful for the extremely unusual, but very timely Chinook that had moved into the area on Christmas Eve. Chinooks rarely occurred north of Red Deer, but when they did, they often brought fierce winds accompanied by a sudden rise in temperatures. Although one would call it a blustery day, they had been spared the dreaded wind.

You came at the right time, she thought, humanizing the Chinook. *Wish you could stay longer.*

She smiled at her antagonistic attitude toward winter. No matter how hard she tried, and despite the number of years she'd spent in northern Alberta, the winter months always seemed to drag on mercilessly. Every year she counted the days from the first snowflake until the day she saw the first fledgling blade of grass daring to present itself through the shallow mounds of snow in her garden.

Levi shifted in his seat and Evelyn found herself quietly watching her friend. His medical knowledge never ceased to amaze her, nor did the privilege he had of watching the birth of new life or the joy of seeing remarkable recoveries from life-threatening surgeries. She was moved by his unwavering commitment to go all the way to Pike Ridge for someone who wasn't even one of his patients. Yet she was not naïve; she knew that being a doctor had its demands, its moments when the question of *why* surfaced, its moments of overwhelming helplessness, defeat, and loss upon the death of a patient. Memories of her stillborn son swept over her and, for a moment, she relived Allen Bailey's comment, "There wasn't anything anyone could do. We couldn't save him." Her sudden quiver reached the tips of her fingers and Levi squeezed her hand, a small frown crossing his face.

"You okay?"

Not now, she silently begged the unwelcome intruder. *Not today.* Evelyn returned Levi's smile and took strength from his concern. "I'm fine."

A comfortable silence settled over them and Evelyn laid her head back, closing her eyes. After a moment or two, she found herself staring out the window. As many books as she had read in her lifetime, nothing provided the words to describe what she saw. For several miles, they had witnessed the sun as it sat on the edge of the distant hills—as though it depended upon them to hold it up. The remnants of a Chinook arch graced the sky, expressing itself in magnificent shades of pink and red. But now, with the sun gone, the orange and yellow hues that had hovered on the distant horizon and stretched before them like molten lava pouring from the heavens were replaced. The aurora borealis lit up the sky.

Levi pulled the car over to the side of the road, carefully avoiding the build-up of ice on the shoulder.

They sat in silence until Levi spoke.

"You're the reader. Have you found the right words yet?" he asked.

Evelyn just shook her head. "It's breathtaking, isn't it?"

Levi hugged the steering wheel. "Did you know that in many northern areas, the borealis is seen as a symbol of approaching doom? These northern lights are often regarded with fear and superstition."

"How can anything so beautiful be thought of with such dread?" Evelyn asked, staring through the front window.

"There's a myth among the Inuit people who live in the higher, northern latitudes that says the aurora borealis is a manifestation of their ancestors. Another myth indicates that it's telling stories of what happened in the past and what will happen in the future."

"Do people actually believe this?"

"Some do."

Evelyn watched in wonder at the beauty in the sky.

Levi broke the silence again. "Fairbanks, Alaska is known as one of the best places in the world to see this spectacle of lights."

"Have you been there?"

"No, but close. Autumn is the best season to see this magnificent display of colour—partly because the nights are getting longer and the pleasant evenings bring people outside to look at the stars—so I took a leave from the office for a three-week hike. I was much younger back then." He gave her a wink. "I didn't quite make it to Fairbanks, but what I saw was worth the sore muscles and aching back. The sky was light green and yellow with pink wisps waving and vibrating across the heavens. It was spectacular! I found out later that some had described what they'd seen as curtains or pillars or pinwheels, and even haloes of light bouncing across the sky."

"Did God create this?"

Levi turned to Evelyn. "Yes, He did," he replied in earnest, and said no more as he put the car in gear and pulled onto the road.

Evelyn welcomed the silence.

Where did that come from? she thought, trying to find an explanation for her question. It startled her, perhaps even frightened her, when she realized her reference to God had sounded personal.

Shrugging off the unsettling thought, she checked her watch. By her calculations, they should be in Pike Ridge within the half-hour. She wondered if Levi was hungry. She was, despite the turkey dinner they'd enjoyed not too many hours earlier.

Turning to ask him, a sudden but appealing thought overcame her. *I really do love him.* She swallowed hard at the very idea of loving again and turned her face toward the road. The idea of another man in her life frightened her, almost to the point of wanting to end her relationship with Levi. Yet she knew he cared for her. After all, there was that kiss earlier in the day. Evelyn felt her cheeks flush at the memory and she smiled shyly.

I think he rather enjoys teasing me—and I think I rather enjoy being teased.

"Penny for your thoughts … or are they worth more?" Levi grinned. "I think I asked you that question once before."

Evelyn tactfully ignored his question. How could she tell him what she'd been thinking? "I was just wondering if you were hungry," she said.

She looked defensively at him when he laughed, then quickly changed the subject.

"Lee, is there any further word on Jake? I can't help wondering if he's ever going to get his memory back. I may be the only one, but I feel sorry for him; he's a very troubled young man."

"That may be the case, but to answer your question, he's being discharged into the care of Ruth Norton the first week in January. Those were the terms the doctors agreed to. Apparently, his physical health is stable. All he needs to do is regain his strength and, of course, his memory."

Evelyn remained silent.

"A nickel this time?" he asked.

Evelyn looked at him, head tilted with a questioning frown.

"For your thoughts."

"Oh, I'm just digesting the whole idea," she said. "Ruth will certainly take good care of him, there's no doubt about that. I'm just thinking about the *old* Jake. Do you think he'll ever get his memory back?"

"Hard to say. Maybe, maybe not. A colleague of mine on the coast had a patient back in the 50s, a father of four. He was involved in an accident with a logging truck in the B.C. interior. The chains holding the logs on the truck broke, and the logs came through the front window, crushing him."

"How dreadful!"

"Yes, it was. The medics at the accident scene never believed he'd survive the airlift to Calgary, but he did. He spent almost six months there, and then another six months at the Veteran's Hospital in Toronto. He'd survived the war, then came home, lost his carpentry business in a fire, and had to resort to travelling across Canada selling incidentals to keep his family together. He survived the accident, but never regained his memory. He only had family pictures to assure him that the four children who called him Dad were really his."

Evelyn fell silent for several miles. Levi had assured her that Jake's accident wasn't as serious as the one that had claimed the Ontario man's memory, and she took comfort in that. She wanted Jake to get better, but she knew if he regained his memory, he'd be fighting an even greater battle. Anger suffocates and destroys—she could testify to that—but she feared his anger would be fuelled by what had happened to him, no matter how innocently it was done.

"Look, there's the sign. We're here."

Evelyn looked where Levi pointed and read,

PIKE RIDGE: WHERE HEARTS ARE WARM
WHEN THE WINTER IS COLD

Evelyn shook her head at the thought of putting *warm* and *winter* in the same sentence. She would never appreciate cold weather, no matter how nice the words made it sound.

Lucy laughed as she kinged her last checker, winning the game. "That's two games out of three, Zaida. Wanna try and tie it?"

Before her grandfather could reply, the front doorbell rang and Trickster raced past Lucy, knocking over the checkerboard, sending red and black discs flying to the floor. Always ready to greet whoever stood on the other side of the door, the tiny dog circled in anticipation while Lucy made her way to the front hall, laughing at the dog's whimsical behaviour. Hoisting Trickster into her arms, Lucy opened the door and gasped.

"You must be Lucy. I'm your Aunt Rachel. Is my elusive sister home?"

Lucy stared, frozen on the spot. Even Trickster's expected welcome seemed diffused by the forthright stranger standing in the melting snow.

"Well, are you going to invite me in, or not?"

Lucy wordlessly stepped aside, her mouth still gaping as Trickster growled a protective threat.

"You certainly look like your mother...at least, you've got her hair." Rachel dropped her backpack on the floor in front of the closet and returned Lucy's stare. "Not sure about your eyes, though. Must be your father's. But then again, I never met him so I can't really say for sure."

Her caustic remark went unnoticed by Lucy, who stood shivering, heedless of the open door. She hushed Trickster into silence as she watched her grandfather embrace the woman who claimed to be her aunt.

32

And they that know thy name will put their trust in thee:
for thou, Lord, hast not forsaken them that seek thee.
PSALM 9:10

Pike Ridge, Alberta
Christmas Day

S itting like a magistrate high on her throne, 75 Amber Lane towered over Pike Ridge, demanding every passerby's attention. The majestic house, with its multiple chimneys and stained glass windows, could not be missed from anywhere on the main street. History seeped from its walls, windows and roof, and folk passing through the small northern town often stopped to inquire about its origin.

Levi pulled up to the curb and leaned across Evelyn to look out her side window. "Have you ever seen anything so…magnificent? I mean, some houses in Vancouver are beautiful, even stately, but this one…well, it's almost regal."

Both stared for several moments, taking in the Christmas-card-like setting. Strands of white lights too numerous to count glittered beneath the snow blanketing the bushes that surrounded the front walk and veranda. Patches of melting snow dripped from the warm lights, revealing those placed lower in the shrubs. A massive front door wreath covered the two panels of stained glass. Draped garlands created arches beneath the eaves of the veranda, and a monolithic Christmas tree filled the front window.

"Can you imagine setting that tree up?" Levi asked. "Apart from nature's own display, I've never seen such a huge tree. Certainly never in a home!"

Taking Evelyn's arm, Levi proceeded up a flight of eight steps to a long walkway. He stopped when Evelyn pulled on his arm.

"Can you imagine this home in the spring, Levi, with the flowers bursting in all directions? And the summer…" She turned to face the car. "The sun sets over there."

She pointed beyond where they'd parked before spinning back to face the house.

"I can see it all now, in spite of the snow, each silver leaf of the jack frost flower looking like a beautiful stained glass painting. The carpathian bellflower would grow over there, in the middle…"

Evelyn indicated the centre of the lawn, where uneven mounds testified to the presence of a garden buried deep beneath the snow.

"… or over there under the shade of the tall ferns, close to the low growing blue waterfall bellflower."

Evelyn's arms reached toward the front of the veranda.

"Oh my goodness, Lee, it would be a painter's delight to sit on this very spot and paint scene after scene in any direction."

She stumbled on the slippery walk and Lee braced her arm with his, smiling at her excitement.

"A lot of these plants will still be green, you know, even now under the snow," she said. "And as the snow melts in the spring, the east side will be bursting with new blooms."

She spun around and pointed to her left.

"Over there under that massive birch, I can see yards and yards of lemon mint, just like in front of my house." She spun again. "And next to the house, crocuses and tulips in the spring and groomed rose bushes in…oh, Lee, how breathtaking it could be."

Levi smiled and watched Evelyn spin like a child who'd been turned loose in a toy store and didn't know where to look first. He had been very conscious of her quiet moments in the car and he'd let her have them. While he'd not missed her reference to God, tempering his smile, inwardly he thanked his Creator for revealing Himself to Evelyn, even more than she realized.

Because he cared for her so deeply, Levi tried to imagine the summer garden as Evelyn had described it. But although he enjoyed gardening and had, in fact, spent many hours in his own garden in Vancouver before moving to Thystle Creek, his enthusiasm could not match hers.

"Maybe you could volunteer as the gardener's assistant this summer," Levi quipped, leading her up to the veranda as he enjoyed the wistful smile on her face.

When he rang the bell, the door chimes swelled like cathedral bells echoing in a tall tower.

"Did you hear that?" he whispered to Evelyn, not taking his eyes off the front door. "They sure can't miss someone who comes calling."

Edna Barnes opened the front door wearing a well-worn apron and wiping her hands on an oversized towel.

Levi hesitated. "I'm—I'm Doctor Morsman. I understand there's a young lady living here who might need my assistance. Can you let the lady of the house know I'm here?"

Edna smiled. "Welcome to my home, Doctor." She acknowledged Levi's uncomfortable response with a smile. "No need to feel embarrassed. This massive home can give the wrong impression. She may be regal on the outside, but trust me, she's very unassuming once you get to know her. Please come in, both of you."

Levi liked his host instantly. Introducing Evelyn as a friend, they were ushered into the drawing room that faced the street and housed the majestic tree he and Evelyn had stared at moments earlier.

"Beautiful, isn't she?" Edna stood beside her guests as they absorbed the grandeur of the tree. "I need help getting to the top—too old to be climbing ladders. But once the lights are on and the star's in place, I spend about two days decorating it, enjoying the memories that each ornament brings."

Edna lifted a tiny bell that hung front and centre on the tree. "This was my mother's. When my sister and I were little children tucked into bed on Christmas Eve, too excited to sleep, she would have my father slip outside and ring the bell by our bedroom window. Then she'd whisper, 'Santa's waiting for you to go to sleep before he comes down the chimney,' and we would dive under the sheets and will ourselves to sleep."

Edna replaced the bell with such tenderness that Levi and Evelyn stepped back a bit, for fear of intruding on a private moment.

"Memories are wonderful, aren't they?" Edna said with a sigh. "But you didn't come all this way to listen to an old lady reminisce. I should explain my delay in taking you to see Angie. She fell asleep a bit ago and I'm loathe to wake her. Poor thing. She's terrified she'll lose the baby and I thought if she had a cup of warm milk and some rest, things would settle down. Hope I'm doing the right thing. Bringing you all the way here on Christmas Day…"

"Don't worry about our being here," Evelyn said, speaking for the first time since their introduction. "The very unusual Chinook we've been experiencing has made the drive uneventful. The wind was strong, but nothing Lee couldn't manage."

Levi nodded. "That's right, Mrs. Barnes, but—"

"Please, call me Edna."

"If Angie's resting comfortably," he said, "we'll leave her be for a little while longer, but I'd like to check things out and make sure that all is well before too long. We can't presume that just because she's sleeping—"

"Perhaps I'll make us some tea and we can enjoy a wee visit," Edna interjected. "That should be enough time for Angie to rest. Would that be okay with you, Doctor?"

The kindness of this matronly woman didn't miss its mark. Levi nodded and winked at Evelyn, who had been gazing at the enormous Christmas tree, daring to touch the assorted ornaments.

"A cup of tea would be wonderful." He nodded his head in appreciation.

"And I've made my favourite English scones. We'll have some jam with them. I'm rather famous for my baking," she confessed with a giggle.

"She's quite the lady," Evelyn remarked, staring at the empty doorway. "And tea and scones sound marvellous. I didn't realize how hungry I was until the last half-hour of our drive." She looked at Levi, head to one side. "Do you think things are okay with our... *your* patient?"

She laughed shyly at her faux pas.

"Well, if she's resting and the contractions have subsided, my guess is that it's nothing but Braxton Hicks," he said. "We'll see after I've checked things out."

Half an hour later, following a delightful cup of hot tea and scones that confirmed Edna's well-earned reputation, Levi and Evelyn enjoyed a brief tour of a home that seemed to have invisible arms wrapping themselves around its guests to make them feel at home.

A quiet cough from the main floor bedroom alerted both host and guests.

"I think Angie's awake," Edna said. "Let me take a peek."

Edna disappeared down a long hallway that had not been included in their tour. Evelyn returned to the front parlour while Levi hovered in the doorway, awaiting his host's return. When she did, Edna motioned for him to follow her.

The grand hallway led to a door at the far end where the warmth of a fire could be felt long before they entered the room. Less than a minute later, Levi retraced his steps and stood speechless in front of Evelyn.

"That didn't take long. Is she okay?"

"Come with me," Levi whispered, mystery cloaking his words.

Abby Waters turned her tear-stained face and looked toward the entrance of the bedroom, and Evelyn gasped.

"Abby!"

She hurried across the room to the young woman, who sat sobbing uncontrollably.

"Hush, hush. Please, Abby, don't cry." Evelyn enveloped her young friend in her arms and rocked her as a mother rocks a weeping child.

Abby's sobs increased. "I—I'm…I can't believe you're here. I can't believe you found me. It's Christmas Day…and you came all this way."

"We didn't know it was you, Abby." Evelyn raised Abby's head and smoothed her hands down the young woman's shoulders and arms. "When Doc Bailey called Lee, he knew he had to come. I just came along to keep him company."

Evelyn fought back her own tears and welcomed Levi's warm hand on her shoulder. Evelyn and Abby accepted tissues from Edna, who stood hovering nearby, wiping her own eyes.

"Edna, this is the lady I've been writing to," Abby explained.

Edna just smiled and blew her nose.

The reunion ended when Abby's eyes filled with panic. "What about Jake? He's going to find out I'm here. If you found me, he will, too. I have to find somewhere else to live! He can't find me. You don't understand. I've got to…"

Abby struggled to stand.

Levi gently stopped her from getting out of bed, then picked up the blanket that had fallen to the floor. "Abby, you can't go anywhere, at least not for a while. I need to check you over and make sure things are okay with you and your unborn child. Then we'll talk about what needs to be done. We're not going to do anything to threaten your wellbeing or your child's, but you have to trust us. Can you do that?"

Abby hung her head and nodded. It was then that Evelyn noticed her hair. Sitting on the opposite side of the bed, she cupped her hand under Abby's chin and smiled. "Your hair's short. It looks very nice."

"Edna cut it for me after I hacked it with my nail scissors."

Everyone laughed and Evelyn squeezed Abby's shoulders with an endearing embrace. "I'll leave you with Edna and Lee while Lee checks you over."

"Please enjoy my home, Evelyn," Edna said. "Afterward we'll have sandwiches made with my homemade bread and a fresh cup of tea."

Evelyn smiled at her host, leaned over, and kissed the top of Abby's head. Then she left her in the care of the ones who could do more for her than a mountain of sandwiches or an ocean of tea.

33

And thou shalt rejoice in every good thing
which the Lord thy God hath given unto thee…
Deuteronomy 26:11

With stealth-like care, Evelyn unlatched the front door. The hour had long since passed midnight. All were asleep at 1151 Aspen Avenue, including Trickster, and Evelyn desperately wanted to keep it that way. Closing the door softly—hoping her dog would not hear it from her bed in B.J.'s room—Evelyn left the front hall in darkness and tiptoed into the kitchen. Laying her coat over the kitchen chair by the back window, she glanced out the window and smiled.

A snowman stood in the centre of the yard, adorned in full snowman regalia and illuminated by a full moon. It seemed to smile at her and, for a brief moment, she longed for the hours she had missed. Then she remembered Abby and turned from the window. Not for a moment would she regret the trip to Pike Ridge. Given the opportunity to relive the day, she knew she would have made the same decision.

Glad she didn't have to climb the stairs, Evelyn slipped through her darkened living room and closed her bedroom door.

Although tired, her thoughts turned to Abby as she prepared for bed. Their long conversation over tea and sandwiches had relaxed everyone, especially when Levi assured them that Abby had, indeed, experienced Braxton Hicks cramping. Mother and child were both fine. He did, however, encourage Edna to keep an eye on her and not let Abby become overtired.

Evelyn smiled as she pulled down her bedspread and fluffed her pillows, a habit she had picked up since Lewis's death. Somehow, fuller and fluffier pillows made her feel less lonely. She shrugged at the distracting memory and returned her thoughts to Edna and her forthrightness in accepting the role of Abby's caregiver.

"You can count on me, Doctor Morsman, and I'll keep in touch with you on a regular basis."

Evelyn muffled a chuckle, remembering Levi's remark over Edna's stalwart acceptance of his request. "I thought she was going to salute me," Levi had jokingly said on their way home.

Both had concluded that Abby could not be in better hands. It had made leaving easier for everyone, although Evelyn had promised a return visit in the very near future. Levi had made his share of promises when he assured Abby that he would give a full report to Ken Crombie and stay in close contact with him regarding Abby's condition.

Jake was another matter. Despite the unexplainable drive she'd felt to help him in the past, Evelyn couldn't deny that her feelings had changed dramatically after Abby's confirmation of the abuse she'd suffered and the story behind Jake's injury.

"When Jake fell and hit his head, I nearly lost it," she had said in a voice so soft that Evelyn had been forced to slide to the edge of her chair to hear better. "I knew I had to turn him over to see if he was still alive— that's how I got the blood on my hands. He moaned, so I knew he wasn't dead, but I knew I would be if I was still there when he came to. So I ran. When I saw you standing at the church steps, I wanted to run right over and tell you everything, but as much as I was afraid, I was ashamed at having to tell you the truth about how Jake treated me."

Evelyn had fought back tears, remembering the argument she'd had with Levi when he'd spoken of the shame an abused women often feels. He'd been right.

"There's nothing to be ashamed of, Abby," she'd soothed. "You've done nothing wrong. Jake's the one with the problem."

"But Evie, you're forgetting one thing," Levi said, turning to Abby. "Jake doesn't remember anything. He's different, Abby. Even Rob says so. Everyone likes him, and Ruth has taken him under her wing until he's back to normal. Seems that his hit on the head may have been a blessing."

Evelyn stretched out on her bed, remembering Levi's later comment while in the car—"I wonder if it will last. I wonder if 'normal' is what Abby's afraid of. She didn't seem too convinced."

Evelyn pulled the chain on her bedside light. Despite the lateness of the hour, she stared into the darkness, having a difficult time falling asleep. Images of Levi floated in front of her. His gentle caring toward Abby. His obvious respect and appreciation for Edna. His profile as he focused on the long, dark drive home. His quiet acceptance of her long, permeating silences. His laugh. His smile. His sly winks.

As sleep slowly settled over her, Evelyn hugged herself and felt the warmth of Levi's arm when he'd walked her down the two flights of steps to the car, which he had taken time to warm up for her. She was in love, and there was nothing she could do to stop the roller coaster ride ahead of her—nor did she want to.

The aroma of freshly baked muffins, Trickster's demanding bark, and a quiet tap on her bedroom door all combined to bring Evelyn out of the deep sleep she'd been enjoying. She turned over, looked at the clock, and nearly jumped to her feet.

9:30! Gracious! She immediately pulled on her housecoat and opened her door.

Her grandmother stood with tray in hand and a gentle smile that warmed Evelyn's spirit.

"Thought you might like to start off your day with one of your father's famous muffins."

Evelyn smiled, accepted the tray, and placed it on the end of the bed. Expecting her grandmother to leave, though not before a good morning hug, Evelyn was surprised when the door closed and her grandmother stood inside, leaning against it.

"My dear, there's something you need to know."

Alarm filled Evelyn and made its way to her face.

"No, no!" she said. "I'm fine, perfectly fine for an eighty-six-year-old woman. And so's your father. I couldn't have been given a better son-in-law had I the opportunity to choose. That's not what I need to talk to you about." She hesitated. "We have another guest."

"Another guest?" Evelyn raised her eyebrows, her curiosity piqued.

"Yes. Your sister arrived yesterday afternoon."

Evelyn sat heavily on the bed, rattling the cup and saucer, spilling coffee onto the tray.

"We had no idea she planned on coming," her grandmother said, "but knowing my granddaughter, I believe the decision was made rather impulsively."

Rachel eased aside the tray and sat beside Evelyn. She took Evelyn's hands in hers and held them for a moment before speaking. Then she lifted Evelyn's face to look into her eyes.

"I felt you should know beforehand. Your sister... she tends to be very... shall we say, ambitious in her mannerisms? Perhaps bold would be a more suitable word." She patted Evelyn's hand. "She and your father are upstairs right now discovering your love of books. Seems that all three of you have that in common. You might do well to approach her first."

Evelyn stood and walked to her bedroom window. The snowman's smile greeted her, but Evelyn did not respond as she had done just a few hours earlier. When she turned around, her beloved Bubi was gone.

Her grandmother's counsel had always proven helpful in the past, at least during her younger years. As she'd struggled in their new life in Pontypool, her grandmother had sat with her, sometimes speaking words of wisdom, sometimes just sitting quietly while Evelyn cried or vented her frustration and anger at her father. Today was no different and Evelyn decided to take her wise advice.

She dressed quickly, drank the now tepid coffee, and took a bite from the muffin before opening her bedroom door.

$$\sim\!\!\!\!\sim$$

"Well, the mystery woman finally appears." Rachel Crawford stretched her legs, but made no attempt to rise.

Evelyn stared, ignoring Trickster's energetic greeting.

"I suppose I should introduce myself. I'm your sister," Rachel said. "Born while you deserted your family, leaving our mother to die without a word from her older child, and abandoning our father to live a life believing you were dead." She paused. "How's that for an introduction?"

Evelyn continued to stare in stunned silence. A threatening voice taunted, *Well, you had to see that coming. She's right, you know.* Evelyn closed her eyes and slowly lowered herself into the sofa opposite her sister, oblivious to Trickster's demanding nudge for her usual morning treat.

"You have every right to—"

"Every right? You bet your sweet petunia I have *every right.* Twenty-six years…"

Joseph walked slowly into the living room, having been summoned by his mother-in-law and warned of the impending confrontation. "Rachel! That will be enough. You are a guest in this home and I expect you to act like one. You invited yourself here and, if your intentions are anything but honourable, I suggest you return home." His voice softened. "On the other hand, if you are willing to be civil, I'm confident Evlyna will share her story, as she has shared it with me and your grandmother."

Evelyn sat numb, afraid to move. She had not missed her father's use of her given name, the name he often used since his arrival. Under different circumstances, she would have smiled at how he seemed to float back and forth between her two names, but not today. Inner turmoil shrouded her thinking.

What *was* her real name, anyway? She felt displaced, uncertain of who she was and where she belonged. She welcomed the warmth of

Trickster lying in her lap—having given up on her unheeded demands—but it did little to settle her growing nausea.

Who is this woman who has invaded my home, my world, my life? She wanted to wish her into oblivion, or at least ask her to leave, but her heart wouldn't let her. This hot-headed, obnoxious woman was her sister; she was *family* and deserved an apology. Evelyn needed to explain. She needed her sister to forgive her.

Her father patted her hand. "Go ahead, Lyna, tell your sister your story. There is nothing you can say to make her any angrier than she already is." Joseph frowned a warning at his younger daughter and said, "She *will* listen."

"So, let me get this straight. Bobby died not knowing you were pregnant. You got rid of the child, married Lewis and had Lucy, lost two more children, and buried your husband when Lucy was a young teenager. Right so far? Oh, and you blame God for everything."

Rachel's callous tone cut into Evelyn more deeply than a knife plunging into a fresh watermelon. She could only close her eyes and nod.

Twenty minutes later, the matriarch of the family handed Rachel a tissue and everyone waited.

"Lucy knows about our Jewish heritage? And Rob, he's your—"

"Her son," Rob finished, his presence having gone unnoticed. "That's right, Rachel. Evelyn is my birth mother and B.J. is her grandson. Lucy is my half-sister and *you* are my aunt, despite the fact that you're a bit younger than I am." He bowed in mock respect. His lighthearted tone and behaviour diffused the tension and the room fell into silence.

Trickster, only half-awake, yawned and stretched, falling off Evelyn's lap. Everyone laughed. Rob whisked Trickster toward the kitchen door and ushered the little dog outside.

"I'll put the kettle on," Rob said. "I'm sure Lucy and Wil will be here soon, and knowing Lucy as I have come to these past months, you two can anticipate a deluge of questions."

Evelyn rose and walked toward her sister, trusting that her unsteady legs would see her safely across the four-foot span.

"It appears we have a lot of catching up to do. Are you planning on staying for a while?"

Rachel embraced Evelyn and held her for several seconds. Neither woman wept. They just smiled and hugged one another.

"Is a year too long?"

Evelyn gasped, holding her sister at arm's length.

"Just kidding."

With one arm around Evelyn's shoulder, Rachel turned toward their father.

"I've arranged for Billy Kennedy to keep the home fires burning," Rachel said. "No, no, Father, he's not baking in your ovens! I've closed the bakery for the holidays and Billy's just making sure the pipes don't freeze. He's going to go over every day until I get back at the end of next week. I made an assumption that when Levi kidnapped you—by the way, where is Sir Levi? I thought for sure he'd be here by now." She fluffed off the matter as though it was no more than an annoyance. "Oh, it doesn't matter… now, where was I? Oh yeah… I thought that once you got here, you and Bubi would be staying a bit longer than you might have planned." She released her sister and shook her head. "Why anyone would want to spend time in this bitterly cold, unforgiving, God-forsaken land is beyond me."

Joseph ignored his daughter's exaggerations. "But my customers—"

"You taught me well, Father. Have no fear. I will make you proud." She turned to Evelyn. "He's such a worrier, this father of ours. Seems he thinks *no one* can bake like he can."

"But our mother could," Evelyn said quietly. "I remember coming home from school to fresh baking when we lived in Toronto. I was the envy of all my friends to have *two* parents who competed for the much-coveted Brock Street Best Baker award. There was a time when…"

Evelyn never noticed her father and grandmother leave the room. The only thing she noticed was the undivided attention of a sister who, until four days ago, she hadn't known existed.

34

And the peace of God, which passeth all understanding,
shall keep your hearts and minds through Christ Jesus.
Philippians 4:7

I miss Christina, Lee. How's she feeling?"

Evelyn sat opposite Levi at her kitchen table, both staring out at the three inches of snow that had fallen overnight. Saturdays often found Evelyn enjoying the morning with Levi and his mother, but today he'd come alone.

"I thought she seemed quieter than usual over the holidays," Evelyn continued, turning to see a frown on Levi's face.

"Frankly, I'm not sure how she's feeling. She has an uncanny way of fooling me." Levi finished the last of his coffee and acknowledged Evelyn's offer for more. "But I'm keeping a close eye on her. Her blood pressure is higher than I'd like and, although she seldom complains, I know she's been suffering with some pretty bad headaches … has been for some time."

"I had no idea. She always seems so upbeat, but I did notice she didn't seem to be herself during the holidays." Evelyn returned from the stove, coffeepot in hand, and poured the fresh brew into Levi's mug. "I never thought of it being anything other than her concern for you when you were away. Maybe a little overtired with all the baking she'd done, but she never mentioned a word about headaches."

"She's been having them for several months now... since the summer. Remember the day of the July picnic, the day you learned about Rob and B.J.? She almost didn't make it to the festivities, her headache was so bad. But she insisted on going and swore me to secrecy. Said she didn't want to spoil the day for anyone. I gave her a strong painkiller and it seemed to work well enough for her to sing a solo at your house afterward."

Evelyn smiled, remembering the proud look Levi had sported when he'd walked into the living room with a tray of fresh coffee just as his mother finished singing.

"I've arranged for some tests at the hospital in Edmonton in early January." Levi took a sip of his coffee and toyed with the muffin crumbs on the plate in front of him. "But despite my concern, she has such peace of mind about everything, including her health. I find her an inspiration... but then I always have."

Evelyn sensed his unspoken worry. She loved his mother and missed having her drop by. Sometimes, when Levi had an emergency, Christina would come alone. Those days often involved a different kind of visit, one that allowed Evelyn the opportunity to open her heart and share what she'd been reading or thinking about, things that often confused her. There was a special something about Christina that Evelyn struggled to define. Her wit, maybe. Certainly her love for her son. But there was something else. As Christina unfolded her life story—her love for her husband, proven through her conversion first to Judaism and later to his belief in Jesus as the Messiah—Evelyn began to experience a profound yearning for Christina's kind of faith, her deep belief... her peace.

"Lee," Evelyn said, looking directly into Levi's eyes, "while you were away just before Christmas, your mother and I had a wonderful evening babysitting little Annie. Lucy, Wil, and Rob had gone to the school's Christmas party and we were left with B.J. and the baby to keep us company." Evelyn struggled with the next thought. "This might sound strange to you, but ever since I met your mother, it's as though she's cast a spell on me."

Both laughed.

"Really! It's true... okay, so I'm exaggerating a little... but from our first cup of tea together not long after your uncle died, to the news that she was moving here from the coast, and even as recently as Christmas Day, she's been able to somehow sense my needs more accurately than I can sense them myself. I can't tell you how greatly she's influenced me."

Evelyn shrugged her shoulders at Levi's raised eyebrows.

"Anyway, on the evening we were babysitting she talked about peace," Evelyn said. "She quoted a verse. *'And the peace of God, which passeth all understanding, shall keep your hearts and minds through Christ Jesus.'* Then she said, *Shalom*."

Levi smiled, tipping the kitchen chair back on two legs. "That would be my mother."

"She's so sure about what she believes in, Lee, that nothing seems to deter her. How does she do it? Here she is, her health in question, and she talks to me about *peace*."

Evelyn surprised herself with the question. She knew Levi would read into her thoughts. The question revealed her own personal struggle, but she felt safe. Never once over the past months of churchgoing had she received anything but gentle wisdom from him when a Sunday sermon sparked confusion or doubt. Never once had Levi pressured her or looked at her in stunned disbelief at a so-called "stupid question." Equal to Christina's, Levi's concern for her spiritual wellbeing was no secret to Evelyn, and he seemed to welcome any opportunity to clarify, encourage, or challenge.

Levi held his coffee mug and stared into the half-finished beverage. He looked long and hard at Evelyn before responding. "My mother's been known to say that Christians can choose to be happy rather than walk among the thorns of worry. But Evie, she hasn't always had the peace you're asking about. When Leah and her grandparents died such a senseless death, my mother's faith in the God of the Jews took a nosedive. She was not alone in that," he added, before continuing in a stronger voice. "When my father made his decision to accept and follow Jesus as Messiah, she again struggled in her faith."

Levi glanced out the window. He seemed more reflective than before.

"But then, I know you understand the battle that goes on inwardly when confusion and rejection go hand-in-hand," he said. "However, your question begs me to tread where angels fear to tread. I have a question of my own."

Evelyn stiffened, noticeably.

"Now, before you go getting upset with me, I'll admit that I'm breaking the unspoken rule of not prying or pressuring. But honestly, you can't blame me for wondering what's going on in your head." Levi cocked his head to one side and smiled. "Peace isn't easy to define or explain, Evie. It comes from way down here." He patted his chest. "Often when someone yearns for peace, it's because something is missing in his life; something, but he doesn't know what. Just yesterday, my mother responded to my hovering by saying, 'I'm enjoying my life and it could be that my time here is limited or that God isn't finished with me yet. Either way, I'm ready to go home.'

"You said she spoke the word, *Shalom*. The Kekchi Indians of Guatemala use the same word. For them, it means quiet goodness free of troublesome circumstances. But the absence of troublesome circumstances is not what the Scriptures focus on. Instead, we learn about peace that isn't touched by what happens on the outside or by the circumstances of life."

Levi paused and Evelyn uttered a frustrated groan, trying to understand what he was saying.

"A person might be in the middle of great trials and still have biblical peace," he finished. "My mother is a classic example. I'm worried about her headaches and she's at peace."

Evelyn sat for a long time before she spoke. When she did, her voice broke. "Is she up for a visit from Bubi and me?"

"I think this new storm will keep most folk housebound for a few days. By then, she'll welcome any face other than mine."

Trickster dropped her toy at Levi's feet, backing up with her tail wagging so hard she almost fell over.

"Think she wants something?" Levi joked.

Evelyn just rolled her eyes and stood up to greet her grandmother, who was coming into the kitchen.

"Good morning, Bubi." Evelyn kissed her grandmother on the cheek as Levi pulled out a chair for her.

"Join us, Rachel, please," Levi invited. "We were just talking about you, hoping to get you over to see my mother soon."

"I would enjoy that very much, Levi…Lee." She corrected herself with a mischievous grin. "We had a splendid visit on Christmas Day after you and Evelyn travelled to see that young woman. How did things turn out?

Evelyn and Levi glanced at one another.

"Fortunately, Bubi, Lee was able to assure her that she was not in labour as she'd feared. We had a delightful time meeting her landlady, who made us a delicious supper before we headed home." With a cursory look at Levi, Evelyn added, "It seems the young lady is in need of a friend. I told her I'd visit again when the weather permits."

Rachel patted her granddaughter's hand and smiled. "That doesn't surprise me, my dear. You will make a good friend for this young lady. Is there no husband or father for the baby?"

Another look at Levi and Evelyn hesitated.

"I am sorry, child, that was a rather personal question. I'm afraid my concern for the young one caused me to speak before thinking."

"Actually, Rachel, she is on her own," Levi offered, "but she's not alone. Edna, her landlady, is a wonderful friend and can't seem to do enough for her. Edna promised to call when the baby is born, sometime late March or early April. By that time, the roads will be better for travelling, although we were very fortunate not to have any problems on Christmas Day."

"We had a little prayer meeting while you were away," Rachel said, smiling at Levi. "Prayer does wonderful things, not just for the one prayed for, but for the one doing the praying. For some unexplainable reason, when prayers are said from the heart," Rachel pointed a finger to her chest, "there is such a peace that comes…such a peace…"

Evelyn sat quietly, listening. She found it a little unnerving that her grandmother would speak of the same thing she and Levi had been discussing just moments earlier.

PART
FOUR

35

And it came to pass in those days,
that he went out into a mountain to pray,
and continued all night in prayer to God.
LUKE 6:12

January, 1970

Yes, he's home now—at least, he's staying with Ruth," Evelyn said, confirming what she had heard from Levi about Jake's release from the hospital.

"And from what I've been hearing," Lucy added, "Ruth's convinced that Jake's a new person. Even if his memory does come back, she thinks she'll be able to help him through whatever ghosts or skeletons lurk in his head."

Sitting in the rocking chair in Annie's bedroom, Evelyn cuddled little Annie while Lucy shook out and meticulously folded a pile of freshly-washed diapers. "If that day ever comes, one can only hope Ruth can follow through on her desires. Jake is a complex person, and not the most likeable at the best of times. He's never responded well to anyone's offer of friendship, and ever since that episode with B.J. on the day of the picnic, he's kept pretty much to himself. We've known him a little over a year now and have yet to see the good side—if there is one."

"That sounds rather ominous, Mother! Do you know something I don't?"

"My dear, I know lots of things you don't!" Evelyn laughed to cover up the uneasy memories of what she and Levi had learned about Jake from Abby.

Several minutes passed with only the sound of the rocker swaying back and forth and Annie's playful gurgles.

"Lucy, I think you were born to be a mother!" Evelyn said, throwing her daughter the occasional side glance. She lifted Annie to her left shoulder, and in doing so changed the topic. "I do believe you thrive on motherhood."

"Yep, that's me: a physically tired, mentally exhausted, husband-neglecting wife, thriving on motherhood."

Both women laughed and Evelyn shook her head at her daughter's dry wit.

Lucy arranged a clean diaper on the changing table and reached for Annie. Moments later, with diaper in place, Evelyn relinquished the rocker to her daughter, kissed Annie on the forehead—being careful to keep her necklace out of Annie's reach—and began the task of folding the remaining laundry that filled the basket beside the dresser.

"Look at this!" Evelyn held up a romper given to her granddaughter by Mae Smytheson. "When Mae gave this to Annie, I thought Annie would be at least a year old before wearing it. Hard to believe how much she's grown since last summer."

Annie had just passed her six-month birthday with all the fanfare of a coronation. For the occasion, Wil had arranged for a teacher friend who dabbled in photography to take pictures of the five-generation family. Evelyn's favourite was the picture of Annie with her maternal great-great-grandmother. The black and white photograph graced the mantle in Lucy and Wil's living room, demanding the attention of anyone who walked into the room.

"Mom, are you more relaxed now that Bubi and Zaida have decided to stay through the winter months?" Lucy asked. She settled Annie to her breast for her afternoon feeding, propping her feet up on the footstool.

"Wil and I noticed how distracted you were over the holidays, but we figured it was all the excitement of Bubi and Zaida surprising you, not to mention Aunt Rachel's unexpected visit."

Lucy's words struck a chord. Evelyn *had* felt the need to be the perfect hostess, living with the idea that she was being studied like one studied a drop of water under a microscope. As a result, she often found herself hovering over her father and grandmother with an unspoken need for approval and acceptance. She knew in her heart those feelings were preposterous, and after they decided to stay longer, her need to make up for the past twenty-five years in three weeks disappeared, along with her need to prove herself. What she didn't realize was how obvious it might have appeared to anyone sensitive enough to the issue. Lucy was one such person.

"Lucy, I'm not sure you'll understand this, but I've struggled with guilt every day for the past twenty-five years. There were days I felt overwhelmed by a surge of such regret that I almost wished they had never come. Does that make sense?" She smiled at her daughter's obvious concern. "I felt the need to make up for the past, for my neglect of them, and at the same time knew it wasn't humanly possible. Plus, I had to deal with the revelation of having a sister I never knew about—and her accusations. She called last night, by the way, to say she'd arrived home safely and all was well.

"Discovering I had a sister only added to my dilemma. In some ways—actually, in many ways—I was very sorry to see her leave. It's funny, you know. You never miss something you've never had, but all of a sudden I *have* something—a sister—and now she's gone."

Evelyn laid her hand on a stack of folded diapers as she contemplated her next words.

"Rachel and I will never be close … for a lot of reasons—our age, our proximity, and obviously, our history. I know she forgives me, but I've yet to forgive myself. I never knew she existed! I never knew my mother had died giving birth to her. But her willingness to forgive me has bridged the gap. Now I just have to deal with *me*." She reached for the final diaper and added it to the stack. "There. All folded. Now all you have to do is put them away."

Changing the subject, Evelyn patted the folded baby clothes and checked her watch. "I should get home. I left your grandfather happily baking in the kitchen, and I want to recapture the memory of coming home from school to the smell of freshly baked bread, or whatever else our baker has been inspired to make." She turned to kiss her granddaughter goodbye. "Memories are wonderful, aren't they, Luce?"

Backing out of the driveway, Evelyn realized that their conversation had drifted away from Jake and hadn't returned. She was grateful for it. Neither she nor Levi had told anyone of Abby's whereabouts, although Evelyn had been tempted to tell Christina.

No doubt she'd faithfully pray for Abby and her unborn baby.

As Evelyn pulled into her driveway on Aspen Avenue, she found herself still focused on the idea of Christina praying and the fact that the idea had come naturally to her.

How about that? she mused as she stomped her feet at the front stoop, smiling at Trickster's greeting from inside the house.

36

Jesus said unto him, If thou canst believe,
all things are possible to him that believeth.
And straightway the father of the child cried out, and said with tears,
Lord, I believe; help thou mine unbelief.
MARK 9:23–24

Pike Ridge, Alberta
Mid-January

Back in her own room on the second floor, Abby reached for the hot chocolate Edna deposited on the small table beside her. She smiled a thank-you as Edna settled herself in a nearby chair, stretched her legs out on the ottoman, and politely sipped her own hot drink.

"Hank's out front shovelling the steps all the way down to the side-walk," Edna said. "Been at it for almost an hour. He'll be ready for something warm soon, so I thought I'd make a pot of cocoa and we could have a hot chocolate and marshmallow party."

Abby laughed at Edna's silliness and leaned back, enjoying the warmth of the mug in her hands. She felt good, really good. In fact, she couldn't remember when she'd last experienced such a sense of wholeness. A visit to Doctor Crombie two days earlier had assured her that she and the baby were healthy, but the visit from Doctor Morsman and Evelyn on Christmas Day had done more for her than any visit to a doctor. Apart from erasing her fear of an early labour, just knowing they were aware of her condition, and location, brought a strange sense of well-being. Their visit had left her feeling that she had a purpose in life; she was having a baby! She didn't allow herself to think of the events around its conception—just its life—and throughout the days since their visit, she'd found herself smiling for no real reason.

Evelyn had promised a return visit, and Abby was not surprised by Edna's warm hospitality; Evelyn would be welcome anytime and could stay as long as she liked. Abby had assured Evelyn that she would continue to write, only now she would be able to include all the pregnancy details she had been leaving out in previous exchanges.

"You're too good to me, Edna. You seem to know just when to spoil me." Abby lifted her mug in the air to prove her point. "And you know when I need time alone. You certainly are fulfilling your promise to Doctor Morsman about keeping an eye on me. How can I ever repay you?"

"Repay me? My goodness, child, do you have any idea how much your presence in this monstrosity of a house means to me? Repay me? Why, you've become the daughter I never had—no thanks to Hank Mason."

"Tell me about you and Hank. Why haven't you two married?" Abby asked, daring to put into words the haunting question that had come to her mind on several occasions. Seeing her two friends squabbling like a frustrated hen and arrogant rooster sometimes made her smile, but more often than not it made her sad.

Edna talked nonstop. An hour later, both women sat staring into the dying fire.

"It just wasn't meant to be." Edna sighed, breaking the silence that filled the room. "I suppose if I believed in the influence of some greater power, like the big guy in the sky, I'd have to think He never intended for us to marry. At twenty-one, Hank wanted to run off and get married and never look back. As if that was going to happen! He had no ties here, not since both his parents died in an awful accident when he was nineteen."

Abby raised questioning eyebrows.

"Sad, sad story. Seems they were on their way home from Edmonton and got caught in a rock slide. It closed the highway for two days, and it was another day before their car was found. They were still sitting upright in their seats. There was talk that they had just turned a curve in the highway and it hit them from above. They didn't have a chance. Hank's answer was to run away instead of dealing with the loss. He has no siblings— neither do I, for that matter—and he seemed to think that if he didn't acknowledge it, the pain would eventually disappear."

Abby watched Edna's face as she willingly shared the old memories, as though they had been stored away too long and needed dusting.

"So, when he asked me to marry him, I told him I'd think about it, all the while hoping he would deal with his parents' deaths—I was smart enough to know that you can't carry that kind of baggage around without it catching up with you. But my logic backfired. After a while, so much time had passed that it seemed the question of marriage wasn't on the table anymore. So we fell into the relationship we have now, and have had for over thirty years. My goodness! That sounds like a long time to wait for another proposal, doesn't it?"

Engrossed in Edna's story, Abby shifted her position, straightening her cramped legs.

"Funny thing is, neither of us ever dated anyone else and Hank never left town. He used his parents' insurance money to open the diner and he's been there ever since … and I've been right here." Edna rolled her eyes and looked around the room. "It's been lonely over the years, but I've accepted it as my lot in life. Until you came along, I didn't think another soul would live under this roof while I was still alive … but here you are!"

Abby leaned across the arm of her chair and reached for Edna's hand. "Yes, I am, and I love you for sharing your home, and your story, with me. Thank you. I hope I haven't opened Pandora's Box in asking about you and Hank."

"Nonsense! What's done is done. Can't undo it now, can we?" Edna stood and slid open the mesh screen in front of the fire. She added two more logs. "That should do it. With all our talking, we almost lost our fire! Hank wouldn't have been too impressed by that."

"Edna, with all your joking about a big guy in the sky, do you believe in God?"

A heavy sigh escaped Edna, overshadowing the crackling of the new flame. She sat down in her chair with a thump.

"Big guy in the sky? That's rather dangerous talk, isn't it? I have to admit I use the term loosely," Edna offered, apologetically. She pressed her fingers to her lips. "I suppose most people believe in God, and that would include me. I think there's something more important than *believing,* though, and that is what you *do* with your belief. I haven't been too active in the *doing* part. I went to Sunday School as a child, even won my share of perfect attendance awards."

Edna closed her eyes and tipped her head in a mock bow.

"But somehow life intervened and God became distant," Edna said, "almost as though He set me on a path and left it up to me to follow through with whatever life handed me."

Edna considered this possibility before continuing, and Abby waited quietly, watching her friend's face as she searched for the right words.

"Yet, when something happens that breaks the pattern, the routine, the norm—call it what you like—I can't help wondering if God isn't as distant as I've thought. Perhaps He brought you here! And perhaps not just for your sake, but for mine! Maybe to remind me of what I once believed a very long time ago.

"When I think about it, I wonder if *I* was the one who put God aside. On the outside, I suppose it would seem that I've managed so far without Him. I'm in reasonably good health, my home is comfortable, and I have a family of friends I've known my whole life who would be here in an instant to help if I needed it. So, to some degree, I'm living a dream that others could only imagine…and with all the appearances of an absent God." Edna faltered before returning to Abby's question. "Do I believe there's a God? Yes, but I'm afraid my faith died a long time ago."

Abby looked at her friend and then chose her words carefully. "I have to admit there have been times when I've felt that God has set *me* on a path and then left *me* alone to deal with all that has happened in my life… especially in my marriage." Her thoughts drifted, as did her eyes, and she spoke more to herself than to her friend. "I tried to be a good wife, the *perfect* wife. I believed with my whole heart that I was the right person for Jake to marry...that God had pointed me in that direction. I believed I could fill the emptiness Jake seemed to have inside and help him with the anger he hid from everyone but me."

Abby turned to Edna, her face expressing her inner struggles.

"I believed God would somehow intervene during the abuse, like a strong arm coming down from heaven and holding back Jake's hand every time he raised it against me. I believed God would help Jake mend his ways and we would live happily ever after." Abby closed her eyes and took a deep breath. "But God didn't intervene. The beatings never stopped. They only increased in frequency and severity and I began to believe that God *had* abandoned me." Abby's eyes filled, despite her smile. "But when I consider how He's taken care of me through it all...He's never abandoned me, Edna! God's never left me alone for a minute! And I doubt very much that He's ever left you."

The fire caught on the fresh logs and they burst into flames, filling the room with warmth. Minutes passed and the tenth-hour chime on the front hall's grandfather clock drifted up the stairs. Abby counted the bongs unconsciously, then slowly smiled. Excitement filled her, warming her more than the fire. She sat up straight and put her empty mug on the side table.

"Look at this fire," Abby said. "Before you added more wood, it was just a bed of hot coals. Had those coals been left to themselves, the fire would have died. But the coals didn't die, they just needed more fuel. Right? They needed to be stoked and prodded and fanned before they could produce the heat we're feeling now." Abby twisted herself around and looked directly at Edna. "You've just said that you were afraid your faith died a long time ago. But I don't think it did! The fact that you've considered the possibility of God leading me to you for *both* our sakes tells me that the coals of your faith are *not* dead. They just need to be fanned, like the coals on that fire."

Abby looked into the flames before continuing, her thoughts directed as much to herself as to Edna.

"Like those coals, sometimes we need to be reminded of what was once important in our lives, acknowledging that something is missing, that something has slipped away, unnoticed."

Abby cocked her head to one side, wondering if her friend followed her line of thinking.

"Our belief in God has to be fanned, Edna, just like those coals, so that our faith can be refreshed and we can be reminded that God is the Supreme Ruler in our lives…no matter what happens to us."

The fire continued to crackle, sending flames shooting up the chimney. Abby sat quietly for a moment before continuing.

"As difficult as it is to understand, sometimes God has to prod us to get our attention. When pain of any sort becomes part of our lives, our faith is tested…mine was, anyway. And as we suffer physically—or emotionally—we suffer spiritually, and in our suffering we begin to think that God has deserted us. In our finite minds, we reason that if He hadn't deserted us, we wouldn't be suffering—in my case, Jake would never have abused me. We reason that if God hadn't deserted us, our lives would be a bed of roses from birth to death. What we tend to forget—maybe it's more than forgetting, maybe it's just not knowing—is that through our pain, through God's prodding, we grow and become stronger, just like the fire. Look at it now!"

Abby pointed to the blazing fire, her own excitement matching the rocketing flames.

"God has never left me!" she said. "He's been with me in my fears and in my low self-worth. He's been with me through these nine years of abuse and as I've sought refuge in your home. Edna, He's been with *you* through your whole life, too, through your disappointments, through the failed expectations you had of Hank, through the life you thought you deserved and never had, even through the life you have now that seems so perfect. Don't you see? He's never left us!"

"You're making it sound so…logical," Edna responded, staring into the fire as though seeing it for the first time. "I suppose if I'd let the coals die completely, the room would get cold…"

"Just like our lives. If we let our faith in God die, we *are* left on our own. The longer we live without God as the source of our spiritual heat, the easier it is for us to ignore Him or, worse, blame Him for all the things that go wrong in our lives." Abby paused. "I remember hearing our pastor speak on this very thing a few weeks before I left Thystle Creek. He said that when we're suffering, when we experience pain, God feels the pain worse than we do. Don't you find that amazing? I mean, how can an invisible God feel the kind of pain we feel when we are hurt at the hands of another? How can God feel the physical pain I experienced when Jake beat me, or the emotional pain of disappointment and rejection you experienced? But I suppose it's because He *is* God and when one of His creation is hurting, it hurts Him even more. When I got a spanking as a kid, I remember my daddy saying, 'This is going to hurt me more than it'll hurt you.' I used to think that he meant his hand would sting more than my bottom."

Abby nodded to acknowledge Edna's laugh.

"It's true, I used to think that. But I know now that it hurt my daddy more when he saw me hurting, even if he was the one inflicting the pain. And he was my earthly father! Can you imagine how much *more* God cried when I cried? I mean, He's God and He loves me more than my daddy could ever love me. I suppose that's the kind of love we mortals will never understand. Am I making sense? I've never put these thoughts into words before and I can't help wondering if I'm rambling on nonsensically."

Edna continued to stare into the raging fire and nodded. "You're making perfect sense, child. Perfect sense."

Abby turned and saw Hank Mason leaning in the doorway, tears flowing freely down his cheeks and into his rough beard.

37

The Lord God hath opened mine ear,
and I was not rebellious, neither turned away back.
Isaiah 50:5

February 17

Tuesday morning brought the worst news Evelyn had heard since the death of her husband.

"She has a malignant brain tumour." Levi took a deep breath before continuing. "It's a slow growing one, but inoperable."

Evelyn gasped, as did her grandmother. Her father bowed his head and closed his eyes.

"They want to do further tests to determine what treatment can be offered, but my mother has refused it all. 'No more tests. No treatment,' she said. And she means it."

"Wha—Why?" Evelyn asked in disbelief, fighting back tears.

"Do you remember the conversation we had a few weeks ago, when I first told you about her headaches? She told me then, and reminded me at the hospital, that she's ready to go home."

"But *I'm* not ready for her to *go home.*" Evelyn's voice quickened. "You need to take me to see her. I need to convince her. *She* might be ready to die, but *I'm* not ready to give her up!"

Evelyn felt her grandmother's hand on hers. Although she knew it was well-intended, Evelyn shook it off.

"Why didn't you see this coming, Lee? Surely your physician's instincts could have spotted this. How could you miss it? You need to convince her to take the treatments. You need to *tell* her to take them." Her voice was demanding, even accusing, and she knew it, but she didn't care. This couldn't be happening. Christina was the best friend she had ever had, and now she was dying.

Her father offered her coffee, but she refused.

"Evie, this is not something that a person can see on the outside. I had no idea…" Levi's muted voice was full of emotion. "Headaches have all kinds of sources…from something as simple as eating the wrong food or not getting enough sleep, to a full-blown disease. My mother has never shown any signs that something existed beyond some annoying headaches."

Levi reached for Evelyn's hands, but she withdrew them and kept them folded on her lap.

"If I thought more could be done, I'd be doing exactly what you've asked," Levi said. "In fact, I would have already done it, but I've talked with the doctors. What they found was the last thing they expected, and it took them by surprise. There's nothing they can do except give her radiation, and Mother has refused."

Levi ended with his head down, unable to continue.

As though sensing the gravity of the conversation, Trickster whimpered at Evelyn's feet. Evelyn bent down and lifted her onto her lap, burying her face in the dog's fur. Trickster didn't move. Evelyn stroked her pet's head, then broke the long silence that had filled the room.

"How much time?" she whispered.

"It's hard to say. According to the report I read, it's at the base of her skull, at the tip of her brain stem, and by all accounts it's been there for some time. It's only these past six months or so that she's been having headaches, and even then, she says they come and go."

"Will you bring her home?" Evelyn asked.

"Absolutely. I have a tonsillectomy scheduled for tomorrow afternoon, but I'll be leaving first thing Thursday morning to do just that. Would you like to come with me?"

"Yes, please … and I'm sorry, Lee. I didn't mean to accuse you. It's just that—"

"No need to apologize. Had you responded any other way, I'd have thought you didn't care." Levi smiled faintly at his own remark. "I know you love my mother, and that speaks volumes to me."

After a prolonged silence, Levi turned to Rachel and Joseph. "My mother believes strongly in God's sovereignty. Of course, she'd rather not deal with this, but she knows God is going to be with her throughout the journey, and that brings her a great deal of peace. When I left her yesterday, she'd just repeated her favourite hymn:

> When peace like a river attendeth my way,
> When sorrows like sea billows roll,
> Whatever my lot, Thou hath taught me to say,
> It is well, it is well with my soul.

"When she was done, she told me she rested in the knowledge that, although the Lord may not take away her troubles, He would see her through them. I could still hear her humming the tune as I walked down the corridor."

Levi turned to Evelyn, leaned on his knees, and took her hands from her lap.

"We've talked about this before, Evie, but I need to say it again," he said. "God is in control of *all* that comes into our lives. Unfortunately, we simplify what happens to us by putting things into two categories: the good and the bad. But as difficult as it may be to understand, it's true. God *is* in control of everything. You *had* to have seen God in action when Rob and B.J. came into your life. Didn't you? But it took some serious not-so-good things to happen before we could all celebrate the finding of one lost little boy."

Evelyn shrugged as she slowly slipped her hands from Levi's. How could she *not* see Levi's reasoning?

"Yes, there are things we'd rather not have happen to us or to the ones we love," Levi continued. "I'm a doctor and I've watched families rejoice at the birth of a baby, never giving any thought or thanks to God who ordained such a gift in the first place. I've seen families fall apart when illness and disease come into their lives, blaming, even cursing God. I've counselled and consoled, but in my heart I know God makes the final decision. I know my mother is in His hands and there's no other place I'd rather her be…nor would she *want* to be."

The rest of the conversation focused on God, and Evelyn felt excluded. She sat quietly, watching as Levi bowed his head, praying with her grandmother and father. Levi had been correct. She didn't understand, but for the first time she wanted to. She was too afraid to say so.

Evelyn closed the front door after watching Levi drive away. Trickster squirmed in her arms and jumped to the floor, begging for attention.

"Sorry, girl, not now."

She walked across the living room toward her bedroom. Before quietly closing the door, she turned a tear-stained face to her father and grandmother. "Why does God make it so difficult to understand Him… or to love Him?"

Rachel nursed a cup of tea as she sat at the desk by the living room window. Her son-in-law had remained in the kitchen doing what he did best, even under a cloud of worry. The aroma of freshly baked cinnamon rolls drifted through the house and Rachel knew that with each kneading of the dough, he was praying.

It had been more than four hours since Evelyn sought refuge in the solitude of her bedroom, and Rachel's concern for her granddaughter grew by the moment. Years may have separated them, but through quiet observation Rachel could see that Evelyn was still as frightened and confused now as she'd been as a child.

She may be a mother—she may even be a grandmother—but she still needs her Bubi.

Rachel rose and stood quietly in front of her granddaughter's bedroom door. As she considered knocking, she couldn't help thinking of what Joseph had said shortly after Levi's departure and Evelyn's seclusion: "How will she deal with this without the Lord's help?" Rachel knew Joseph harboured a great desire to explain the decision he and Evelyn's mother had made years ago, an explanation he hoped would lead his daughter to a realization of the Messiahship of Jesus. Rachel couldn't fault him for that; her heart carried a burden equal to her son-in-law's, but his question struck a nerve as she debated intervening with Evelyn. Who was she to think she could counsel her granddaughter on such matters? Who did she think she was to answer such a question? After all, she'd struggled for years over the decision Joseph and Hannah had made, even long after Hannah's death.

The year Evelyn's sister had turned nineteen had been the turning point for her. Playing the role of Mary in the local Christmas pageant, the younger Rachel had cradled a baby Jesus in her arms and recited Isaiah 9:6.

> For unto us a child is born,
> Unto us a son is given:
> And the government shall be upon his shoulder:
> And his name shall be called Wonderful, Counsellor,
> The mighty God, The everlasting Father, The Prince of Peace.

It was as though her granddaughter had recited the verse just for her, and it was then that she understood Jesus was more than just a good man, more than just a prophet, more than just a name that a Jew was forbidden to use except as a curse. She remembered thinking that a filter had been removed from her ears, a filter that had been sifting out the truth every time her daughter or son-in-law had tried to tell her about Jesus. But when her granddaughter had recited from the Old Testament, from a book she had read many times before, she had understood the whole truth for the first time, and God had become more than the lofty and impersonal God she had followed all her life. The virgin birth had been God-ordained. She'd finally understood that Jesus was God's Son, the Messiah to the Jewish nation.

Rachel remembered her conversation with her son-in-law and granddaughter later that evening.

"I *felt* God. It was as though He touched me and I could see and hear for the first time. The blinding scales on my eyes were gone and my ears were no longer blocked." She'd paced in front of them, knowing she sounded like a mad woman, yet also knowing, through their smiles and tears, that they understood. "My senses came alive! I could feel warmth—the kind you feel from the morning sun as it rises in midsummer—and it surrounded me and held me like *my* Bubi used to do when I was a child, when I was afraid. And then…then came a hush, a comforting silence as calmness enveloped me. It was as though God's strong arms held me as He filled me with a love I'd never felt or known before. Finally I heard what I've refused to hear for so long: I heard *Yeshua* speak my name."

Rachel looked at Evelyn's closed door and sighed through fresh tears. *Only God can help you understand, my little Evlyna. He may use me, or not. Either way, He has to open your heart first. He has to remove the filter from your ears.*

As God poured out His wisdom, Rachel understood that her granddaughter would come to Him when she was ready and in whatever fashion He had chosen for her. She would wait and trust God to do His perfect will in her granddaughter's life.

But please, God, let it be soon!

Her decision made, Rachel's thoughts turned to her other granddaughter, her namesake. Young Rachel had called weekly since returning to Pontypool and reopening her father's bakery. Her letters described in exaggerated detail the line of people waiting for her to flip the closed sign every morning.

"Looks like Papa has lost his prominent position as the town's baker now that I've taken over!" she had written.

The comment had brought smiles to everyone's face except Joseph's, and Rachel had to assure her son-in-law that all would return to normal once he said his goodbyes to Evelyn and returned home.

Which may be later rather than sooner, she thought wistfully. And that suited her just fine.

With a fresh cup of tea, Rachel settled herself at the desk. With pen and paper in hand, she began a letter to her granddaughter:

> My dear, dear Rachel,
>
> We miss your smiling face and your sometimes intolerable humour. Did I just say *intolerable*? Forgive me, dear child, but sometimes you are so unpredictable! But God has a way of making us smile during dark days, and you are one of His chosen instruments of laughter. Your happy face is needed in a tired and sad world, especially today. We learned some very disturbing news this morning concerning Evelyn's dear friend, Christina...

38

Yea, though I walk though the valley of the shadow of death,
I will fear no evil: for thou art with me.
PSALM 23:4

March 2

Christina Morsman had been home from the hospital for over a week when, feeling surprisingly well, she asked Levi to call Evelyn and invite her over for lunch. She needed a visit from her friend. Equally so, she needed to have a party.

It was Christina's turn to make fresh muffins, but her preference and specialty won out. She placed a plate of *schnecken* in front of Evelyn and responded to Evelyn's smile with a smile of her own.

"I learned years ago that when you make bread, if you make a little extra dough, you can turn it into this delicious sweet roll." She took a bite, wiping the corners of her mouth with her linen napkin. After a sip of tea, she continued. "But I also learned over time that the correct proportion of ingredients is approximate. There are probably recipes out there for the less brave, but it's typically measured by the eye: a coating of butter, a layer of brown sugar, a dusting of cinnamon, a good sprinkling of chopped nuts, and a hungry audience waiting for its unveiling."

"Delicious," Evelyn replied, sampling Christina's baking just as Levi popped his head into the kitchen. His surprise visit had no doubt been inspired by her guest and Christina was not duped into thinking otherwise. What he probably didn't realize was that these precious moments were exactly what Christina had hoped to encourage.

Levi stayed long enough to enjoy his mother's baking and then bid his farewell. "Patients await. I must take my leave." He bowed in mock humility. "I rest knowing that you fine ladies will have no difficulty passing the time. And Mother, be assured I will be arriving home with Rachel and Joseph at 5:30 sharp."

"My father and grandmother?" Evelyn's shocked reaction did not surprise Christina.

"Indeed! And Lucy and Wil and Rob and little Annie and B.J. will all be coming for dinner once those men close up their classrooms for the day. Did you really think we were just going to sit around and talk?" Christina winked at her son and smiled at her friend. "I intend to fill this house with lots of laughter. We have potatoes to peel, carrots to scrub, and a bowl of red jelly to make for all those under ninety!"

Levi saluted his mother, bowed to Evelyn, and left both women to carry through with his mother's planned dinner.

"Oh, Levi!" Christina called to her son as he reached the front door. "Don't forget Trickster."

"Trickster? Christina, this house will be bursting enough. Do you really want to add Trickster to the mix? Are you sure about all this? I mean, are you up to the work, not to mention the confusion?"

Christina handed Evelyn an apron and tied her own around her waist before replying. "Evie, I'm fine. There will be a day when I won't be, and when that time comes, my entertaining days will be over. But until then, I'm trusting the good Lord to give me strength to create some wonderful memories." She patted Evelyn's cheek, as she often did. "Now, let's have some tea and these wonderful rolls before I crack the whip and put you to work."

Two hours later, peeled potatoes and sliced carrots sat in water waiting to be cooked. Other vegetables awaited their turn on the stove and a prime rib roast sizzled in the oven, surrounded by onions and parsnips.

"I think some fresh tea is in order," Christina announced as she put the kettle on. "After all this work, we deserve another treat. Don't you think so, Evie?"

Hearing no answer, she turned from the stove to find that Evelyn had left the room. Curious, she went looking and found her sitting at the piano.

"Do you play much?" Evelyn asked as she slid across the stool and took the tray of teacups and warm scones from Christina.

"Not like I used to. My hands don't move as well as they once did. I'm afraid I'd insult the artist of any song I might play—or should I say, attempt to play. Octaves don't come easily anymore." Christina smiled and stretched her thumb and baby finger across the keys to show her limitations. "When I'm alone and there's just me and God, I sing and play for Him, but not for human ears."

"Would you play for me?" Evelyn asked with a pleading look.

"Very well, but remember, *tolerance* is the word of the day."

Settling herself in the middle of the piano bench, Christina prefaced her song with an explanation. "When I was a child, my father used to play this song over and over. I think it's ingrained in my mind for eternity."

Christina began to play and sing. She closed her eyes and lost herself in the words.

> I come to the garden alone while the dew is still on the
> roses,
> And the voice I hear falling on my ear the Son of God
> discloses.
> And He walks with me, and He talks with me, and He
> tells me I am His own;
> And the joy we share as we tarry there, none other has
> ever known.

Her hands moved across the keys, stretching and reaching, and by a miracle from heaven, the music was flawless. Evelyn slid beside her with all the stealth of a child tiptoeing into a room full of adults, hoping not to be seen.

He speaks, and the sound of His voice is so sweet the
  birds hush their singing,
And the melody that He gave to me within my heart is
  ringing.
And He walks with me, and he talks with me, and he
  tells me I am His own;
And the joy we share as we tarry there, none other has
  ever known.

Both women sat quietly for several moments, their shoulders leaning into each other before Christina spoke.

"The words are exquisite, aren't they? I thought you'd like it, knowing how much you love your garden. Do you ever think God is present as you weed it?"

"No, never," Evelyn whispered.

"Well, my dear, not only is He present, He's trying to talk to you through His creation. He gave you that love, you know—the love for His flowers. Not everyone can appreciate such beauty, not as you do. It's as though He handpicked you to take care of what He created."

Evelyn stood up abruptly. "Christina, how can you be so—so *gracious* when you speak of God, knowing you are…"

"Dying?" Christina swung her legs around the piano bench and joined Evelyn on the sofa. "Evie, my Father in Heaven loves me more than you can possibly imagine. How could I *not* be gracious with all that He has done for me—for all that He has given me—like your friendship? He is the most loving God one could ever worship. His love is unfathomable. He is my refuge and my strength. Even if He chooses to sap all the strength from my body, I know He loves me more than I can put into words."

She leaned back on the sofa with a freshly poured cup of tea. "I know you must be struggling with my illness. There are times, especially at night, when I struggle." Christina smiled and nodded at Evelyn's response. "Yes, my dear child, I struggle. But have you ever known a child who hasn't had issues with a parent? In the end, the parent's love proves that only the parent knows what's best for the child. That's God's kind of love. Only He knows what's best for any of us … including you, my dear."

A timer went off in the kitchen and Christina excused herself, only to return moments later.

"I don't understand that kind of love," Evelyn said, resuming the conversation.

Christina silently thanked God for a quick answer to her prayer.

"Nor can anyone. God is holy." Christina turned toward her friend and spoke softly. "When a person is open and receptive to God, His holiness will be experienced as *agape* love. It's not the kind of love we humans are equipped to understand. It all comes down to one word: faith. *'Now faith is the substance of things hoped for, the evidence of things not seen.'* That's found in Hebrews."

Evelyn frowned. "You quote the verse so easily … as though you live it every day."

"Ah, but I do! That's the secret of faith, the base for what makes life worth living: trusting an unseen God on a daily basis, no matter what. But there's another side to faith and trust."

Evelyn's look encouraged Christina to continue.

"It's easy to have faith in things we can touch and see. It's harder to have faith in things you can't see. Let me tell you a story …" Christina settled back on the sofa and Evelyn pulled the ottoman closer for Christina's outstretched legs. "When I was a young married woman living in Vancouver under the dark cloud of a 'mixed marriage,' as society tagged it, I had a very dear friend, Maybelle McGeachie. Maybelle was a Gentile, born and raised in Scotland, who moved to Canada as a young married woman. I was a converted Jew raised in the interior of Northern Alberta—two people whom you would never have expected to become friends. But we did.

"She was five and a half years older than me and lived with her husband in the same apartment building that Jacob and I lived in. In the early months of our friendship, we shared the trivia of life: our recipes, the best places to buy groceries, our burning desire to have children, our husbands' idiosyncrasies … all over hot tea and cinnamon raisin toast."

Christina's eyes sparkled as she spoke of her friend, sipping her tea with her usual slurp.

"As the months grew into years, we became best friends. Of course, we both had other friends, but we shared something special. Our husbands would often shake their heads at our silliness. While they'd be trying to solve the problems of the world, we'd be reading *Pride and Prejudice*, curled up under the same comforter eating popcorn, crying and laughing over the love between Elizabeth Bennet and Mr. Darcy! There was just something between us that no words could define. We had built a bond, a trust in each other... and then the unthinkable happened."

"She died?" Evelyn asked, barely able to frame the words.

"No, my dear, she didn't die." Christina patted Evelyn's hand reassuringly. "She moved back to Scotland. I was devastated. She was my best friend. No one was ever going to replace her in my life. No one ever could. You see, Evie, we had come to depend upon each other through a deep trust, a trust that grew over many years and many trials. Naturally, our husbands were at the centre of our worlds, but this was a *woman* thing. When she moved away, the visual contact was gone, and had we not worked hard at maintaining it—despite the ocean that separated us—our friendship, our faith, and our trust would have been gone, too.

"Jacob gave me an unexpected gift when I turned sixty. He sent me to Scotland to see Maybelle. Her husband had passed away five years earlier and she had settled into a new life, living alone. What an amazing time we had. Laughing, crying, eating... oh my, how we ate! We went to the live theatre in London, and once we even skipped through a child's hopscotch on the sidewalk. We shared ten wonderful days." Christina smiled, lost in a memory that had been buried for fifteen years. "It was as though we'd jumped back in time and were young again. Our bond had never broken; the trust was still there. I didn't know that it would be the last time I'd see her on this earth. She passed away the following year."

Christina stared at Evelyn, believing she knew what was going through Evelyn's mind.

"Evie, a loving relationship is built on trust, and sometimes when life throws you a curve, you have to work harder at a relationship to keep it alive. Although Maybelle and I couldn't see each other, our relationship continued to be strong. We had a history together and it was built on a wonderful trust."

Christina rose to head for the kitchen, but turned to look at Evelyn.

"We are truly blessed when we have a Maybelle in our lives, someone we can completely trust, despite distance or oceans." Christina smiled. "That's the *seeing* part of trust. But you know what's an even greater blessing? When we have faith and trust in God, whom we have *never* seen, and know in our hearts that He's always with us...that no ocean is wide enough to separate us."

Before redirecting her steps to respond to the ring of the front doorbell, Christina turned to her young friend for a second time.

"I'm not afraid of dying, Evie. I'll not be walking through that valley alone. I have faith in my unseen God to be with me all the way. Am I afraid of the process? I wouldn't be human if I wasn't. But of leaving this world to be with my Lord... 'For me, to live is Christ, but to die, is gain.'"

She paused to give Evelyn time to think on the verse she had just quoted.

"Read Isaiah 53 and ask God to reveal Himself to you," Christina said. "I believe with my whole being that God is on the doorstep of your life. All you need to do is listen for His still, small voice. Sometimes it's a gentle breeze, sometimes it's a whisper, and sometimes it's a quiet hush."

Christina returned to the sofa and kissed Evelyn on the cheek. "Come on, let's have a party."

She looped her arm in Evelyn's and walked to the front door to begin an evening of building new memories.

39

But thou art a God ready to pardon, gracious and merciful,
slow to anger, and of great kindness, and forsookest them not.
NEHEMIAH 9:17

March 8

Sunday afternoon found the Sherwood home unusually quiet. Evelyn welcomed the solitude, not because she was tired of the noise and confusion—although the house never lacked for either—but because she wanted to reread Abby's letter. She had not heard from Abby since replying to her last letter a month ago, and Friday's letter had released her of a growing concern.

Two fresh cups of coffee and a mug of hot chocolate had been delivered to her father, son, and grandson, who were enjoying a tour through Lewis Sherwood's family albums. Had Lucy been with them, she would have been in the midst of the action, filling in the blanks and adding her own interpretations with the who, what, where, when, and why of each treasure. Left to themselves to digest the pictures, Rob and her father had welcomed the fresh brew. B.J. had jumped up enthusiastically, as though he'd been given a week off school, when offered the hot chocolate. Evelyn had heaped a mound of marshmallows on top, much to the young boy's delight.

With her grandmother napping in her room, Evelyn poured her own cup of coffee and settled herself with the letter at the kitchen table.

> Dear Evie,
>
> Hi … sorry I've taken so long to write back. No excuses, but my intentions were good!
>
> I know I've said this before, but I can't tell you enough how grateful I am for you two visiting me on Christmas Day. When I first saw Doctor Morsman, I panicked a little, wondering what he would say to me, or worse, if he was obligated in any way to reveal where I was living. But when you walked through the doorway, I almost cried. Well, actually, I guess I did cry, didn't I? To see your face and … well, words fail me now, as they did then. I'm just so grateful that you came with Doctor Morsman. It's amazing how God works in our lives. When we least expect it, He just pours out His blessing and love. You were just that to me.

As she had when she first read it, Evelyn paused at this statement. Abby's words reminded her of the conversation she'd had with Christina a few days earlier about God's love and the way He works in people's lives. Even this morning's sermon had touched on the very subject.

Setting Abby's letter aside, Evelyn searched out her Bible. She had scribbled the pastor's reference to a verse in Nehemiah on the edge of the church bulletin and slipped it into her Bible. She knew it would take several readings for her to understand any of it and, even then, it would be a stretch. Of that she was certain. But her determination to learn always motivated her.

The loose piece of paper fell from the inside of her Bible and Evelyn quickly picked it up and read it. She found Nehemiah 9:17. Her journal was never far from her Bible, and she turned to an empty page to summarize her thoughts.

March 8. The pastor talked about the Jews, or the children of Israel, in his sermon today, about their rebellion
and how they refused to listen to God or remember the
miracles He had performed in the past. But God did
not desert them, even when they built a golden calf and
worshipped it.

She turned from her notes to the Bible and copied word for word
into her journal:

"But thou art a God ready to pardon, gracious and
merciful, slow to anger, and of great kindness, and forsookest them not." It seems to me that God has more
patience than we deserve. I'm a Jew and I've rebelled
and refused to listen to… what did Christina call it? The
still, small voice? The whisper? The hush?

Evelyn stared out the window at the sun making itself known, despite the falling snow.

*Yes, I am a Jew. Yes, by the Bible's standards, I have rebelled and refused
to listen.*

She thought of the number of times Lewis had tried to reach her
about God's love and forgiveness, and the number of times she had refused to listen.

Now, where do I go from here? She knew the time was coming when
she would need help with all the notes she had accumulated over the past
year. *Should I ask Levi? Christina?*

"Papa?" Evelyn whispered. As she closed her Bible and turned her
attention back to Abby's letter, she knew she had the answer to her
question.

As much as Edna and Hank try to convince me that
I'm wrong, I live in constant fear that Jake will dis-
cover where I live. I'm sure they're right—that I'm safe
here—but my nightmares, not just the ones that come

when I'm sleeping, but the nightmares I've lived, make that possibility very real. I'm comforted by their friendship, though. Stunned, in fact, that they care so much about me, a total stranger, and that they want to help so much in any way they can.

Evie, I want to tell you something...about the abuse. For years I believed Jake when he told me I was responsible. That I needed to be a better wife. That as my husband, he had the right to do what needed to be done to make me what I needed to be. That he needed to keep me in line. His *required discipline*, he called it. I believed him, and even if there were moments when I doubted what he said was true—when the beatings were severe, but secretive because he always made sure the *evidence* was invisible—I never had anyone to tell. My mother would only have said, "Hang in there, things will get better." I never had a close girlfriend, not after Holly died. Even when she was alive, Jake never let us hang out together. And even if he had, I'd have been too ashamed to admit what Jake was really like. Besides, my self-esteem was so low that I believed I deserved the beatings. I was pretty much on my own and Jake preferred it that way. In fact, he kept it that way. He's not friendly at the best of times—most of Thystle Creek knows that. He doesn't even try to hide his meanness.

Do you remember the night we first met—Lucy had a party for Josh and Jennie so everyone could thank Rob and B.J. for saving their lives? You were so kind to me. You asked me lots of questions about where I came from and my life in Quebec, things I liked to do, like reading. Just friendly stuff people ask one another when they first meet. But I knew Jake was watching us and I knew he wouldn't be happy about your interest in me. It wasn't long before he interrupted us and took

me away from you. Remember? He didn't leave me
alone for the rest of the evening, and I have to say he
was some unhappy when you arranged for me to work
at the Emporium.

Evelyn recalled the night. Lucy had invited Jake and Abby to the
party because they were new in town, and Lucy had learned they were
friends of Rob. It had been an innocent act on Lucy's part, one she soon
regretted. It wasn't long after the party that Evelyn's observations of Jake
had been proven correct. He was a loner. Controlling. Suspicious. And he
had a distinct look in his eye—one Evelyn recognized: Jake was an angry
person. As he'd steered Abby away from her that evening, Evelyn recalled
thinking that she'd like to stay in touch with Abby. She'd sensed Abby
needed a friend. She'd been right.

Life in Quebec was no different. Before Holly got sick,
Jake found fault with everything I did. No matter how
hard I tried to be perfect, to do everything exactly as
he wanted and expected, it was never good enough. I
wasn't Holly. In the beginning, it was verbal—shouting, name-calling, abusive insults. Then it increased to
punching and slapping. After Holly died, Jake would
become…well, ballistic, almost evil. At times I wondered if I'd live through the night, because when night
came, the monster in Jake woke up and I was its victim.

I would never put in writing the things he did to
me, things that no wife—no woman!—should ever
have to endure. When the hours of rage subsided, he'd
have what he called his *make-up party*, and I'd have to
turn my mind off to endure even the slightest embrace.
How I never became pregnant then is only through
God's grace. You know, Evie, it wasn't until we moved
to Thystle Creek and I met you that I began to realize
I was wrong in accepting this twisted life. I can't really

say how or when it happened, but you gave me the motivation I needed, even though you may not have realized it. You became my friend. You encouraged me to work at the Emporium. You encouraged me to be my own person. As I've told you before, you helped me rediscover my self-respect, and in doing that, I found the courage to leave.

Well, there you have it. You are the only one who knows what Jake is really like. If what I've heard is true and the old Jake has disappeared, well, I can only pray that it remains that way. Because if the old Jake ever reappears, I'm in deep trouble.

I have to go now so I can mail this letter before I go to work. And don't worry, Hank has cut my hours to just twelve a week and I'm doing just fine. I've started a new life here in Pike Ridge. With only four more weeks before my due date—unless Baby decides otherwise—I anticipate Edna taking on the adoptive grandmother role, which suits me just fine. By the way, please tell Doctor Morsman that I'm seeing Doctor Crombie weekly now, and please say hi to him for me.

Keep in touch,
Abby

Evelyn jumped at the ring of the front doorbell. Even though she'd read Abby's letter through once before, what she'd read had again disturbed her beyond words. The last thing she needed at that moment was company. Shoving the letter into her skirt pocket, she made her way to the front hall. She smiled and glanced at the staircase when she heard Trickster thud to the floor in the library, no doubt leaping from her chair to greet the unknown visitor with her robust energy.

Evelyn opened the front door and stared at her visitor. There stood Jake Waters, banging snow from his boots. An immediate flashback of her visit with Abby and the letter she'd just read left her speechless.

"Excuse me. Are you Mrs. Sherwood?"

Of course she was Mrs. Sherwood. Why would Jake be asking her that?

Five, six, seven seconds passed and Evelyn continued to stare.

"Perhaps I've got the wrong address," Jake continued. "I'm looking for Rob Adams. I was told he and his son live with Mrs. Sherwood. Mrs. Evelyn Sherwood. I was sure this was the correct address." He stumbled with his explanation.

The awkwardness continued until a gust of wind sent snow blowing into the front hall.

"Yes, I'm Mrs. Sherwood. Please, come in."

Jake stepped inside the front door.

Snow dripped from the toque Jake held in his hand. Its removal had uncovered his greasy and dishevelled shoulder-length hair. His moustache, badly in need of a trim, sparkled with frozen droplets and his jacket, still covered with fresh snow, shrouded his upper torso. His look would have been intimidating had Evelyn not known who he was.

"I'm Jake Waters."

Trickster reached the bottom of the stairs and froze. No barking. No tail wagging. Just a deep guttural growl that quickly turned into violent barking.

"Trickster! Wh—what in the world?" Evelyn reached for her dog, but Trickster leaped away and circled Jake's legs, snapping at his pants.

"Seems she doesn't take well to strangers," Jake offered, twisting in circles as he kept an eye on the dog.

"Trickster, stop that! Come here."

Evelyn reached down to pick up the dog, unknowingly dropping Abby's letter to the floor.

Jake reached out to pet the dog only to jerk back at Trickster's bared teeth.

"Quite the guard dog you have there," he said.

Trickster continued to growl with such ferocity that Evelyn feared even she would be nipped accidently.

"Would you excuse me for a moment? I think it best if I put this little creature outside."

Evelyn turned and left Jake staring at the last page of Abby's letter.

"Hey, Evie, what's all the noise abou—" Rob froze mid-flight, causing B.J. to bump into him. "Jake!"

Rob continued down the stairs, more slowly now, with his son hovering close behind.

"Hi, Rob. Hope I'm not intruding." Jake smiled at B.J. who just glared back at him. "Thought I'd look you up, now that I'm better...at least physically. The doctors said it would be good for me to reconnect with people—with some friends who know me. Said it would help in restoring my memory, and I thought of you."

Returning from the kitchen, Evelyn quickly picked up the dropped letter lying two feet from Jake on the hall floor. She sighed in relief; it appeared Rob had arrived at just the right moment. Neither had seen it.

"Rob, I was about to come and get you, but I had to deal with Trickster first. I've never seen her behave like that before. I'm sorry, Jake. She's normally very good with strangers. Must have been all the snow and your heavy coat that startled her."

Evelyn knew her excuse was lame, but she let it go. Signalling for B.J. to follow her, she suggested the two men visit in the living room while she made a fresh pot of coffee.

She picked up the envelope from the kitchen table and placed the now carefully folded letter inside.

How could I have been so careless? Good thing Rob came down when he did. Evelyn closed her eyes, shaken by the thought of what could have been a disastrous outcome.

"What's *he* doing here?" B.J. whispered, his voice trembling.

Evelyn crouched down to embrace her grandson, searching for the right words to help abate his obvious fears. "It's okay, B.J. Jake is still sick and he doesn't remember things."

"Like when he was mean to me?"

"That's right. You know he had an accident. Well, that accident left him unable to remember a lot of things, like who he is and what he's done.

Doctor Morsman encouraged your daddy to visit him in the hospital. That's the only way Jake knows they have a history."

B.J. glared at the kitchen doorway. "Well, I still don't like him. He gives me the creeps."

Evelyn followed his stare and said nothing.

Jake slipped his toque over his hair, pulled up the collar of his jacket, and walked slowly away from the Sherwood home. He turned slightly and saw Rob and Evelyn watching from the living room window.

He waved.

"Fools," he muttered through a forced smile. *Am I good or what?* He chuckled at his answer. *Yeah, I'm good. Real good.*

He headed toward his truck, parked down the street in a place where he'd sat unseen for several nights watching, waiting, planning. With a sweep of his hand, he cleared the snow from the windshield, climbed in, and spun his tires on the ice as he pulled away from the curb.

"So we're friends are we, *Mr. Adams?* You said to come again, did you, *Mrs. Sherwood?* Well, we'll just see what you do with my next visit."

Jake turned up his radio and pounded out the beat from the current rock band on his steering wheel.

"Yes, siree! We'll see what they do with my next visit. People don't mistreat Jake Waters and not pay."

His smile grew as he thumped out two words to the beat of the music: Pike Ridge, Pike Ridge, Pike Ridge.

40

The wicked watcheth the righteous,
and seeketh to slay him.
PSALM 37:32

March 12

The kerosene-soaked charcoal had served its purpose. Although intense heat sent rippled waves into the air, there was no smoke—not until several logs, intertwined with the latest newspaper, found a home in the centre of the hot coals. A sudden *pop* and the new smoke disappeared as flames burst into life, thanking their benefactor for renewed life.

No one had heard it.

Melting snow along its path, the fire moved along the alley wall, slowly, perniciously devouring everything in its path. Crates of dried packing straw and barrels of empty cardboard containers fell victim to its insatiable hunger until the flame's new life was threatened by lack of food. In a frenzy, the fire twisted in the wind, swishing, swirling, searching for anything to sustain it. Like a ravenous animal whose life-threatening hunger drove it to madness, the flame defied its own death at the hands of melting snow and leapt across the damp ground to strike its next victim. Quietly, maliciously, the fire crept up the wooden door until its planks succumbed and fell, opening a new path to further appease the flaming devil.

Jake watched from across the road, hidden beneath the cover of darkness. His faint smile grew into a detestable laugh, but he shook it off out of fear of discovery. He watched until the flames leapt over the puddles of melting snow to lick the back door of the Emporium.

Let's see you get out of this one, Josh, my boy. He crushed his half-finished cigarette under his shoe and headed toward his truck, parked two blocks away. The thought of making Josh Graham pay for hiring his wife had festered and grown since the day Abby and Evelyn Sherwood had connived against him to get her out of the house. The final straw had come last August with his wife's promotion to store manager while he continued the menial task of pulling weeds and grooming strawberry plants on Ruth Norton's farm.

No one makes a fool out of me and gets away with it.

He glanced over his shoulder and, in the twilight of the setting sun, confirmed that the Emporium was the price Josh would pay for messing with him. When he saw Josh's car parked on the north side of the building, he grinned. *Two for one!* He took a quick detour to snip the building's phone lines. If Josh was inside, there was no getting help now!

As he climbed into his truck, he turned his thoughts in another direction.

Your turn's next, Evelyn Sherwood. You with your little secret will pay… dearly.

He turned the ignition key and headed west out of town before looping back to the farm, back to his sanctuary, back to the woman who had given him refuge. "If only you knew, dear Mrs. Norton… if only you knew."

Free from prying ears and curious eyes, Jake gave in to his laughter. Loud. Insidious. Victorious.

It was an innocent mouse, whose demise Josh Graham had laboured over for days, that first alerted him to the fact that something was wrong. In the confined office, the mouse ran right across his feet and then back again, once, twice, three times crossing his foot without regard for its potential fate.

"You strange little creature, you. For days I've tried to send you off to mouse heaven, yet here you are running right in front of me as though a monstrous cat was licking at your heels."

He stopped the one-way conversation with his annoying little intruder and listened. A faint noise. He shook his head and returned his attention to the elusive mouse. It ran in circles right under his desk as if it had lost its way.

"Something's scaring you senseless."

The noise came a second time and he opened his office door.

Smoke from under the storage room door was quickly filling the store. The unseen flames had yet to reach the stack of yard goods piled in a neat row on the shelf nearest the door, but Josh knew it was just a matter of time. He could only imagine the damage in the storage room, but did not take time to consider it fully. He couldn't.

He slammed shut his office door and ran to the phone. The line was dead. He opened the door a second time, but could no longer see the front door of the store. Slamming the door once more, he took off his jacket and shoved it along the crack at the bottom, backed into the far corner, and crouched near the floor. He could not get out. He was stuck. He had no window. He had no means of communication. He had no escape.

Despite his efforts to keep the smoke from filtering into his office, it crept past his jacket, moving like an amoeba on a mission: forming, reforming, shaping, and reshaping as it slid across the floor, growing to encompass the whole room. One look at the tiny rodent, who had sought escape in the same corner he had, told Josh that he needn't set further traps.

Memories filled his head and he heard his best friend calling him.

"Josh! Josh! Where are you?"

It had been another fire. Another lifetime ago.

"Louie? Is that you? I—I can't see! The smoke's too thick. I'm over near the embankment, pinned under a tree. I think my leg's broken."

A choking cough. Another.

"Hang on, son, I'm coming… "

Another cough, then a fourth. A fifth. His thoughts became irrational. *Jennie will wonder where I am. I need to call her.*

Josh reached for the phone and lifted the receiver to his ear. "Jennie? Jennie?" He squeaked his wife's name, but only a rasping gurgle echoed in his head before blackness finally consumed him.

Jake swerved along County Road 7, laughing with the excitement of a little boy on his first rollercoaster ride. Flashing lights coming toward him tempered his reverie. He pulled to the shoulder just as Pete Cannington's truck raced past him.

"Happy firefighting, Pete," Jake said, his sarcasm bouncing off the interior walls of his truck. His exuberance rallied as he envisioned the results of his labour.

He pressed down hard on the gas pedal, spinning his tires on the shoulder of the road, twisting, jerking his truck onto the icy pavement. Defiant and reckless, he turned off his headlights and aimed his truck precariously down the centre of the road, his speed accelerating and his laughter reaching the snow-covered fields.

Moments later, he pulled his truck into Ruth's driveway. Turning off the ignition, he squared his shoulders and wiggled his head from side to side to release the tension. He replaced his victorious gloating with the innocence and charm his landlady had come to believe was the new Jake Waters. He had to come up with a reason for why he'd missed the roast beef dinner he'd been promised—and he had to do it quickly. Ruth was hurrying toward him, apron flapping in the wind, arms flailing.

Hmm, I wonder what could be the problem.

Jake suppressed a smile.

41

The Lord will perfect that which concerneth me:
thy mercy, O Lord, endureth for ever:
forsake not the works of thine own hands.
PSALM 138:8

Levi pulled off his latex gloves, turning them inside-out as he pushed open the doors of the operating room. Never had he been so relieved. He hurried down the short corridor toward the waiting room, removing his surgical tunic and head covering. Handing them to a passing nurse, he turned the corner and found Jennie Graham and Evelyn sitting quietly in two vinyl chairs. He was glad the lateness of the hour had spared them the normal anxious buzz such a small room created. The room stood empty apart from the two women.

Jennie's head rested on the wall behind the row of chairs and her hands twisted a tear-soaked tissue. Evelyn sat next to her, aimlessly flipping the pages of a magazine. Seeing Levi approach, she gently touched her friend.

Levi took Jennie's hands, nodding as he spoke. "He'll be fine. He took in a lot of smoke and I had to perform a bronchoscopy... sorry, I had to take a look in his lungs and airway to make sure he didn't inhale anything dangerous." He paused. "The long and short of it is that Josh's lungs are clear, something we can be very thankful for. He was very fortunate. I think…I *know* my report would have been very different had he been in his office much longer. He did well to stay close to the floor. It probably saved his life. He's going to be fine, but he'll be hoarse for a while."

"Can I see him?" Jennie requested quietly, gently.

"Of course, but keep in mind I had to give him something for the bronchosc…the procedure. He'll probably want to sleep." Levi laughed. "Actually, with what I gave him, he'll be lucky to finish a sentence. Go on in and see him."

Levi signalled for a nurse to take Jennie to her husband.

Evelyn sighed and Levi put his arm around her shoulder. "You okay?"

Both knew the question had more to it than concern for Josh's well-being. Ten years had passed since the death of Lewis Sherwood in the June forest fire of 1960. Levi had not known Evelyn then, but he did know that this small waiting room was where Evelyn had received the most devastating words a spouse can hear: "I'm sorry, he didn't make it."

"I'll be fine," she said. "Knowing Josh survived the fire is—"

"A miracle?" Levi suggested.

"—is incredible," Evelyn countered with a smile. "Miracles are not in my language just yet, although I have to admit, Doc Bailey's decision to drive through downtown rather than take the back road home from Ruth's place may have saved Josh's life."

"No, Evie. Not *may have*. It *did*. Had Allen taken the shortcut, I'd have given Jennie a different report. Breaking the front window allowed the smoke to filter outside. That simple act contributed to Josh's survival."

Evelyn's eyes filled in spite of her smile. "But Allen *didn't* take the shortcut, and you *didn't* have to give Jennie bad news. That's what counts. Is there any thought as to what caused the fire?"

"It's too early for that. In the morning, Bryan Benson and Pete Cannington will sift through the back lane and storage room for an answer. The fire seems to have started in one of those two places. Fortunately, that's where it stayed. And I'm sure you're more aware than I that those two men have years of experience in fighting fires. They'll come up with the cause."

"Pete found Louie under the tree and dragged him out, risking his own life." Evelyn never took her eyes off Levi. "I'll be forever grateful to Pete for bringing Louie home."

Sensitive to Evelyn's memories, Levi gently moved the subject in another direction. "According to Doc Bailey, as he was coming into town from the east, he noticed the red taillights of a truck heading out of town. Although the streets were quiet, he didn't give it much thought. It may not mean a thing, but he did mention it to the powers that be."

Moments later, Jennie appeared and Levi insisted she go home and get some rest. He assured her once again that Josh would be fine and would be able to go home soon. Evelyn looped her arm in Jennie's, smiled one more time at Levi, and then, whispering words of encouragement to Jennie, left Levi standing in the middle of the waiting room. He watched the two women until they turned the corner at the far end of the corridor.

Heading for his office to write his report on Josh's accident, he couldn't help but mull over the unanswered question Evelyn had put to him. If it wasn't an accident, who would want to do that to Josh?

42

My son, eat thou honey, because it is good;
and the honeycomb, which is sweet to thy taste.
PROVERBS 24:13

March 17

The Tuesday morning following the fire at the Emporium found Evelyn enjoying a cup of hot apple cider and watching her beloved dog burrow tunnels in fresh snow. Although it was a school day, the previous night's weather had resulted in cancelled classes, forcing a much-coveted snow day. She smiled at the terminology. "Aren't all days in March snow days?" she'd teased B.J.

The small table by the back door offered a quiet spot, away from the hustle and bustle that came with a household of four adults and a child. But not for a moment did she wish it otherwise. She had been alone for two years since Lucy had married.

Two years too long, she thought, scanning the backyard for Trickster.

Without the busyness that most weekday mornings brought, her house remained asleep. Even her father, who from years of habit rose before the sun to turn on his ovens, remained in his room. Evelyn doubted if he was asleep, but she left him to his solitude and took advantage of the quiet.

She loved the early morning hours and found herself reading scripture more at this time of the day than any other. She felt that her current readings penetrated her mind and heart more fully when she read them in the morning than when she read them at night. Thus, she considered herself a morning person.

She sipped her cider, remembering the past week's Sunday service. Josh had been in church and Evelyn had watched and listened while people shook his hand and others pounded his back in pure joy. Pastor Cribbs had acknowledged him in the service, offering a prayer of thanksgiving for his safety. Evelyn had listened, wondering at how different the service had been when Lewis had died saving Josh. As though sensing her thoughts, Lucy had slipped her hand in hers and squeezed it gently without looking at her.

Evelyn recalled the pastor's verse of the morning—Psalm 138:8—and she turned to it, smiling at how easily she was able to navigate the book. *"The Lord will perfect that which concerneth me: thy mercy, O Lord, endureth for ever: forsake not the works of thine own hands."*

Such verses created questions that continued to multiply in Evelyn's mind.

Did God perfect my life with Lewis's death? Is Levi part of the perfecting? Will God ever forsake me? Will my father…

She paused. Her father. On Christmas morning, she and her father and grandmother had crossed the communication bridge and she'd shared her life journey: Bobby's death, giving up Rob as an infant, marrying Lewis, and all that her life had entailed as his wife. She learned that her grandmother had become a believer in the Christ of the New Testament not very many years ago, living with the regret that her own daughter never lived to see that happen. Her father had started to explain why he and Evelyn's mother had made the same decision when Evelyn was a young teenager. But B.J. had bounded down the stairs shouting "Merry Christmas" just at that moment and had dashed toward the presents under the tree. Evelyn remembered having had mixed emotions, wishing her father's story could have been heard while at the same time feeling an overwhelming thrill at seeing B.J. and Annie together on Christmas morning for the very first time.

Evelyn's thoughts turned to her daughter. Lucy had survived a tumultuous childhood, but the early years following Lewis's death had all but destroyed what was left of their relationship. Silence, apathy, indifference. They had seldom spoken in those years, only out of necessity.

> Ships that pass in the night, and speak each other in
>   passing,
> Only a signal shown, and a distant voice in the darkness;
> So on the ocean of life we pass and speak one another,
> Only a look and a voice, then darkness again and a si-
>   lence.

Longfellow's poem describes those years, she thought with threatening sadness. *But Lucy survived, and I survived!*

Evelyn smiled. Their relationship had *changed.* How or why, she didn't bother to consider; it just changed, especially since Lucy had married Wil, and even more so since Annie's birth. If the truth were told, she welcomed the noise, confusion, and excitement that resulted when Lucy and her family dropped by to disrupt her lonely days.

And the surprise visits from Christina and Levi... Evelyn's smile broadened as she thought of their friendship, her eyes searching the snow-covered garden for her dog. Yet as her thoughts turned to Christina, a cloud of despair threatened to engulf her and she began to wonder how much longer she would have Christina in her life.

I owe her so much. Evelyn capped her pen and closed her journal. *Bubi asks about her every day.*

Her smile returned as she thought about the sweetness of both women and their influence on her life.

Evelyn pushed back her chair and took another glance out the window in search of her over-enthusiastic dog before deciding to invite Christina over for tea, hoping it would be a good day for her, a day free of headaches. She opened the cookbook her father had given her for

Christmas—one that contained a selection of his favourite recipes, along with some of her mother's. Handprinted with the precision of a seasoned lithographer, each page had been bound into a beautiful book sporting a waterproof cover. She held the book to her chest for a moment, remembering her mother, remembering the smells of her baking, remembering her father's bakery—not the one in Pontypool, but in their first home, the home that held all her happy childhood memories.

Reverently turning the pages, Evelyn read recipe after recipe, enjoying the anecdotes her father had included along the way. Words of wisdom. Scripture verses. Memories. Tips for making the best pastry, the best dough, the best *challah* bread, potato *latkes* and *schnecken*. Evelyn smiled at the Jewish recipes and marvelled at how her father had instinctively included them in the book despite his decision to repress his Jewish heritage.

I wonder if he did that just for me. Maybe even for Lucy, Evelyn considered as she turned page after page of the precious book.

The inclusion of scripture verses intrigued her, and for the first time since receiving the book she noticed the Old Testament Scripture Cake recipe. She read it through. Butter, Judges 5:25. White sugar, Jeremiah 6:20. Eggs, Isaiah 10:14. Flour, 1 Kings 4:22. She marvelled at how the author of such a recipe had given up his heritage in order to follow the One he believed to be the chosen one of Israel. She continued reading the references, noting the ingredients, but focusing on the parts of the Bible that included both the Old and New Testament. Luke 13:21, 1 Kings 10:10, Leviticus 2:13, Genesis 43:24. When she read Proverbs 24:13, her curiosity piqued. She laid the book aside, opened the Bible sitting beside her empty mug, and read aloud, "My son, eat thou honey, because it is good; and the honeycomb, which is sweet to thy taste."

"Watcha doin', Nana?"

B.J. stood in the kitchen doorway, wiping sleep from the corners of his eyes.

Evelyn jumped and dropped her Bible on the floor. Before she could bend over, B.J. was at her feet, handing it up to her. "Is there something in the Bible about honeycomb? I love honeycomb. My daddy used to take me to the market back where we used to live and buy a chunk of it, but I had to make it last all week. That was hard."

Evelyn smiled at her grandson's innocence. "I'm sure it was. Honey is very good. Bears especially like it," she quipped and kissed the top of his head. She placed her Bible on the table and turned to the task of making the cake she had just read about.

"Where's Trickster?" B.J. asked. "I woke up and she wasn't there."

"What? Oh my goodness, I got so wrapped up in my reading, I forgot about her. The poor thing is probably shivering outside the door, too cold to even bark. Do you mind bringing her in, B.J.?"

Without hesitation, B.J. eagerly opened the back door only to find the snow undisturbed on the back step and walkway.

"She's not here, Nana."

"She must still be having fun digging those tunnels through the snow, although I'm surprised she wants to stay out for so long. It's quite cold this morning." Evelyn went to the back door and called, "Trickster! Come on, girl! Get your treat!"

Nothing.

"Come on, Tricks. It's too cold out there."

Nothing.

"I think I heard your daddy getting up," she said, turning back to her grandson. "Why don't you run upstairs and get dressed? I'll get my coat on and go get her. She seems to be having far too much fun to notice how cold it is. When she's all dry and sleeping by the fire, you and I can bake a very special cake. We'll invite Lee and Christina over and have a party. Would you like to invite Aunt Lucy and Uncle Wil and little Annie, too? Uncle Wil will be home today, since there's no school."

The lilt in her voice did not match the thumping in her heart. Where was that dog? And why hadn't she come when she heard her favourite word—*treat*?

43

The Lord hath made all things for himself:
yea, even the wicked for the day of evil.
PROVERBS 16:4

Tying her scarf tightly around her head against the growing wind, Evelyn made fresh footprints in the snow that had fallen while she'd buried herself in her cookbook.

"Trickster! Come on, girl. It's cold out here. Tricks…Trickster!"

Evelyn walked further into the yard, calling her dog with increasing anxiety.

Deep into the garden, under Lewis's favourite tree, a mound of snow caught Evelyn's eye—more because of the red stain on it than because of the recognizable shape.

"Trickster!" Evelyn yelled. She leapt across the deep mounds that had been created as Levi faithfully shovelled a path.

Falling to her knees, Evelyn stroked Trickster's fur, brushing away the accumulating snow with trembling hands, her racing heart fearing the worst. She gasped as her hand struck something sharp. A piece of a broken arrow protruded five inches from the dog's left side, and Trickster whimpered. Evelyn bent closer, brushing off the snow. She carefully lifted Trickster into her arms, desperately fighting for control, wondering if this was a time to pray. But did God hear prayers from the likes of her? Would He listen to prayers for a wounded pet?

Trickster's eyes rolled as she tried to lift her head.

"Easy, girl," Evelyn whispered.

Evelyn held her dog close to her chest as she struggled to stand from her crouched position. Overcoming the mounds of snow, she noticed something that made her blood run as cold as the Arctic winds. To her right she saw the beginning of a faint trail of footprints leading away from where she had found Trickster. Following them with her eyes, she traced them toward the back fence where they disappeared.

Horror filled her as she stared at the impressions in disbelief. A groan from Trickster jolted her back to the moment. She turned and raced through the snow, trusting she would not fall, screaming for her son.

Evelyn burst through the back door and found Rob standing at the counter, coffee mug in hand, sharing stories with his grandfather.

"Trickster's been shot with an arrow! The snow...it's covered with blood. I don't know how long...please, we need to get help!"

Evelyn gently placed Trickster on her mat inside the back door and fell at her side, weeping.

Rob picked up the phone, made the call, and turned his attention to Evelyn.

"Lee's on his way right now. He'll call the vet, but he said not to move her, just to keep her warm." Rob accepted a blanket from his grandfather and gently enveloped the shivering dog, whispering soothing words in an effort to quieten the injured animal.

"Rob, it's all my fault. I let her out for just a few minutes and then forgot about her. I was reading my new recipe book..." Evelyn turned to her father, who sat with B.J. in his arms, rocking him quietly. "It was the one you gave me for Christmas. I forgot about Trickster being outside. It wasn't until B.J. came downstairs and asked where she was that I remembered."

Evelyn's voice broke. Her tears poured freely as she sat stroking her dog.

Her grandmother bent down beside her and caressed her head. "It's not your fault, child. Whatever evil person has done this…he's the one at fault."

Trickster whimpered and tried to sit up.

"Shhhh, girl, lie still." Evelyn wiped her face with her sleeve. "We'll get you fixed up and you'll be romping in the snow again before you know it." She soothed her dog, conscious of the blood oozing from the wound, taking care to avoid brushing her hand against the piece of arrow.

Christina and Levi arrived within minutes and found a sombre family hovering over the wounded animal. When Levi bent down, Evelyn fell into his arms and wept.

"Why would anyone do this?" she sobbed. "She's just a little dog, Lee. Just a little dog that loves everybody." Her words filled the room and fanned everyone's growing despair.

Suddenly Evelyn yanked herself free from Lee's arms and stood up. With wide eyes and a voice filled with rage, she pointed to the backyard window.

"Go and look at the end of the yard, Lee," she snapped. "Go and see what I saw and tell me I'm wrong. Please, tell me I'm wrong."

Evelyn sank onto the chair that moments earlier had been her solace, her sanctuary, and stared out the window, sobbing uncontrollably.

Minutes passed. Christina busied herself by making fresh coffee and offered a cup to Evelyn, who refused it with a wave of her hand and a weak smile. Joseph continued to comfort his distraught great-grandson and Evelyn's grandmother hovered over her, assuring her of Trickster's eventual recovery.

"After all, she's still a young dog and will heal quickly," Rachel said. "Remember early Christmas Day when she stepped on a pin buried deep in the carpet? My goodness, how she carried on. After Lee pulled it out, she ran around without so much as a limp."

"This is different, Bubi." Evelyn looked into Trickster's eyes. "She's hurting and I don't know if she's going to—"

"Doctor Clarington's here, Evie," Christina announced quietly.

The veterinarian hung his coat and hat over a kitchen chair and moved swiftly to Trickster's side. Levi was still outside with Rob and Wil, who had just happened to come over to shovel the front walk.

Evelyn remained in her chair, watching the three men as they made their way to the back of the yard, then turned and returned to the house. When they came in from investigating the scene, their faces confirmed what Evelyn had seen: someone had come into the yard and shot Trickster, then left by way of the back fence.

"From what we can make out," Wil volunteered after acknowledging Charles Clarington, "someone came in from the side gate. It seems to have been intentionally propped open. Looks like the person intended to leave the same way he came in, but something spooked him. Did you hear her bark, Evie?"

"No." Evelyn hugged herself with the sweater her grandmother had wrapped around her shoulders. "If Trickster had barked, I'd have heard her." She kept her eyes fixed on the snow-covered yard rather than watching the vet work on Trickster. But a sudden yelp made her jump to her feet.

"That confirms our suspicion," Levi continued, distracting Evelyn. "Trickster must not have seen or heard the person who shot her."

"Easy, girl," Clarington spoke softly. "Evelyn, any idea of how long ago this happened?"

Evelyn hesitated. "I put her out about half an hour ago and I forgot about her." Her eyes filled with tears again and overflowed onto her face. "I forgot about her," she whispered. "If only I'd remembered…"

Rachel put her arm around her granddaughter's waist.

"It may have been fairly recent, Doc," Wil volunteered. "If our guess is right, whoever did this must have thought he'd planned it perfectly, but he wasn't prepared for Evie's interference when she called Trickster. He left in a hurry."

Trickster yelped again and everyone stopped talking.

"I need to get her to my office," Clarington said when he finished his exam. "It's quite possible the arrow punctured her jugular vein, and I don't want to pull it out here. Right now it's acting like a plug in the proverbial dam. If I pull it out now, she's liable to bleed out." He turned to Evelyn. "I'm sorry, Evelyn, but I can't make any guarantees. Once I put her out, I'll have a better idea of what I'm up against. I'll need to do an x-ray to see if there's internal damage before I can stitch her up. And there's always the chance of infection, especially if the arrow was old. It's hard to say right now, but from what I can see, she's getting weak from the loss of blood. Lee, can you give me a hand?"

Evelyn stepped aside while Levi and Clarington gently lifted Trickster onto a blanket and carried her sling-style to the veterinarian's van. She watched them lift Trickster carefully into a crate in the back of the van, then nodded in understanding when Levi motioned that he would go with the vet.

B.J. came to the doorway and hugged her waist, smothering his face in her apron. His sobs shook his body and Evelyn bent down to hold him as she watched the van pull away.

"She'll be fine, B.J. You'll see. When Levi gets back, he'll tell us that she'll be her old self again in a few days, barking at the front doorbell, chasing her squeaky toy, and begging for more treats."

It was all Evelyn could do to control her own tears. For the sake of her grandson, she wanted all those predictions to come true. She forced her hovering doubts into a deep part of her mind, not giving them any credence, at least not in front of her weeping grandson.

44

He that hateth dissembleth with his lips,
and layeth up deceit within him;
When he speaketh fair, believe him not:
for there are seven abominations in his heart.

PROVERBS 26:24–25

March 18

That was a nasty fire at the Emporium last Thursday night, wasn't it, Jake? Everyone's so thankful Doc Bailey came along when he did. He was here for dinner, you know—the one you missed. Good thing he left early, otherwise things may have turned out very badly for Josh."

Ruth chatted nonstop as she flipped strips of grease-soaked bacon in her cast-iron skillet. Small beads of sweat lined the nape of her neck as she busied herself over the wood-burning stove. She seemed oblivious to the heat and the small curls of hair that fell loose from her salt and pepper up-sweep. Ruth was not overly concerned with making a fashion state-ment—evidenced in her wearing the same simple house dresses Monday through Friday. Nor was she particularly obsessed with health concerns, her full figure accenting her personality and often revealing rolls of flesh bouncing with every laugh. And she laughed often.

"Seems that Pete and Bryan—you've met them, haven't you, Jake? Or maybe you don't remember." She fluffed the pointless question off with a wave of her greasy fork. "Anyway, seems that Pete and Bryan think someone deliberately set the fire. Can you believe that? Arson! The word has such an awful sound to it, doesn't it? They found a pile of charcoal in the back alley right behind the store. Even the phone line was cut. Why would anyone do such a thing?" She paused in her rambling. "More bacon, Jake? I've cooked enough for an army. My Stanley loved his bacon. Every Saturday—just like today—we'd cook half a pound of bacon and eat it between the two of us. Isn't that sinful?"

Jake smiled out of politeness, devouring the food Ruth piled on his plate. He couldn't care less what Stanley had eaten on Saturdays, or if the two of them put away half a pig. His thoughts were on Ruth's remark about the fire.

I should have been more careful. Now somebody's going to start snooping.

He polished off his toast and coffee, thanked his guileless host, and headed for his room on the second floor.

It had been a little over two months since he'd been discharged from the hospital, since Ruth had offered to take care of him. He grinned at how stupid some people could be. He remembered how he'd felt on the day he was discharged; he couldn't get out of the hospital fast enough, for fear that his restored memory would be discovered. Lucky for him, Ruth had been a convenient pawn. He'd plotted, contrived, and waited, and she'd come along at just the right time.

Plan my work and work my plan, he'd jokingly thought, lying in the solitude of his hospital room. He'd listened to the rhythmic beeping of the machines attached to him and, like a lullaby, the beeps ironically soothed his growing rage when the flashbacks became more frequent. His hatred toward Rob for taking Holly from him. His jealousy and resentment when Rob and B.J. left Quebec and headed west after Holly's death. His manipulations in convincing Abby to go west, too, all under the delusion that he wanted a "fresh start." The rage that drove his passion to get even with Rob, at any cost. The ultimate moment had come when he'd remembered what Abby had done to land him in the hospital. Those beeping monitors had done little to contain his fury.

When visitors had been permitted to see him, he'd put on award-winning performances. Pretending to like Rob, repressing the years of hatred to a dark corner of his mind. Smiling with false gratitude with each visit from Ruth, quietly believing there was a fool born every minute. Tearing up when the doctors told him he was physically fine, laughing inwardly when they suggested the small possibility that his memory might never return.

Little did they know, Jake thought, closing the door to his room and flopping onto his unmade bed.

And then there was Abby, who the police believed had "intentionally and with malice" harmed him. Poor, vulnerable Abby. A sinister smile spread across his face as he stretched his legs and locked his hands behind his head. He remembered the night all too well.

How dare she try and leave me!

His mother had tried the same thing when he was seven. He could still remember the smacking, the begging, and the final thud when his mother had hit the wall in his parents' bedroom. The muffled cries had seeped through his fists, balled against his ears as he'd lain curled up in his bed with the blankets pulled over his head. He'd willed his mother to stop crying. The silence that finally followed had unnerved him, and yet the following morning his mother stood in the kitchen preparing his father's breakfast as though they'd just returned from a relaxing and fun-filled holiday. Apart from her swollen eye and slight limp, nothing had been said. Life had continued and he'd eventually grown deaf to the sounds that threatened his sleep.

He'd lost something for his mother in those years—a feeling that never found a word. Love, maybe? He'd come to believe that the fighting and beatings were her fault. If she had just shown more respect to his father, if she had not tried to leave that first time, if she'd just obeyed him…On the other hand, Jake's admiration for his father had deepened as he watched and listened and learned how to keep a wife in line.

His only defense for his actions was that it had worked for his father, and it would work for him.

"She was—*is*—my wife," he spoke quietly into the empty room, cringing at his mistake. "And she'll pay for what she did to me."

From his position on the bed, he watched the wind blow the weather vane on top of the drive shed. The arrow spun around and around like a branch caught in a swirling eddy. Jake sat up and walked to the window. As though under the vane's hypnotic spell, he counted the spins—one to the right, three to the left, one to the right, two to the left and back again. Over and over the arrow twisted and jerked at the mercy of the wind. Minutes passed as Jake continued to stare until he became conscious of his fists: opening, closing, tighter, tighter; opening, closing, tighter, tighter.

His neck veins bulged and his breathing quickened as he thought of what Abby had done. Then he remembered his plan and shoved his hands into his pockets, as though to hide any evidence of his turmoil.

Two down and one to go.

"Plan my work and work my plan." He chanted the words for encouragement and it worked. So far he'd been successful. Abby was the only one left. He could taste the revenge, fuelled by his visit to Evelyn Sherwood's home the previous week.

In defiance of the wind, the weather vane stopped spinning.

No one can stop you from doing what you want, not even the wind. His smile grew as he associated his own will and purpose with the metal appendage high in the sky. *We both have something in common. We will get our own way.* The motionless arrow pointed west and, in his twisted thinking, Jake took it as a sign: *Go west, young man, go west.*

Jake laughed aloud. He saluted the wooden rooster sitting atop the arrow and turned from the window. The wind blew again, but Jake didn't see the arrow resume its spinning, back and forth—one to the right, three to the left, one to the right, two to the left and back again.

The noise of Ruth's vacuum cleaner drifted up the stairwell and through his closed door, and Jake's thoughts turned to his earlier conversation with his landlady.

Why did I ever use Ruth's charcoal to start the fire?

Behind the barbeque in the basement, the three unopened bags had been too irresistible. He had only used one, but knowing his overly industrious host, she probably had counted the number of bags left from the previous summer.

Her suspicions would be aroused soon. He needed to replace it, and quickly.

Ruth watched Jake spin his tires on the patch of ice in front of the garage door and race down the long driveway to County Road 7. The back end of his truck swung recklessly from side to side, leaving a cloud of fresh snow in its wake.

"He acts like the devil himself is after him!" Ruth shook her head and turned from the upstairs window to continue her weekly cleaning. She dragged the vacuum cleaner along the upstairs hall and stopped outside Jake's room.

Must have been in a hurry, she concluded when she saw the open door. She never intruded on his privacy, assuming he kept his own things in order, but the open door revealed quite the opposite.

The unmade bed, piles of clothes scattered on the floor, and pants hanging from the knob of the open closet door all suggested he needed a little help, if not a reminder that cleanliness was, indeed, next to godliness. Wondering if he would consider it an intrusion, she lingered in the doorway, remembering the first week Jake had come home from the hospital.

He'd been quite pleasant, laughing over her silly jokes, carrying wood in from the back porch, even offering to dry the dishes, which she had emphatically refused. One day during the third week following his release, he'd trampled through the deep snow into the woods behind the house. He had been gone for several hours. "Just to think," he'd told Ruth when she expressed concern on his return. He'd told her not to fuss so much, but she just smiled and told him that she enjoyed having someone around to fuss over. Then she had placed in front of him a slice of warm apple pie and a heap of ice cream.

By the end of February, the "new Jake"—as she had repeatedly called him to those who inquired—had slowly begun to disappear. It worried her, yet she brushed off the concern, attributing his behaviour to growing frustration that his memory had not returned. In some ways she felt sorry for him, and it was for that reason—and that reason alone—that she decided to show some Christian love and clean his room.

After she found a home for his strewn clothes, Ruth put fresh sheets on his bed. She gathered up a pile of loose papers heaped in the corner of the room and removed a badly soiled towel from under the small night table, dropping it into the waste basket. A roughly folded map of Alberta caused her to pause and study it before refolding it and putting it on the dresser.

When the floor was finally clear of the clutter, she pulled the vacuum into the centre of the room and resumed the task she had started after breakfast. Humming a nameless tune, she pushed and pulled the vacuum across the floor, contentment oozing from her pores. She loved her home, and sharing it with a troubled young man gave her a sense of purpose in life. She missed her husband and the long winter nights sometimes proved unbearable. She would help Jake—even if the old Jake returned, she decided. She'd long-since convinced herself that she could help him solve his problems.

Surely they can't be that *bad,* she thought, extending the vacuum under Jake's bed.

A sudden noise startled her. Something had caught in the foot of the vacuum and she quickly switched the machine off before pulling it out from under the bed.

Lying sideways, half in and half out of the foot nozzle, was a slender piece of wood. Tiny feathers protruded from the end that hung from the attachment. Ruth pulled on it gently until it fell off in her hand. Checking for damage, and confirming that her vacuum was still intact, she turned her attention to the wood. Turning it over in her hands, it didn't take her long to recognize what she was holding. Her curiosity heightened, she searched the room for the answer to the riddle. Leaning against the window, a makeshift bow stood on its point behind the heavy felt curtains.

"It seems I've found your partner," Ruth spoke to the piece of broken arrow she held in her hand.

She stood and stared out the window in the direction Jake's truck had driven with such haste and, for the first time since her initial visit to see Jake in the hospital, a nagging doubt surfaced.

Ruth returned the bow to its hidden location, placed the broken arrow back under the bed, removed the clean sheets, and recreated the dishevelled scene she had found twenty minutes earlier. She would leave things as they were, but she would watch and listen...and she would be very cautious.

45

To every thing there is a season,
and a time to every purpose under the heaven:
A time to be born, and a time to die.
ECCLESIASTES 3:1–2

March 19

Really, Lee? She's going to be fine?" Evelyn's eyes filled with tears. Ruth Norton set her cup down slowly in its saucer and watched her friend. Her unexpected afternoon visit had been well received, despite the fact that Lucy and Annie had arrived moments before her. She had been enjoying crumpets with Evelyn's grandmother and father—who had graciously bowed when Evelyn had introduced him as not only the creator of the crumpets, but of the recipe—when Levi's phone call interrupted their casual visit.

Ruth turned to Lucy. "Who's going to be fine and why is your mother crying?"

Before Lucy could reply, Evelyn hung up the phone and reached for her daughter's hand.

"She's fine!" Evelyn said. "She's going to be just fine! Lee just heard from Doctor Clarington. Apparently, it was touch and go for awhile, but there's no infection and she's eating."

Rachel whispered a sincere "Thank you, Lord," and her son-in-law excused himself on the pretence of getting something in his room. Neither Rachel's comment nor Joseph's hasty departure were missed on Ruth.

Ruth cleared her throat with feigned impatience. "Would someone please indulge this nosy friend with the answer to *who* is going to be fine and, if they're fine, why you are all in such an emotional state? Why are you crying, Evelyn?"

"Trickster had an accident on Tuesd—

"An accident? Mom, tell Ruth what really happened."

Summarizing the attack on Trickster, Evelyn concluded, "Doctor Clarington couldn't promise us anything. He didn't want to give us false hope, I suppose." Evelyn acknowledged her grandmother's smile. "He said she was one lucky dog and that, had the arrow been removed prematurely, or worse, had it struck an inch lower… well, we won't go there. Unfortunately, the arrow did do damage to some ligaments in her neck and shoulder that will affect how she walks, so she'll have a little bit of a limp. But that won't slow her down any." Evelyn blew her nose. "Sorry, Ruth, but that dog is so much a part of our lives now, I can't imagine what I'd… what *we'd* do if she'd…"

Evelyn left the sentence hanging and blew her nose a second time before smiling at her friend.

Ruth returned the smile, but said nothing. Her mind was elsewhere… in a bedroom in her house, in a room that housed a man who, Ruth now began to realize, was anything but what she thought he was. In her mind, she could still hear the rumbling of Jake's truck when he'd returned late the previous night. When she'd left for her visit with Evelyn, his truck had still stood where he'd parked it. Ruth remembered thinking, *I want to ask him to leave*, but knew she would be too afraid to do it.

"I know one little boy who'll be ecstatic," Lucy remarked as she sat Annie in the high chair, opened a jar of pureed apricots, and began spooning it quickly into Annie's open mouth. "When can she come home?"

"Levi said she needed to stay for another couple of nights, but we can pick her up on Saturday morning."

The back door opened and a little boy, covered in snow from hat to boot, stood at the opening with a long face. Closing the door slowly, he dropped his lunch pail on the floor and looked at Trickster's empty mat. His sad eyes told the story and his sigh touched everyone in the room.

"B.J., I heard from Doctor Morsman. Trickster's okay. We can bring her home on Saturday."

It took a few seconds before the news registered, but when it did, B.J.'s squeal of delight could have broken the sound barrier—or so it appeared to Ruth, who was unaccustomed to children, never having had any of her own. She watched as B.J. stripped himself of his snow-soaked jacket, mitts, and boots and all but bounced across the kitchen floor with a joy that couldn't help but bring a smile to her lips, despite what she knew about Jake, despite what she knew he had done.

Not long after B.J. settled himself at the kitchen table with hot chocolate and one of his Zaida's crumpets, Ruth stood to leave. Embracing Evelyn and Rachel, she thanked them for the afternoon. She took delight in having met such an interesting woman as Evelyn's grandmother. She shook Joseph's hand, extending her compliments once again on his baking, and smiled at Lucy, who sat by the window cuddling her sleeping daughter.

Bending down in front of B.J., Ruth cupped her hand under his chin and told him she was happy that his dog was fine. Then she took her leave. She had to go somewhere, see someone…and she didn't know where or who. She just knew she had to tell someone what she'd found under Jake's bed the day before.

46

He that hath a froward heart findeth no good:
and he that hath a perverse tongue falleth into mischief.
PROVERBS 17:20

Early evening, Pike Ridge, Alberta
March 19

S he's gotta be. They gave me her address at the post office," Jake lied as he signed his name on the guest register of Wind-in-the-Pines Motel.

"Like I said, there's no one here by the name of Abby Waters. Never has been."

The stocky motel owner's defences were aroused and Jake knew it. He backpedalled and took a deep breath before asking his next question. "What about Abigail Evans or Abby Evans?" Jake tried his wife's maiden name, smiling as he laid his money on the counter and accepted the key to his motel room.

"Did you say Abigail? We did have an Angelina Abigail. I remember the name. Seemed strange to me that someone would name their child two names that were so similar."

Jake waited, suppressing his impatience while the man speculated on his wife's name.

"She called herself Angie," the man offered, then fell silent. "Who are you, anyway?"

"Oh, I'm sorry." Jake turned on his charm further. "I'm her brother. We both came west at the same time, but took different paths."

His smile grew and his speech accelerated at his ingenuity. Like a cat ready to pounce on its unsuspecting prey, stealth-like Jake wove his words as he lured his victim into his grasp.

"She came north and I went to the coast. But there's no work there and I thought maybe I'd have more luck getting a job in a small town. We lost track of one another and the last I heard she was here in Pike Ridge. I can see why she'd like living here. Seems like a pretty friendly town."

"Her brother! Well, why didn't you say so? I'm Vincent Craig." He extended his hand toward Jake. "But you can call me Vinnie. Angie did say she was from the east. Quebec, right?"

Jake nodded and continued to smile, afraid if he spoke his voice would betray him. His heart pounded in his ears and perspiration dripped from his armpits, staining his t-shirt. He dared not speak. Inwardly he wanted to shout, to grab Vinnie by the throat and pound him to a pulp for providing his wife sanctuary, no matter how innocently it was done. He clenched his teeth through his smile and stared at the short, unkempt man whose large belly, tobacco-stained shirt, and grimy pants spoke of a lethargic lifestyle.

An innocent victim caught in the web of Jake's devious plot, Vincent Craig continued to expound on the virtues of the "sweet little lady" who had kept to herself and finally landed a job at the local diner. Jake fought the bile rising in his throat. *Sweet little lady*. His disdain went unnoticed.

"She stayed with me for just a month. Money ran out, I guess, but lucky for her she got the job at the diner. Hank Mason—he's the owner—introduced her to Edna Barnes, and Edna let Angie move in with her. Nice lady, Edna..."

Jake tuned Vinnie out as if he had an *off* button and Jake had pressed it. He really didn't care about Hank owning the diner or about how nice Edna was. Jake cared about nothing other than finding Abby, and nothing was going to prevent him from enjoying this moment, certainly not

Vinnie's small talk and town trivia. He'd imagined it for weeks, ever since his memory had returned. He knew he'd find her...he just never knew it would be this easy. All he needed was an address.

Right here in Pike Ridge, working at the diner, living with Edna Barnes. Life couldn't be kinder, Jake thought, mimicking the man he'd left in mid-sentence with the excuse of being anxious to see his sister.

He all but skipped to his truck, like a child whose premeditated thievery had gone unnoticed. Pushing over a pile of maps that had fallen from the sun visor, he climbed in and gave one last cynical look in the direction of the motel. Vinnie had been a fool.

Out of habit, Jake pounded the steering wheel as the reality of where Abby had been hiding registered.

She didn't go home after all, Jake thought as he headed for town. His anger mounted each time he opened and closed his fist. *Less than three hours down the road, living a quiet life, unnoticed. Well, that's gonna change, wife of mine! Your life's gonna change in a big way.*

He wasn't the least bit worried that someone might find out he wasn't her brother. By the time that happened, he'd be long gone and "Angie" would be history. The use of his wife's alias fanned his passion for revenge, and if revenge had a taste, Jake wallowed in its succulence.

Jake sat in the truck on the side road, away from the main flow of traffic, away from the curious eyes of any passersby. He watched people come and go from the diner, but he never saw Abby. His rage built and he wondered if he should pay a second visit to Vinnie, but the thought of tipping off his true identity stopped him. He needed a drink.

Reaching under the driver's seat, Jake pulled out a well-used flask. He tipped it to his mouth and swore. Not a drop. A second curse as he threw it on the seat beside him. *Coffee will have to do,* he thought, glaring at the empty flask, and then grinned maliciously as he pulled his truck onto the main road and parked in front of Hank's Diner.

"Think you can get away from me that easily, do ya? Well, guess again." Abandoning all caution, Jake spoke the sinister words aloud as he climbed over a mound of snow by the curb.

He pulled open the door of the diner and heard a bell ring over his head.

It's me, Abby, he thought cynically.

The diner sat empty except for two men. One sat fiddling with an empty mug, reading the local newspaper. He didn't look up when Jake entered the diner. The second, a fat man with a chef's hat and grease-stained apron, was slouched over on a stool behind the cash register; he raised his head in the direction of the door when the bell rang.

Jake took a booth at the opposite end of the room, away from the fat man's curious stare. He waited, anticipation growing like an inferno in his lower gut. Instead of Abby, a waitress wearing the nametag "Maggie" plopped a menu in front of him. With her chewing gum pushed into her cheek, she said, "Coffee?"

Jake ordered the daily special and a coffee, breathing a sigh of relief when the waitress left without giving him the expected third degree. Aware that people living in a small town knew one another, it wouldn't have taken much for someone to realize he was a stranger in town. Fortunately, Maggie seemed more intent on chewing her gum and taking his order than busying herself with nosy curiosity.

Jake's privacy was challenged, though, when he accidently made eye contact with the man behind the register. Sporting a worn and wet cigar, the man strolled over to Jake's table.

"New in town?" he asked.

Jake covered his annoyance by extending his head. "Yep, name's Johnny…Johnny Brewer."

Two can play the alias game, he chuckled inwardly.

The man hesitated before wiping his hand on his apron and accepting Jake's attempt at politeness. Without a doubt, he was the owner.

"What brings you to Pike Ridge?" the owner asked, causing Jake to pause in their mutual handshake.

"Looking for work. You must be the owner. Hank Mason?"

"In the flesh."

"Maybe you know someone around here who needs a handyman?"

"Nope."

"Really?" Jake pulled back. There was something about this burly man; he hovered over Jake like a lion hovers over its kill. "Seems the motel owner on the other side of town must have his wires crossed. Told me if anyone could help me, it would be you."

"He's wrong."

Hank turned and disappeared into a back room, leaving Jake fuming at his belligerence.

47

But evil men and seducers shall wax worse and worse,
deceiving, and being deceived.
2 Timothy 3:13

March 21

Levi and Ruth stood at the open door of Jake's bedroom. The room
was empty of Jake's belongings. The bed remained unmade and the
garbage pail lay tipped on the floor. A crumpled bath towel was
strewn over the sheets, but nothing else remained to indicate someone
had been living in the room.

"Not very tidy, was he?" Levi commented.

"He doesn't know the meaning of the word!"

Ruth walked into the room as one who was reclaiming something
that had been stolen from her. She walked straight to the window and
pushed back the drape.

"It's gone!" She turned around, anger flashing in her eyes. "Lee, there
was a bow leaning against *this* wall behind *this* curtain, and it's gone!"

She lifted the corner of the bedding that lay on the floor and bent
down on all fours.

"I'm telling you, Lee, there was a piece of broken arrow under this
bed. It got caught in my vacuum on Wednesday when I tried to surprise

Jake with a clean room." She accepted Levi's help in standing up. "He's gone, I tell you, and he's taken everything with him. Must have emptied it out while I was visiting Evelyn on Thursday. I guess it's been like this for two days. It's just taken me this long to figure things out. The door's been closed and I didn't want to open it until someone was with me."

Levi stood in the centre of the empty room and circled it slowly. "You're sure it was an arrow?"

"Absolutely! There's no doubt about what I saw. Stanley made a set of bow and arrows with the intent of bringing home some rabbits, until I told him I'd leave him if he so much as *thought* of killing one."

Levi smiled, trying to imagine how that conversation had gone.

"Ruth, was there anything else out of place on Wednesday...anything that seemed strange?"

Ruth walked around the room, arms folded across her midriff. She pursed her lips and shook her head. "Nothing. Only dirty clothes, a dried-up orange peel, and candy wrappers scattered on the floor. There was a map of Alberta on the floor and a dirty rag covered in black soot was shoved under this night table." Ruth tapped her finger on the top of the table, shaking her head in disgust. "Seemed he didn't know how to use a garbage pail. My goodness, when I think of what I did for that young man..."

"Did you say a map of Alberta?"

"Yes, I did. I didn't think it unusual, though it was folded strangely."

"*How* strangely?"

"It didn't follow the natural folds, but I did notice that Thystle Creek, Pike Ridge, and Edmonton were circled. Seems to me he was trying to learn the area."

"Pike Ridge?" Levi whispered the words, his anxiety building by the minute.

"Yes. Why?"

"Ruth, I need to get back to town. Can you call Evelyn and tell her I'm on my way to see her?" He paused. "Is the map around anywhere?"

Ruth stripped the sheets and covers on the bed, shaking them loose. "There's nothing here. Appears he's taken it with him. Is there a problem, Lee?"

Levi stared at Ruth before answering. "I'm afraid so, Ruth—very afraid. I need to get to Evelyn's."

Leaving the room, Levi turned to take one last look around, and saw the rag.

"Did you say the rag had soot on it?" he asked.

"I think so. It's hard to say, but it smells like kerosene or charcoal or... oh, my heavens! Lee, you don't think Jake..."

Levi scooped up the rag and turned it over in his hand. "Ruth, Jake's not coming back here, you can be sure of that. You can feel very safe."

"Safe?"

"Yes, safe," he repeated as he raced down the stairs to the main floor.

48

For my thoughts are not your thoughts,
neither are your ways my ways, saith the Lord.
Isaiah 55:8

W e need to be careful with her, B.J.," Evelyn cautioned while she scrambled eggs and milk in a large mixing bowl.

B.J. sat on the kitchen floor cuddling Trickster, who licked B.J.'s face in obvious adoration.

"She still has stitches that won't come out for another few weeks. Doctor Clarington said that exercise is good for her, but we aren't to let her run around too much, especially in the deep snow."

Evelyn poured the eggs into a heated frying pan, seasoned them with salt and pepper, and then covered the pan with a lid.

Slicing several tomatoes into thick rings, she continued, "She certainly loves the attention she's getting, but we can't spoil her."

For a second, she saw the irony of her words, since *spoiling* Trickster was exactly what she would be doing. But she shrugged the thought off as she took an onion from the fridge and sliced it.

Trickster squirmed in B.J.'s lap when Rob came into the kitchen, her tail wagging in anticipation of yet more attention.

"Good morning, everyone. Smells good in here, Evie." Rob kissed his mother on the cheek. "And welcome home, you little ball of fluff! Do you know how worried we all were about you?"

Rob bent down to greet Trickster, cracking the knee joint in his left leg. Trickster's ears went up and she cocked her head to one side.

"I'm just getting old, girl, that's all," Rob laughed, tousling the dog's head before standing to his full height.

"Old? You know the meaning of old?" Rachel, the family matriarch, stood in the middle of the kitchen doorway. "Let me tell you about old..."

Everyone laughed.

Evelyn paused in buttering the toast and greeted her grandmother with a hug.

Always beautiful. Always quick, Evelyn thought. "You smell nice," she whispered into her grandmother's ear before continuing the task of preparing breakfast.

She put the plate of toast on the table, poured fresh coffee for her father and son, and set a pot of hot tea under a tea cozy on the table for her grandmother. After the addition of a plate of fried tomatoes and onions, a bowl of hot scrambled eggs, and orange juice for everyone, she called B.J. He reluctantly released his hold on Trickster, watching her scrunch her blanket into a heap, then curl up in the middle of it. She was asleep before Rob finished saying the morning grace.

"She walks funny, Nana. Maybe I should carry her for a while, until she's better." With a longing side glance at Trickster, B.J. accepted his eggs and reached for a slice of toast.

"Did you ever hear the story of how a caterpillar becomes a beautiful Monarch butterfly?" Joseph asked his great-grandson.

Evelyn and Rob exchanged looks at the mention of butterflies.

"It was a butterfly that took B.J. down the embankment last summer," Rob explained, watching his son put a hearty layer of peanut butter on his toast. "He gave us quite a scare, but it all worked out as God would have it: *perfectly.*"

"My daddy told me that a caterpillar spins a silky house called a chry—chrysalis on a milk pod," B.J. continued after a mouthful of toast.

"He said that when it opens up, a beautiful butterfly flies out. I went looking for one and I fell." Another bite ended B.J.'s summary of the accident.

"Well, let me add to your daddy's story," Joseph said. He laid down his fork and knife, folded his elbows on the table, and leaned toward his great-grandson. "When a caterpillar spins its cocoon, or chrysalis, and goes to sleep for a while, it's growing wings. But then, I bet you've already figured that one out."

B.J. nodded as he drank his orange juice.

"When God decides that it's time for the butterfly to spread its wings and fly, it squirms around in its silky little house until it pushes its way out and flies to the nearest branch. When it gets there, it sits and rests until a breeze dries out the moisture on its wings. Then it flies away."

B.J. sat mesmerized by the story.

"Did you ever wonder what would happen if someone saw the butterfly squirming around inside its cocoon and decided to help it by opening the silky house?"

B.J. just shook his head.

"The butterfly would not be able to fly," Joseph said.

"It wouldn't?"

"No. It needs to stretch its wings inside its little house and strengthen them so that when God says, 'It's time to fly,' the wings will be strong."

"So," B.J. said, "if I carry Trickster around all the time, I wouldn't be helping her any, would I? Sort of like opening the butterfly's silky house."

Smiles circled Evelyn's breakfast table and her heart burst with pride.

"You're absolutely right," Joseph told him. "Trickster needs to walk, even though it might be hard for her. It will keep the muscles in her legs strong. When her wound heals, she'll be back to chasing her squeaky toy or stalking the squirrels or searching you out when you play hide-and-seek."

"I like that story about the butterfly, Zaida. Do you have any more stories like that?"

"Let's go hide in my favourite room after breakfast…"

"My Nana's library, right? That's my Nana's favourite room, too!"

With breakfast over, Evelyn and her grandmother watched the storyteller and his young follower head for the coveted "favourite room," Evelyn's father resting his arm comfortably across his great-grandson's shoulder.

"I can only imagine what he's thinking," Rachel commented as the two disappeared from the kitchen.

"Well, I know what I'm thinking," Rob remarked. "I've got a stack of tests to mark before Monday. Oh, the joys of being a teacher." He kissed his mother and thanked her for breakfast. "I'll come out from under in a few days!"

The two women laughed as they watched Rob leave the kitchen, mimicking the weight of the world on his shoulders.

Evelyn smiled at her grandmother. "My life has changed so much since last summer." She stood staring at the empty doorway. "I sometimes look at Rob and B.J. and fear that this is all just a dream, that I'll wake up and still be living a life void of them."

"Ah, but it is *not* a dream, my little Lyna. You *do* have a wonderful life, filled with love and a precious family." Rachel carried the dirty dishes to the counter as she spoke. "And finding your father again is part of that life. Your father's whole life has changed, too, since finding you. You have brought him *shtik naches*—great joy."

Evelyn smiled, not just at what her grandmother had said, but at how she had said it. Yiddish had been part of her home when she was a child. Hearing her grandmother use it on occasion brought back memories that had been buried too long.

"All he needs now is to see you embrace the Messiah."

Her grandmother's last sentence startled Evelyn. It seemed so direct, so bold, so defining… and yet so full of love. Evelyn knew it was meant as a challenge—a challenge as only her Bubi could give.

"I read a verse recently that may describe me," Evelyn began tentatively, resting with her hands in the soapy dishwater. "I believe it's in Isaiah. '*The Lord God hath opened mine ear, and I was not rebellious, neither turned away back.'* When I visited Christina not long after her diagnosis, she challenged me, much like you. She told me to read Isaiah 53. I did, and then I read the whole book! I didn't understand most of it, but I did get a few verses. That was one of them."

Trickster stirred in her sleep, interrupting the flow of conversation.

"I think she's still groggy from the medication." Evelyn watched Trickster repeat the circling, prodding and then flopping in her bed to resettle herself.

"Do you remember any other verses?" her grandmother asked as she dried the last dish.

"I'm afraid I'm not good at memorizing words I don't understand, but yes, I do remember another one: *'For my thoughts are not your thoughts, neither are your ways my ways, saith the Lord.'* I remember that verse because it made me think a lot about Lewis and his death. I've harboured so much anger at God for not protecting him that it's prevented me from seeing God's hand in my life. And if I throw into the mix my life before I met Lewis, well, I'd pretty much given up on Him...and assumed He'd given up on me."

Finishing the dishes, Evelyn removed her apron.

"You know, Bubi, when I found Trickster lying in the snow bleeding and almost dead, I actually prayed for the first time. But I never believed God would listen to me or that He would pay attention to a prayer about a wounded pet. I guess I was wrong on both counts."

Standing almost a foot shorter than Evelyn, Rachel grasped her granddaughter's hands. "You, my dear, sweet child, are on the threshold of a wonderful journey. Your father and I have prayed for this moment for a very long time. As have Lucy and Wil and your dear friends, Christina and Levi. Especially Levi. He loves you, you know. *Dos hartz hot mir gezogt*—my heart told me...and my heart never lies."

Evelyn blushed at her grandmother's frankness. "I'm not there yet. I know I've said that before, but I do feel closer. Much closer."

"Are we talking about loving Levi or about acknowledging the Messiah?"

The phone rang, startling both women, who laughed at themselves for jumping at the intrusive noise.

"Evelyn, it's Ruth," the voice on the other end of the line said. "Lee was just here. He asked me to call you to say he's on his way over. He said it's urgent, Evie…very urgent."

49

Though I walk in the midst of trouble, thou wilt revive me:
thou shalt stretch forth thine hand against the wrath of mine enemies,
and thy right hand shall save me.
PSALM 138:7

Unable to think clearly, Evelyn appreciated Levi's efforts to bring some calm to a grave situation with fresh coffee for everyone, and a pot of tea for Rachel and his mother. Having been given the news concerning Jake beforehand, Evelyn agreed with Levi that it was time to talk to the family about Abby.

Lucy and Wil arrived with Christina, whose dark circles and quiet demeanour told Evelyn that headaches were robbing the older woman of sleep. Evelyn embraced her longer than usual before releasing her. Annie reached her arms out to Evelyn and, under different circumstances, Evelyn would have taken her granddaughter and held her close, cuddling and cooing words of delight into her hair. But she wasn't able to trust her emotions and instead suggested that Lucy settle Annie in the playpen that had become a permanent fixture of the living room.

Working hard to conceal his own emotions, Levi sat down with the group of seven adults in the living room and described the Christmas Day trip—meeting Edna Barnes, discovering that the young pregnant patient had been Abby Waters, hearing about the man named Hank Mason, a dear friend of Edna's and a guardian angel for both Edna and Abby.

Finally, with halting speech, Levi described, in limited detail, the abusive life Abby had been living for over nine years. When he finished, an unsettled feeling permeated the room. Rob's stunned look paralleled Lucy's gasp, while Christina shook her head in horror and Evelyn sat in silence, rehashing in her head the words Abby had shared with her in her last letter.

"We've respected Abby's wishes to keep her whereabouts a secret," Levi continued. "She lives in constant fear that Jake will find her."

The group brooded in a lengthy silence, gradually absorbing what Evelyn had been unable to share.

"It's like sitting *shiva*," Joseph quietly whispered to Rachel.

Evelyn's father and grandmother had been included in the family gathering at Evelyn's request, and they had sat through Levi's monologue with growing concern. Never having met the young woman at the heart of the disturbing news, they quietly absorbed the gravity of the situation.

"I was in contact with Abby long before our Christmas trip," Evelyn spoke in a monotone, ignoring the reaction of her daughter and son. "She wrote me last September, or sometime in the early fall, telling me she was okay, but that she would never be able to return to Thystle Creek. She didn't mention the incident between Jake and her; she only asked me to keep our connection quiet, and I agreed. She never told me where she lived." She looked at Lucy and Rob, silently begging for their understanding.

"What kind of man is he?" Rob exploded, raking his fingers through his hair. "I thought I knew him! From our years of growing up together, I've known Jake's always been a little volatile. His temper often got him into trouble, but never like this. This...this time he's stepped over the line."

Rob shook his head and went quiet, his head bowed, his fingers clenched together between his knees.

"How could I have been so foolish, so careless, Lee?" Evelyn's question only added to the stress of the moment. Her voice oozed with anger at herself and an unsettling distaste for the young man she had befriended but since learned to fear. "The letter on the floor…I thought no one saw it. Rob, when you and Jake were talking, I saw it lying at Jake's feet. At first I was shocked—I didn't know I'd dropped it—and then I felt relieved that it had gone unnoticed, never considering the possibility that Jake had read some of it."

Evelyn twisted her hands in her lap as she spoke.

"Don't blame yourself, Evie," Levi said. "Jake's a manipulator. He knew exactly what he was doing by coming to your house. Dropping the letter wasn't…"

Again Levi's efforts to console Evelyn went unheeded. "Where is he now?" Evelyn asked. "How long has he been gone from Ruth's?"

"We don't know where he is, and Ruth's not sure when he actually left. His bedroom door was shut all the time—except for Wednesday when he left in a hurry, according to Ruth. She found the door open and, under the misguided act of *helping,* attempted to clean Jake's room. That's when she found the piece of arrow."

Evelyn stood up abruptly. "What an evil man!" she whispered, then regretted saying the words. Tears fell on her cheeks. "I'm sorry. I shouldn't have said that. I just can't imagine such malicious behaviour. And what about Josh? Did the rag really have charcoal on it?"

Levi sighed. "Before I came here, Ruth and I checked her basement. Seems she took advantage of a sale as the season ended last year. She bought three bags. There were still three there, but one was a different brand than the other two and she knew she'd bought three the same."

"We need to contact the police," Wil interjected. "This guy sounds like a loose cannon."

"I think Wil's right, Lee," Rob agreed.

Silence again fell over the room, like a black shadow moving across the floor, devouring everything in its path. Lucy shivered and pressed her arms close to her chest. Rachel leaned into her son-in-law's shoulder and closed her eyes. Evelyn paced and Christina sat quietly, watching her best friend.

Levi stared straight ahead before breaking the silence. "It's quite possible that Jake's headed for Pike Ridge."

Evelyn gasped.

"I'll call Edna and suggest she ask Hank to stay with her and Abby until we know where Jake is," Levi said. "We don't know how long he's been gone, but he's definitely moved out of Ruth's house."

"Lee, we need to get to Pike Ridge." Evelyn stood up and headed toward the hall closet.

"No, Evie. *We* don't need to go to Pike Ridge. Rob, Wil, and I will go. You need to remain here. There's nothing you can do to—"

"Lee, I need to be with Abby. She's counting on me." Evelyn burst into tears. "I can't desert her, Lee, we—we have a friendship, a…an understanding." She took the tissue offered by her daughter. "Lee, she's almost ready to have her baby and we don't want her to lose it…"

Evelyn's words held more meaning than she had voiced and everyone in the room knew exactly what she was saying…or not saying.

Levi stopped Evelyn from pacing and held her in his arms, wiping her tears with his thumbs. "Evie, nothing is going to happen to Abby or the baby. Rob, Wil, and I will drive to Pike Ridge today and bring her home. As soon as we get to Edna's, we'll call the police and tell them everything we know. They'll take it from there." He held Evelyn at a distance and spoke with the confidence the moment demanded. "We'll let the police worry about Jake."

Heading west, with the winter sun threatening to disappear behind the distant mountains, Levi kept his foot steady on the gas pedal. His two passengers never said a word; they didn't need to. Levi knew he was well over the speed limit, but he had no choice.

Edna hadn't answered the phone.

50

The God of my rock; in him will I trust:
he is my shield, and the horn of my salvation,
my high tower, and my refuge,
my saviour; thou savest me from violence.
2 SAMUEL 22:3

The doorbell awoke Abby from a sound sleep. She had been content with reading her favourite book and drinking the hot chocolate Edna had insisted on making before she left for an overnight visit with her sister three miles east of Pike Ridge. Not long after, Abby had fallen into a restful sleep, oblivious to the ringing of the telephone.

It must be Hank, she thought, stretching her legs. She shifted the afghan to one side, patted her tummy, and whispered to her unborn child, "Let's go see Uncle Hank."

Making her way down the hallway, Abby recalled the last thing Edna had said before leaving: "I'll be home by supper tomorrow, but if you need *anything*, just give Hank a call. He knows I'll be away, so he'll be checking in on you when he closes up for the night." Abby had nodded in appreciation, assuring Edna that she would be fine.

She thought of Hank and smiled at the gentleness of the man whose very presence in a room raised eyebrows and brought apprehensive stares.

He's nothing but a puppy dog in a guard dog's body. She almost laughed out loud at the suitable comparison.

The first thing Abby noticed as she reached the top of the staircase was the dimly lit entryway on the main floor. The sun had almost set behind the mountains west of Pike Ridge and the rainbow of colours filtering through the stained glass transom window over the front door slowly evaporated. Scrunching her nose in disappointment, Abby stopped at the top of the stairs, hoping to catch the last shimmers of light. Experience had taught her that, with the winter sun gone for another day, dusk would settle quickly over the white landscape.

I can't believe I slept half the afternoon away, she thought, frustrated with herself. She flicked on the light switch, filling the staircase and lower hall with light.

The second thing Abby noticed was the silhouette of a man, barely visible through the frosted bevelled glass door. *Hank, you're an angel in disguise,* she smiled, acknowledging her burly friend's unnatural doting. Arriving at the foot of the staircase, she noticed the time on the grandfather clock in the front hall—4:20. That was strange. The diner didn't close for another four hours.

Abby opened the front door, and her world came to a crashing halt.

"J—Jake!"

"Hello, Abby—or should I say *Angie?* How nice of *Vinnie* to help me find you."

Abby froze.

"I noticed sweet Edna has gone off with a suitcase in tow—just the kind of convenient information one learns when one watches." Jake squinted his eyes over an artificial smile, obviously pleased with himself. He leaned his left hand on the doorframe, pressing his right foot against the bottom of the door. "Would that mean we have this lovely house to ourselves?" he asked, his smile gone.

Jakes didn't wait for an answer. He stepped inside, pushing the door open with such force that it banged the inside wall, rattling the bevelled glass.

Unprepared for the sudden thrust against the door, Abby stumbled backward, knocking the hall table that housed Edna's hurricane lamp, sending it crashing to the floor.

"Well, well, looky here. I can see you've been busy." Jake poked Abby's belly several times, first with one finger and then with his full hand, pushing her into the hallway.

Abby's voice shook with fear. "You're wrong, Jake. It—it's your baby." Never had she imagined Jake would think such thoughts about her.

Jake ignored her. He moved like a snake, slithering slowly, insidiously, closer and closer, ready to inject its deadly venom. She could see his pulse banging in his neck. *Thump. Thump. Thump.* It matched her own. *Thump. Thump. Thump.* Hers was fed by growing fear, Jake's by festering rage. She wanted to believe he wouldn't harm her, not in her condition. She wanted to believe that with her whole being, but deep inside, she knew better.

"There's been no one else…honest! The baby's yours, Jake! It happened—"

Jake swung the back of his hand hard against Abby's face, knocking her backward into the wall.

"Don't insult me, you little tramp! You think I'm *that* stupid?"

Jake's rage grew like an ocean wave reaching tsunami proportions, and he struck a second blow.

Twisting her body to protect the baby, Abby fell forward, her hands and knees landing on the broken lamp at her feet. Her hands, now pitted with glass shards, took the brunt of the fall. She writhed in pain, struggling to gain her balance, but her feet crunched over the glass, piercing her heels. Her socks offered no protection.

Jake pounced again. Punching, two, three, four times until his foot landed in Abby's midriff, knocking her fully to the ground. Writhing in agony, she rolled into a fetal position and held her stomach, oblivious to the glass. She willed the pain to cease, praying the kick did not harm her child—praying that God would strike her husband dead.

"Please…the baby…please don't hurt the baby." Abby gasped, fearing the worst for her child. "I can't stand up, Jake…please, I'm hurt."

"Hurt, are we?" Jake asked, heedless of Abby's condition and the blood oozing from her hands and feet. "Let me tell you about pain."

Jake grabbed Abby's hair and pulled her to her feet.

Abby screamed, feeling faint as chunks of glass gouged the bottom of her feet. Like a small animal fighting to escape the clutches of a bird of prey, she struggled to free herself from Jake's grasp only to have Jake yank her hair even harder.

"You're not going anywhere. Not this time."

Jake half-dragged, half-pushed Abby down the hall as if he knew exactly where it led. Finding the kitchen, he forced Abby to a chair and began pulling apart the kitchen drawers, letting the contents crash to the floor.

Through blurred vision and escalating fear, Abby watched, knowing her husband all too well. He was on a mission and it wouldn't be long before she found out exactly what that mission was. Her baby squirmed inside her womb as though sensing its mother's distress and fearing for its own life.

Abby's maternal instincts surfaced in defense of her child.

She glanced toward the kitchen doorway and tried to calculate how she could get to the front door without Jake getting there first. Even if her feet let her stand—which they wouldn't—even if she could make it out of the kitchen—which in her heart she knew she couldn't—she had no shoes, no coat, and no way of avoiding the glass scattered across the front hallway. Blood soaked her socks and she knew she had pieces of glass embedded deep in the soles of her feet. She couldn't run. There was no escape.

Like a caged animal, loose but trapped, she watched her husband until he suddenly stopped, his frenzied search over. He'd found what he'd been looking for, and Abby held her breath.

When he turned around, Jake held a ball of twine. If she had considered attempting an escape, dared to make a move, every possibility was now eradicated. Never before had Abby seen such an evil look. Never in all the years Jake had abused her had she seen such devilish pleasure saturating her husband's face.

51

The Lord is my strength and song, and he is become my salvation:
he is my God, and I will prepare him an habitation;
my father's God, and I will exalt him.

EXODUS 15:2

W e'll stop at the diner and connect with Hank Mason before going to Edna's," Levi informed Wil and Rob as they passed the Pike Ridge town sign. "It would be good to have someone like him in case we run into Jake, though it's highly unlikely we will. I'm not going to pretend to be anything I'm not, and I don't want you two to get hurt."

"Jake's not going to hurt me, Lee," Rob said. "We've known each other for too many years. Maybe all he needs is to be reminded of—"

"Rob, you admitted yourself how shocked you were when the evidence showed him to be capable of causing the near-death of Josh Graham, not to mention the attack on Trickster," Levi interjected. "Let's just be prepared."

The three men fell silent, and thirty minutes later Levi pulled to a stop in front of Hank Mason's diner. He flicked off the car lights and glanced in the front window, where a half-dozen patrons were still enjoying their evening meals.

It's late, Levi thought, realizing the drive to Pike Ridge had taken longer than anticipated. For a brief moment, he regretted promising Evelyn that he would bring Abby home that same day.

Hank Mason looked up as three strangers walked into his diner. Not one to assume all men were friendly, Hank watched as they approached Maggie, then boldly headed in his direction. He frowned, groaning his displeasure. What he didn't need was a trio of strangers taking up his time.

Come in, sit down, and eat, he thought. *And don't bother me.*

He glanced impatiently at his watch and closed his eyes, fighting fatigue. It would be another two hours before he could flip the closed sign, and he was behind schedule. The Sunday special had yet to be prepared, the lunch dishes still sat stacked by the sink awaiting his attention, and Maggie had informed him as soon as she'd arrived for work that she needed to leave an hour early. Something about a surprise party for one of her kids, he remembered, annoyed at himself for resenting her early departure. After all, she had taken on more hours in Abby's absence, and hadn't he left her alone for half an hour to check on Abby? But he was the boss, wasn't he? He didn't need permission to drive out to Edna's, even if it was just before the busy supper hour.

Hank heaved a sigh as he considered the night ahead. His absence had set him back and, working through the supper hour, he'd battled guilt at feeling relieved when Abby hadn't been able to open the door.

"I'm just out of the tub, Hank, after a long, lazy bath. Don't want to catch a chill," she'd said, assuring him behind the unopened door that he could rest with a clear conscience.

As the men stopped in front of him, Hank pushed aside his thoughts of Abby and braced himself for the inevitable questions. How far is such-and-such? Is there a place for skiing nearby? He hated that question.

He was not prepared, however, for the questions his latest visitors posed. Their conversation lasted less than five minutes before Hank summoned Maggie and told her that an emergency had come up and that he had to close the diner immediately. He asked her to lock the front door behind him, finish with the current customers, and shut down the kitchen. He assured her that he would return later to get things ready for Sunday, trying to alleviate the concern spreading across her face.

Wil climbed into the back seat of the car with Rob, leaving Hank to join Levi up front. That suited Levi just fine. Something Hank had said in the diner had bothered him and he wanted clarity. He backed the car onto the main street and headed west.

"So you think this Jake guy could be coming here?" Hank asked in a tone that demanded an immediate answer.

Levi threw a quick look in Hank's direction, taken aback by the man's abruptness, then glanced in the rear-view mirror.

"It's hard to say," Levi began. "All the evidence points to Jake as the arsonist who started a fire that almost killed someone. We also think he needlessly brutalized a dog. But we only have suspicions, nothing concrete. We're just being cautious and think it best for Abby to come back to Thystle Creek where we can keep an eye on her."

"What about the police?" Hank asked. "Rumour has it they think she's somehow responsible for putting that no-good husband of hers in the hospital."

Hank's distaste for Jake didn't surprise Levi. No doubt Abby had shared her story with him, too.

Wil leaned forward, resting his elbows on the back of Hank's seat. "Hank, Jake's got a reputation in Thystle Creek ... and not a particularly good one at that—"

"I'd like to get my hands on him for five minutes," Hank interrupted, his right fist pounding into his left palm.

Wil pulled his body back from the seat and turned a startled look at Rob. "I don't think it would take much for the police to change their whole approach to Abby's involvement in Jake's injury. Once we share our suspicions, they'll likely want to bring him in for questioning."

On the outskirts of town, with Edna's house looming ahead, Levi asked Hank to explain what Abby had said when he'd checked on her.

Rob and Wil exchanged glances while Hank reiterated what he'd told the three back at the diner. "I rang the bell and waited. Longer than normal. I just figured Abby was upstairs and needed time to come to the door. After a few minutes, I rang the bell again and heard some rustling before Abby spoke through the closed door."

"Did you think that strange?" Rob asked.

"A little at first, until she explained the reason. Then I never gave it another thought."

"And her exact words were?" Levi pressed Hank.

"She said, 'Sorry, Hank, I can't open the door. I just had a long, lazy bath and don't want to get a chill.' Those were her exact words, I think. I told her I understood and that she should call me if she needed anything. I turned and went down the stairs, climbed into my truck, and drove back to the diner."

Hank's words settled over the three men as the darkness grew around them. Night had come as each man digested Hank's story.

"Makes sense to me," Wil finally said. "It's dark and cold and what woman would want to stand by an open door after having a long bath? Especially if she's pregnant."

A twitch of a smile crossed Levi's face at Wil's intuitiveness, and then it was gone. "That's the whole point, Wil. What pregnant woman—particularly two weeks from her due date—would take a long, lazy bath alone in the house and away from the phone? What if the long, hot bath relaxed her so much that she fell asleep? What if she fell getting in or out of the tub? A woman that pregnant has a severely limited sense of balance. In fact, I recommend my mothers-to-be not to bathe in their last month at all. I'm quite sure Ken Crombie would have made the same suggestion." He turned back to Hank. "Did you notice anything unusual about the house? The windows, the lights? Were any lights off that Edna would normally have on?"

Hank sat in deep thought for a long time before turning to face Edna's house. Levi pulled up to the curb and left the car idling.

"You see there?" Hank tapped on the window, pointing with a thick, calloused finger. "By the front door, the long windows on either side? Edna always has a light on that shines through. The light comes right outside onto the veranda."

"Would Abby know about that? I mean, about turning on the light?" Wil asked, staring up at the darkened house.

"She wouldn't need to *know*," Hank replied, abruptly.

"Because?"

"Because the light comes from a lamp that's on all the time," Hank responded with obvious impatience, acting as though Wil was some kind of a stupid schoolboy, unable to understand the obvious.

Wil opened his mouth to defend himself, but Hank cut him off.

"Edna loves that lamp. I think it's ugly, but it's her lamp! It's got glass globes in the bottom and the top's covered with hand-painted flowers." Hank looped his hands in a figure eight, trying to demonstrate its shape, then gave up. "Been sitting on that table just inside the front door since Edna was a little girl. It's never off, day or night, so Abby wouldn't need to turn it on. It would already be on." He raised his voice slightly to make his point. "But it wasn't on today. Come to think of it, the only light I could see was from down the hall, from the kitchen."

"Something just doesn't feel right," Levi concluded, turning to face the others. "The house is too dark, and even if Abby has retired for the night, I'm quite sure she'd leave on some kind of light downstairs, just in case she had to get up. But there's nothing, not even on the second floor. It's as though—"

"Look!"

The others followed Rob's pointed finger, watching a light shift across the first floor windows like an apparition moving from room to room. The four men watched, saying nothing. For several minutes the light seemed to float in midair, its high point flickering to the ceiling.

Then it suddenly went out.

"It's a flashlight," Levi whispered, following Hank's example. "Hank, how well do you know the inside of Edna's house?"

"Been comin' and goin' for over fifty years … since we were just kids."

"Where's the back door?" Levi asked

"Which one?"

Levi stared. "Which one? How many are there?"

"Three all together. The main one's off the kitchen at the back of the house. You get to it from that side." Hank pointed to the left of the house. "Edna had me build a walk from the front of the house to the back. It follows the flowerbed. There's another one off the sunroom on the east side, but it's closed up for winter. Too cold in there, even though the winter sun warms it some. The other door is never used. It leads to the basement from the outside. Edna doesn't like going into the cellar at the best of times and usually calls me when she needs something from down there...or if a coon or squirrel manages to get in. There's no way she'd ever go into the house that way."

"What are you thinking?" Rob asked, joining Wil as the two leaned their elbows on the back of the front seat.

"I'm not all that sure. Just trying to put some logic into something that doesn't sit right with me," Levi said, squinting his eyes as darkness filled the car. "We need to do something. Now."

He waited for a response while all four stared at the house.

"I have a key," Hank said quietly.

52

The eyes of the Lord are in every place,
beholding the evil and the good.
PROVERBS 15:3

Very well done, Abby, very well done."

Jake smirked as he shoved Abby away from the front door and pushed her back into the kitchen. She stumbled under Jake's forceful push and would have fallen on her stomach had she not braced herself against the desk in the hallway. The blood had dried on her hands and arms, and although the bleeding had stopped from the wounds in her feet, glass remained embedded in her heels. She found walking unbearable, but would not reveal the pain to Jake, knowing that was exactly what he wanted. Nor would she tell him about the cramps that had crept into her lower back over the past half-hour.

When the doorbell had rung, Jake untied her from the kitchen chair where he had forced her to sit with arms tied behind her back and feet crossed. The visitor had startled them both and Jake had demanded to know who it was. When Abby told him about a friend coming by to check in on her, he'd laughed.

"You get rid of your friend, or I will," he'd threatened.

And Abby had. But not without praying that Hank would figure out her coded plea for help. *Remember, Abby,* she'd recalled Doctor Crombie saying. *No baths in your last month. It's too dangerous. No matter if Edna's in the house or not, no bathing.* As Abby had stumbled toward the front door, doing all she could not to step on broken glass, she rehearsed over and over in her head exactly what she would say. *A long, lazy bath. A long, lazy bath. A long, lazy bath.* She had tried to sound calm but hoped Hank would understand, or at least repeat it to someone who would.

Jake leaned against the kitchen counter, cleaning his fingernails with a knife he'd taken from Edna's knife block.

"You know, Abby, I've been thinking. We could start all over again. Fresh start, no Evelyns or Ednas or Emporiums to interfere with our lives." He glanced up from his manicure and narrowed his eyes. "Just you and me, but no baby to make three." He walked slowly toward Abby and sneered. "We'll make our own kid ... and have fun doin' it."

Jake ran the tip of the knife along Abby's arm, now retied behind her back. This time, Jake anchored the knots to the chair so she couldn't squirm to avoid his unwanted advances.

"Jake, please, you've got to listen to me. This is your baby. Yours and mine. I know you think otherwise, but you're wrong." Abby looked down at her swollen belly. "It's your baby, Jake. Yours!"

Jake pressed the tip of the blade into Abby's forearm and dragged it down to her elbow. He pressed it just enough to draw a fine line of blood, watching as Abby winced.

He leaned in close to her face. "If I hear you say that one more time, you'll have a lot more than a scratch."

Jake followed Abby's eyes to her stomach and pointed the blade against her belly. "We need to dispose of this problem before we can ever start again." He eyed her menacingly and she blanched, knowing he would stop at nothing in his bid for control.

"Jake ... please ... don't. I promise, I'll never say it again."

"Say what again?"

"That the baby is yours." As soon as the words were out, Abby knew she'd fallen into Jake's trap.

Jake ripped her blouse open to reveal her bare, swollen belly.

"Jake! No!" Abby screamed as he slid the blade softly down the centre of her stomach.

"You said it again, Abby dearest, and now you'll see what happens when you disobey your husband, when you run off after trying to kill him."

"I didn't try to kill you, Jake! I just tried to stop you from hurting me. You fell backwards…it wasn't my fault. I didn't—"

Jake's hand slapped hard across Abby's face. "Don't you lie to me. You plotted and planned—you and your friends. You all thought you'd get rid of me, didn't you?"

Jake hit her again in the stomach and she doubled up in agony.

"Please, Jake, don't…"

"Please, Jake, don't." Jake's imitation of Abby plea dripped with sarcasm. He leaned over her with the fiendish delight of a mad dog hovering over its victim, ready to tear flesh. "Do you know what happened to Josh?" he whispered, his breath hot on Abby's cheek as he stroked it with the edge of the knife. "I set fire to the Emporium and your friend almost died. Dear sweet Ruthie said, 'Good thing Doc Bailey came along when he did or Josh wouldn't have made it.' I didn't know he was inside until I saw his car, and when I did, I went back and cut the telephone lines." His eyes widened and he laughed with excitement, then abruptly stopped. His eyes narrowed and his voice changed. "Plotting against me like he did, he should have died…showing the world my wife is better than me. Well, he paid plenty."

Abby released her breath when Jake picked up a flashlight and left her to wander through the house. Surely she hadn't heard right. Surely he hadn't set fire to the Emporium? She tried to distract herself from Jake's insane behaviour by counting the minutes between what she now knew were contractions.

She jumped when Jake returned, holding the gold braided cord that had held back the curtains in the drawing room. She stared wide-eyed as Jake swung it around at his hip.

"And poor Trickster. Poor, poor Trickster." Jake pulled up a chair and straddled it, facing Abby. "She's no more. Gone. Poof!" He flicked his fingers in the air, taking the cord with them. "Into the wind...with the pull of a bow and arrow. Dropped like a dead weight."

Had she heard right? Josh? Now Trickster? Abby could hear distant screams, but it took a moment for her to realize that they were her own. She shrank from the horror of what Jake had done and the things to which he had openly confessed, heedless of the pool of water that had settled on the floor beneath her chair.

Jake jumped back, laughing. "Whoa! Looks like I won't need to help nature along."

He spun, a frenzied laugh puckering his face. His laughter echoed throughout the darkened house; his perverse levity spun him in circles, sending him whirling, dancing in front of Abby until he met the fist of a wild man.

It took but one blow to send Jake rocketing to the floor. Hank Mason stood spread-eagled over Jake, an elephantine monster ready to heave him against the kitchen wall.

"Go ahead, you worthless piece of trash. Move a muscle, any muscle. And if you do, I'll have the greatest pleasure in my life throttling you."

Jake never blinked.

53

For his anger endureth but a moment; in his favour is life:
weeping may endure for a night, but joy cometh in the morning.
PSALM 30:5

March 20

Abby shielded her eyes from the morning sun as memories of Jake's madness filled her head. As much as she tried, she couldn't forget the knife or his threats to harm the baby. Minutes had merged into hours as his abuse continued until, by the merciful hand of God, she'd seen him fly through the air as though a bolt of lightning struck him. She remembered seeing Hank hovering over him and Wil's concerned look as he'd cradled the phone to his ear all the while yelling at Hank, commanding him not to hit Jake again.

She could still feel Rob's gentle arms wrapping around her like a blanket warmed from the heat of the sun. He'd carried her into her bedroom. She remembered the sirens, the police, Edna telling everyone what to do. Part of her had wondered where Edna had come from, but her confused mental state prevented logical reasoning. And then there had been the pain, the excruciating pain, and Doctor Morsman's voice commanding her to push. Then a baby cried and the pain was gone.

"She's beautiful," Edna whispered as she laid the infant in Abby's arms.

Both women stared at the newborn baby and said nothing for several seconds.

Abby's eyes glazed over. "I—I broke your lamp," she faltered, then burst into tears. "I couldn't help it. He pushed me, or I stumbled. I don't remember. But it's broken, all over the floor."

Abby's body heaved with sobs as she clutched her baby to her chest.

"Don't you worry none about that old lamp," Edna said, smoothing hair from Abby's face. "I never did like it, just pretended to. Always wanted to get rid of it. Now I don't have to. Rob cleaned it up and put it in the trash."

Abby reached out her free arm to hug Edna, and only when Edna finally released her did Abby feel better. "I'm so sorry. I can't seem to stop crying." Abby tried to smile through the fresh tears pooling in her eyes. "When did you get home?"

"I came as soon as Hank called and said, 'Get home now! Abby's having her baby.' I think I broke every traffic law in the book. I even prayed that you'd be okay until I got here. How about that? This old woman praying! And, you know, I think He heard me."

Edna leaned over the baby as it squirmed in Abby's arms. "My, she's some beauty! Takes right after her mommy. Can't say I've ever been so moved by the birthing of a young'un."

"Doctor Morsman said he was grateful for your help." Abby welcomed Edna's attempt to fluff her pillow, and willingly accepted her help as Abby shifted her baby to her breast.

"She's a natural!" Edna smiled as the baby did what babies do best. "You both are! I've been around plenty when they were born...enough to know a natural when I see one. I'm the town's midwife, without a degree, you know!"

Edna bowed slightly at her own accolades.

"And a very good one at that," Levi concurred as he joined the two women. "How's she doing, Abby?"

"Fine, I think. I'm kind of new at this." She smiled through a wince of pain. "My hands are pretty useless, though. I hope these bandages won't be on for long. It's hard to do much with my hands."

All three looked at the bandages on Abby's arms and feet and the room fell quiet. Her feet were wrapped in bandages up past her knees. The slivers of glass in her hands and knees had proven to be especially difficult to remove—more so than the pieces in her heels. It had required the aid of Edna's magnifying glass for Levi to find them all.

"Unfortunately, your hands will be sore for a while. As will your feet," Levi said, putting his arm around Edna's shoulder. "But I understand you're not going anywhere anytime soon, according to this wonderful friend you have here. Evie will be happy to hear that you are being cared for with so much love."

"Oh, hush," Edna said. "How could you not love this sweet thing… and this wee baby is a bonus. She sure came into this world with three men at her beck and call." Edna jerked her head in the direction of the hallway, snickering at her own comment.

As Levi left the room, laughing at Edna's foreseeable tattling, Edna leaned closer and whispered, "Abby, those two young men walked up and down that hallway as though the child's safe arrival depended on how long and how fast they could pace. And poor Hank, he just sat holding his hands over his ears until this little one made herself known. When she cried, he raised his head and tears just poured down his cheeks. Then all three of them laughed, clapping one another on the shoulders and hugging one another. You should have seen them! A bigger display of love I've never seen! "

Abby listened to the detailed report, laughing at how Rob, Wil, and Hank would react once they knew how detailed she'd been. "I guess I owe them a lot."

"You were in a bad way, child. Had all three not been here, I don't know what Hank would have done to Jake. Rob and Wil had to hold him back, or we might've been visiting Hank in prison for a long time."

"Where's Jake now?" Abby asked quietly.

"Where he should be. In jail. And you can be sure they're gonna throw the book at him! Arson, attempted murder on two counts—your friend, Josh, and this wee child—and kidnapping." Edna shook her head in disgust. "Hank stood guard over him while Wil called the police. They were here in minutes and took him away. Good thing for him, too. Left in a room alone with Hank for much longer, he might have been carried out in a bag."

"Hey…up to visitors yet?" Rob asked sheepishly, interrupting Edna's story. He poked his head into the bedroom. Seconds later, two more eager faces joined him as the threesome jostled for space in the doorway.

"Are you men comin' or goin'?" Levi laughed, pushing his way into the room.

Abby smiled as she caressed her daughter, now sleeping contentedly in her arms. "Please. Come see what I've got."

Rob, Wil, and Hank slipped shyly into the room and leaned over the sleeping infant like misfit intruders.

Levi held Abby's wrist. "Strong pulse. A good sign, considering what you've been through." He cringed. "Sorry, Abby, once a doctor, always a doctor." He smiled sympathetically as he laid her arm on her tummy and turned his attention to the baby.

"Has this wee bit of a thing got a name yet?" Edna asked, watching Levi hold a stethoscope to the sleeping baby's chest.

Abby looked into the face of her daughter and smiled before responding. "*Weeping may endure for a night, but joy cometh in the morning'* …Joy. Her name is Joy."

After promising to bring Evelyn to visit once spring made travelling easier, Levi walked to his car. He was tired. The day before had been long, but the night had been longer. He welcomed Wil's offer to drive home, gladly handing over the keys. As he opened the rear door, he watched Rob glance repeatedly over his shoulder after a long goodbye to Abby.

He'd make a good father for Joy, Levi thought, smiling as he considered the implications.

Levi climbed into the back seat, planning to sleep most, if not all, of the way home. Church would be over when they arrived in Thystle Creek and he wanted to be alert; Evelyn would have a million questions.

He fell asleep smiling.

54

For I know the thoughts that I think toward you, saith the LORD,
thoughts of peace and not of evil, to give you an expected end.
JEREMIAH 29:11

E velyn sat between her grandmother and father in the same pew she had been sitting in since she'd started attending church the previous summer. Each time she turned her head in either direction, she welcomed a smile, a nudge or even a hug around her shoulder. She stared ahead and smiled.

They love me!

She now knew without a doubt that nothing could ever have stopped them from loving her. Her heart filled with joy and an overwhelming desire to announce to the world that she had been forgiven.

She tried to stay focused on what Pastor Cribbs was saying, but her mind kept drifting. Her thoughts plummeted to the deep places of her heart and she dared to close her eyes. As clearly as if he were sitting beside her, she could hear Lewis whisper in her ear: *"This is what it's all about, Evie girl. Forgiveness. Trust. Faith. It's all wrapped up in a love like no other. This is God's love you're feeling. God's forgiveness. Not just Bubi's or your father's. It's God's, and He's just waiting for you to accept it."*

Is this what I've missed out on, Louie? she thought, opening her eyes at the revelation. *This kind of love?*

And she could almost hear his answer: *"You betcha your sweet life, Evie girl."*

Oh, how she missed him! She'd loved him but had never really been able to express it, not the way she should have. She'd let the black clouds of anger and fear hover over their lives. Yet Lewis had loved her despite all of it. Now she understood how.

God gave you the love, Louie. If only I had listened.

"The greatest and most demanding act of love is forgiveness, and only God knows how to truly forgive," a voice said.

Evelyn snapped to attention as Pastor Cribbs's words filled the auditorium. She felt as though he was speaking directly to her. Like he had been reading her mind, their eyes met.

"*'Blessed is he whose transgressions are forgiven, whose sins are covered. Blessed is the man—or woman—whose sin the Lord doesn't count against him—or her—and in whose spirit is no deceit.'* These are words directly from Psalm 32:1–2, with some of my own thrown in for good measure."

Pastor Cribbs averted his eyes and turned to the congregation. Holding his Bible close to his chest, he spoke softly. "It's possible for the Lord to look at us without seeing our sins because, when He forgave us, He removed our sins as far as the east is from the west. Look that up in Psalm 103. Now, that's love, folks."

Evelyn immediately wrote the two references on her bulletin, then turned her full attention to the pastor's words.

"Forgiveness is something we all want, and we all need, at some point in our lives. It's a valuable gift that cannot be easily secured or easily granted. Yet, forgiveness is as essential to life as the air we breathe; it frees us from our past, from those things that haunt us. It gives us hope and promise for the future. It is for *forgiveness* that Jesus Christ—the Messiah for the Jews and the Saviour for the Gentiles—came to earth to suffer and die for all mankind. Check it out in John 3:16–17. But it doesn't end there, folks."

Pastor Cribbs paused and Evelyn held her breath. He stretched himself to his full height, then stood on his tiptoes and extended his arms above his head. "He rose from the dead!" Excitement filled his voice for a brief moment before he leaned his elbows across the podium and whispered, "But if we reject Jesus, we reject His gift of forgiveness and the opportunity to step out of the darkness into His light."

Evelyn felt her father's hand on hers. She looked down at it and placed her other hand over his. She didn't raise her head; she just felt his love. She remembered his words and their conversation from the night before when they had discussed Levi's call.

"God is in all of this, Evlyna, as much as you may find it hard to accept," he'd said. "He was right there in the middle of everything young Abby was going through. It may be hard to understand and harder still to imagine, but every time Jake struck her, he struck Christ and Christ felt the pain for two... for Abby *and* for Jake."

"Why didn't God stop him?"

"Because God lets us make our own decisions. Sometimes they're good ones, sometimes they're so bad that God weeps tears that would fill an ocean. He was crying right along with Abby."

"Did God cry when Lewis died, when our babies died, when Bobby died? Did He cry then?"

"Yes, He did. And it broke His heart. But we have to trust Him with our lives. We must never forget that even though we don't know the fullness of God's plan, He has one for each of us, a plan that will give us hope and a future. He says so in Jeremiah."

Pastor Cribbs's closing remarks pulled Evelyn from her memory. "God gives us a hope, a promise for the future. Read Jeremiah 29:11."

She smiled at how God had been working in her life over the past twenty-four hours, how He'd directed her father to share the same verse that He'd directed Pastor Cribbs to share with his congregation.

What was it that Louie used to say when he described God? She thought for a moment and then whispered the word: "Awesome."

Both her grandmother and father smiled.

Wil pulled the car into the driveway and honked the horn. Levi sat up, amazed that he'd slept the whole way home. Pulling on his boots, he opened the door and waved. A gust of wind warned of an imminent storm and he thanked God for their timely arrival before it hit.

Lucy held Annie at the front window, standing beside her grandfather while Christina and Rachel hovered behind them. B.J. held Trickster and waved the dog's paw in a greeting that brought a round of laughter from the three men.

Levi watched Evelyn's face as he made his way to greet her. He had prayed for her constantly, even as he'd fallen asleep on the way home—even now, as he approached her. He knew what the Scriptures said about being unequally yoked, and there were times when he'd wanted to rip the pages right out of the Bible. But he trusted God fully and he knew God never made mistakes.

Evelyn smiled and gave him a long hug in the middle of the doorway, despite the winter wind and the fact that others might see.

"We have to talk," she whispered. "There's something very important you need to know. Something you've been waiting to hear for a very long time."

Levi shut the door behind him and embraced the woman with whom he planned to spend the rest of his life.

EPILOGUE

The Lord is my shepherd; I shall not want.
PSALM 23:1

Edmonton, Alberta

June 4

Evelyn's body jerked at the clanging of the metal door as it closed behind her. The automatic lock slid into place and she stood motionless, waiting for the guard to lead the way. Her shoes clicked on the cement floor; she smothered a nervous laugh, wishing she'd worn quieter shoes. The thought unnerved her, considering her surroundings and how foolish and unimportant such a thing was. Distant voices echoed on the walls as she walked, head down, toward the door at the end of the hallway. Operating the coded entry, the guard waited as a buzzer rang and the door swung open. Holding the door, he wordlessly ushered Evelyn into a long room before returning to his original post.

The door closed and the lock fell into place. Although others in the room mingled and waited, Evelyn felt alone. The surroundings intimidated her. Thankful that Levi had offered to accompany her to Edmonton, she now wondered if it was a mistake having him wait in the car.

She paced nervously as she considered her predicament, anticipating how Jake would react when he saw her. Had she done the right thing in coming? Would she say the right words? Would he be receptive to them?

Conscious of her racing heart, Evelyn took several deep breaths and studied her surroundings.

A long table divided the room and a thick glass partition extended to the ceiling, separating prisoners and visitors. Individual cubicles measuring no more than three feet wide housed straight-back metal chairs, and two-way telephones provided the only means of verbal communication. Evelyn quickly realized that anything she had to say to Jake would be heard by everyone on her side of the room.

Four guards stood against the wall behind her, each one observing the movements of the visitors who mingled aimlessly, waiting, and the thought of a fishbowl crossed Evelyn's mind. On the other side of the room stood their counterparts, each with legs separated, hands behind their backs, staring straight ahead. She studied them and very quickly determined their role: they would be watching the prisoners, paying close attention to each word and reaction.

Evelyn shivered. Studying the sterile room had unnerved her further.

Before she had opportunity to consider leaving, a buzzer startled her and another automatic door opened at the far end of the room. Secured in handcuffs, Jake Waters appeared on the other side of the glass partition. Two guards escorted him to the metal chair in front of the table. Instinctively, Evelyn followed suit and sat opposite him. She folded her hands on the table, closed her eyes, and took a long, deep breath, searching for courage. She sighed, realizing it was useless for her to feign courage, and when she opened her eyes Jake was staring at her, his hands free of the handcuffs and a smirk slowly stretching across his mouth.

He picked up his telephone and Evelyn tentatively did the same.

"Never expected to see you here," he laughed. "Welcome to my new home." He extended his arms in a grandiose gesture.

Sarcasm soaked Jake's words and unnerved Evelyn even further. She knew he had received a heavy sentence and would be in prison for a long time, but the blatant disregard he showed for his circumstances threatened to strip her of any courage that remained.

"Jake, I'm sorry things turned out this way."

"Hey, don't be sorry for me. I messed up and got caught. If I'd been more careful, I wouldn't be here today. I'd be sippin' tequila in Tijuana." He laughed at his own joke. "But there's an old saying floating around this big house—'You do the crime, you do the time.'"

Evelyn struggled, not knowing where to begin. Jake's attitude stunned her. Her thoughts spun like unruly kites fighting the wind…soaring, swirling, spinning. She looked into his eyes, hoping to see something, anything that would indicate remorse, but she saw nothing. Instead, images flashed before her: Josh lying in the hospital, Abby with all the signs of a violent beating, the near murder of little Joy and, by no comparison of importance, the near death of Trickster.

"Why *did* you do it, Jake?" Her voice cracked. "Josh, Abby, the baby? And why did you hurt Trickster? She's just a little dog."

"She growled at me," Jake said unemotionally, as if the four words exonerated him of any wrongdoing.

Startled by his lack of remorse, Evelyn stared at him. "Why did you set fire to the Emporium? What did Josh ever do to you except provide a job for your wife when you needed money? And hurting Abby—"

"Abby?" Jake ignored Evelyn's reference to Josh. "Everyone has pity for Abby…everyone has pity for Abby." Bitterness surfaced which Evelyn had never seen in him before. "But what about me? Look what she did to *me*. I had to have brain surgery!" Jake hissed, cursing his wife. "I was in a coma for months and then had to deal with forgetting half my life."

He cursed again, then lowered his head before continuing. When he did, Evelyn could almost see the hatred in his eyes.

"She left me for dead! If she had been a better wife, I wouldn't be here right now."

"Surely you can't blame Abby for your predicament. She was just defending herself and she ran out of fear of you, her husband! Everyone knows you've got a history of hurting her. Can you blame her for running away?"

Jake shrugged, sloughing off the accusation. He stretched his legs and pushed back from the table, immediately drawing the attention of the guard closest to him.

"And what about the baby?" Evelyn asked. "She's—"

"That kid's not mine!" The words came so suddenly and with such venom that Evelyn shuddered. "You think I wouldn't know if I made a kid?" Jake yelled.

He winced under the pressure of a strong hand on his shoulder. The guard warned him that a second outburst would end the visit.

Trying to calm him, Evelyn spoke softly, requiring Jake to press the receiver closer to his ear. "Jake, the baby *is* yours, but I'm not here to debate little Joy's paternity. My questions came from a lack of understanding, that's all. I came today because I want to share something with you, something that has changed my life and could change yours, too, if you're open to it."

Five minutes later, Jake pushed back his chair and stood up. His face expressed little emotion but his eyes exuded a hatred so vile that Evelyn pulled back from the glass.

"I'm not interested," Jake hissed. "If there's a God, He's nothing but a fiendish devil who's taunted me all my life. I'll take my chances on the wider berth. The one you're on is way too narrow. I'm not interested in joining you or the likes of Rob or Josh, and certainly not Abby. I've had enough of them in this lifetime; I don't need them for eternity, whatever that entails!" Jake leaned on the table and spoke as though the glass partition did not exist. "Tell that so-called wife of mine to send me whatever papers are needed to end this fiasco of a marriage once and for all. I'll sign them, and good riddance to her! It was a mistake from day one."

Jake threw the receiver onto the table, turned and never looked back.

Evelyn watched Jake's retreating back. Walking toward the exit, with a guard on either side of him, he exuded defiance. She wiped a tear from her cheek and sat for a long time, trying to imagine the pain and sorrow God experienced as Jake turned his back on Him.

In her recent studies, she had discovered something that had weighed heavily upon her for days: God could change Jake's heart just as easily as He could have changed her heart. But He didn't. For whatever sovereign reason, God left Jake to suffer the consequences of his own choices, and the pain of that decision grieved God far more than it grieved her or would ever grieve Jake.

She pushed back her chair and walked toward the exit, to freedom. The very thought of the word deepened her sorrow for Jake.

By his own choice, he'll never know the true meaning of the word, she thought sadly, turning back for one last look at the now-empty room.

Freedom, she thought with a final push on the last exterior door that led to the parking lot. *I'm no longer a prisoner of my own making.* And although she still felt sorry for Jake, she marvelled at God's love for her.

The grey prison walls retreated with each step she took, but as free as she felt, her heavy sadness for Jake persisted. Could she have done more? Was there something else she should have said? Evelyn rubbed her eyes and looked down.

Did I say the wrong things?

She sighed, unconsciously placing one foot in front of the other as she put distance between herself and the prison.

BE STILL AND KNOW THAT I AM GOD.

Evelyn caught her breath. Over the many months of her search for God, she had come to recognize that still small voice. Warmth filled her. God didn't speak audibly, but rather through one's circumstances. The thought brought her comfort and assurance that God had been with her while she'd endured Jake's animosity. *God* had given her the words to say; they were not her words. She shuddered at the thought of trying to reach Jake on her own.

What a failure that would have been, she thought, acknowledging her human frailties. God *had* spoken through her circumstances and she *had* done all she could do. She could not *make* Jake listen. She could not make Jake *want* what she had found. She could not *force* Jake to understand how his anger denied him the peace she had taken so long to find. Jake's heart was cold, and there was nothing she could do about that. He was in God's hands.

The sun's rays filtered through a crack in the clouds and Evelyn shielded her eyes from the glare. A flock of Canada geese flew overhead in a perfect V-formation. Evelyn looked up as their honking filled the sky. She whispered the first verse of a poem she'd learned as a child:

> Their honking is heard across the sky,
> Stretching their wings,
> In perfect form they fly,
> Never faltering.

Evelyn leaned on a short fence separating the parking lot from the grassy yard. The warmth of the sun felt good.

Before entering the parking lot, she contemplated further the childhood poem.

> Do they know where they are going?
> They follow without fear,
> They trust their leader, soaring,
> Never doubting.

She watched the geese, the rhythm of their beating wings, their strength, their confidence in their leader. She smiled through her tears and felt one with God's amazing creatures. She had a Leader now, too— One she could follow without fear, without guilt, without regret. A Leader she could trust, never doubting. A Leader who cared for her as no human ever could. She would never look back again … not anymore. What good would that do? She could not relive those years, could not undo the pain she had caused her family, could not erase the sorrow that had seeped into their lives. She would keep her eyes ahead, focused on the One who had waited patiently for her to come and find Him.

Evelyn Sherwood wiped her tears as though erasing the pain of a lifetime. She walked across the pavement and, with renewed strength, slowly approached the one waiting in the car.

Spring is in the air; my garden will be breaking through the soil... and I have a wedding to plan.

And he said, Go forth, and stand upon the mount before the Lord. And, behold, the Lord passed by, and a great and strong wind rent the mountains, and brake in pieces the rocks before the Lord; but the Lord was not in the wind: and after the wind an earthquake; but the Lord was not in the earthquake: and after the earthquake a fire; but the Lord was not in the fire: and after the fire a still small voice.

1 KINGS 19:11–12

APPENDIX

ABUSE

"When you are abused, you retreat to a place in your mind where you don't hurt. It may appear to be a calm facade, but it is never calm! It is more likely a wall in your mind to hide behind, to be safe for a while, to not feel anything—good or bad...Depression can be all-consuming, yet somehow safe, a place to retreat to without permission...The physical abuse was bad enough, but at times, knowing it was coming, I'd wish it done and over with. It was easier to take than the emotional abuse. That was another matter. It was constant, always present, always in my head. Very destructive. I can so relate to Abby. Thank God I am healed and have forgiven...but honestly, I guess healing is an ongoing process. I'm still working on it as God continuously reveals Himself and helps me grow. *Then Came a Hush* was another opportunity for healing. Never have I read a book that was so heart-wrenching."

—*the voice of a victim*

Among its many definitions, Collins English Dictionary & Thesaurus defines abuse as "an evil, unjust or corrupt practice." It goes further to define abusive as "brutal, cruel, destructive, hurtful, injurious"[1] and notes that it comes in many forms.

Physical abuse is often the most easily recognized form of abuse, and it can be seen by outward markings on the body. Sexual abuse constitutes sexual contact between an adult and anyone younger than eighteen, between a significantly older child and a younger child, or between non-consenting parties, regardless of age. Emotional abuse can be the most difficult to identify because there are usually no outward signs. Bullying is a form of abusive behaviour characterized by intimidation, threats, or humiliation and can be just as damaging as other forms of abuse. Self-inflicted violence (SIV) is another form of abuse, which can be disturbing and difficult to understand, and is done to release unbearable feelings and pressures through self-harm.

Victims of abuse need support, protection, and prayer. Abusers need to be held accountable. They also need prayer.

VÉLODROME D'HIVER

When the Germans invaded the northern half of France in 1940, including Paris, the area became known as Occupied France. At that time, about 350,000 Jews lived in France, and under the driven madness of Adolf Hitler, several plans were immediately set about to reduce this population. One such plan was Operation Spring Breeze (*Opération Vent Printanier*).

On July 16–17, 1942, a Nazi-decreed raid and mass arrest was carried out by French policemen and gendarmes. Four days prior to the raid, the director of the city police ordered the raid to be carried out with speed and without "pointless speaking and without comment." (In 1995, French President Jacques Chirac apologized for the role the French policemen and civil servants played in the raid.)

In the early morning hours of July 16, 13,152 Jews were arrested (5,802 were women, 4,051 were children). They could only take with them a blanket, one sweater, a pair of shoes, and two shirts. An unknown number escaped after being warned by the French Resistance. Some

---

1 "Abuse." *Collins English Dictionary & Thesaurus* (Second edition, 2000), p. 7.

were hidden by neighbours. Some benefitted from a lack of enthusiasm, whether intentional or not, on the part of police officers. Most families were split up and never reunited.

Needing a place to hold those arrested, the Nazis took over the Vélodrome d'Hiver, an indoor bicycle racing track and stadium in Paris, not far from the Eiffel Tower. The glass roof was painted dark blue to avoid attracting enemy planes. With the windows screwed shut for security, the temperature inside the building became intolerable. There were no lavatories. (Of the ten available, five had sealed windows to prevent escape, and the others were blocked.) Water and food was supplied by the Quakers, the Red Cross, and the very few doctors and nurses who were allowed access.

After eight days of unimaginable and inhumane treatment, the Jews were taken to Drancy, an incomplete complex of apartments and apartment towers that became an internment camp, and from there they were shipped by rail to Auschwitz for immediate extermination. Only four hundred survived.

The incident became known as the Vél' d'Hiv Roundup (Rafle du Vél' d'Hiv) and accounted for more than a quarter of the 42,000 Jews sent from France to Auschwitz in 1942.

YIDDISH

Yiddish is a High German language originating with the Ashkenazi Jews. It is written in the Hebrew alphabet and is spoken in Orthodox Jewish communities around the world. It is the home language learned in childhood in most Hasidic communities, where it is used in schools and in many social settings.

Between 1939 and 1945, Yiddish was nearly wiped out when six million European Jews died in the Holocaust. The majority of Jews who escaped Europe and made it to Israel or to the United States soon learned the local language and made Yiddish their secondary tongue.

Currently, Yiddish is enjoying a rebirth. Several citizens use it as their main language and it is receiving attention from the non-Jewish scholarly community. Many universities worldwide offer courses and even degree programs in Yiddish linguistics.

Yeshua (yehSHOO-ah)

In Hebrew, the word *Yeshua* means "salvation" or "he saves" and was likely the name used throughout Judea by Jesus' parents, siblings, and followers. Probably the Aramaic pronunciation, *Yeshu* (YEHshoo) was used in the rough regional dialect of Galilee. *Yeshua* is used today by Messianic Jews, Hebrew Christians, and other denominations who wish to use Jesus' Hebrew name. The English name "Jesus" is a derivation from the Greek *Iesous* and the Latin *Iesus* and identifies the Messiah to English-speaking people.